"SHE NEEDED HIM"

He wanted to oblige her. Damn, did he want to oblige her.

Casually, Stan moved closer to her until he invaded her space, and her alarm thumped louder with every beat of her heart. He left himself wide open to her, relishing each tingle she felt, absorbing each small shiver of excitement—and letting it excite him in return.

Reaching out, he brushed the side of his thumb along her jawline, up and over her downy cheek, tickling the dangling earrings that suddenly seemed damn sexy. "Maybe you need the iced tea," he murmured, his attention dipping to her naked mouth. Jenna never wore lipstick, and he liked the look of her soft, full lips glistening from the glide of her tongue. Oh, yeah, he liked that a lot. "You feel . . . warm, Jenna."

Her breaths came fast and uneven. "I've been . . . working."

And fantasizing. About him.

STAR QUALITY

LORI FOSTER
LUCY MONROE
DIANNE CASTELL

BRAVA

KENSINGTON PUBLISHING CORP.
http://www.kensingtonbooks.com

BRAVA BOOKS are published by

Kensington Publishing Corp.
850 Third Avenue
New York, NY 10022

All Kensington titles, imprints, and distributed lines are
available at special quantity discounts for bulk purchases for
sales promotion, premiums, fund-raising, educational, or in-
stitutional use.

Special book excerpts or customized printings can also be
created to fit specific needs. For details, write or phone the
office of the Kensington Special Sales Manager: Attn. Special
Sales Department. Kensington Publishing Corp., 850 Third
Avenue, New York, NY 10022. Phone: 1-800-221-2647.

Brava and the B logo Reg. U.S. Pat. & TM Off.

ISBN-13: 978-0-7582-1008-1
ISBN-10: 0-7582-1008-6

First Brava Books Mass-Market Printing: December 2008
First Brava Books Trade Paperback Printing: May 2005
10 9 8 7 6 5 4 3 2 1

Printed in the United States of America

ONCE IN A
BLUE MOON

Lori Foster

One

Lunacy, that's what they'd call it. Pure, plain, lock-em-up-and-throw-away-the-key lunacy. And all because of a stupid moon—the second *full* moon in July. If anyone knew, they'd label him crazy for sure. Not that he planned to tell anyone. He'd tried that once as a kid, and everyone had had a freakin' shit fit, so no more.

But damn it, why now, when he had a full week of landscaping work, a book deadline, and a newspaper interview to get through?

As Stan Tucker walked down the clean sidewalk of Delicious, Ohio, enjoying the fresh air and bright sunshine of July, he did his best to block the voices. Not much of a problem there since most people's thoughts were boring as hell. Grocery lists, appointments, and work woes vied with guilt, jealousy, and self-pity. It amazed him that mankind didn't have more important things to think about.

He ran a hand through his hair, mussing it worse than half a day's work and uneasy breezes had already done. Dirt and noticeable sweat stains covered his shirt, and dried mud clung to his boots. But despite his occasional celebrity status, he still worked hard, and if the interviewer didn't like it, he could take a hike. His publicist would snarl and groan, but Stan just plain didn't care.

As he passed people on the sidewalk, more voices battered his already fractured senses. Stan narrowed his eyes, again tuning them out. It didn't take much effort to put their private thoughts, their personal conversations, on hold, but it bugged him that he had to bother. He'd hoped that moving to Delicious, away from the crowds and human congestion, would help. But thanks to the approach of the full moon, the second in this month, he'd become privy to the introspection of all who got close to him, and not a one of them had a thought worth hearing.

Disgusted, he shoved open the fancy, etched-glass double doors of the small bookstore, The Book Nook, owned by Jenna Rowan. The bookstore was across Jonathan Avenue and up one building from his garden center. Stan owned several acres that backed up to Golden Lake, with his home next door to the garden center. A short jaunt would take him to the town square and the fancy fountain erected by the citizens long before he'd moved in.

Thanks to the apple trees growing wild around the lake, the town's structures had some whimsical names, including the Garden of Eden Salon, Johnny Appleseed Museum, and Granny Smith's Apothecary. Old Orchard Inn, a charming but outdated B&B and restaurant, used the apple trees on their lot for daily fare offered to the guests. In the afternoon you could smell the scents of cooking applesauce, apple pie, and apple cider.

Stan appreciated the novelty of Delicious as much as the laid-back, easy pace.

The second he entered The Book Nook, chilled, conditioned air hit his heated face and the scent of fresh cinnamon got pulled deep into his lungs. Stan liked The

Book Nook, every tidy shelf, polished tabletop, the scents, the colors . . . and the proprietor. Yeah, he especially liked her.

As usual, his gaze sought out Jenna, and he found her toward the back aisle, stocking new books on a shelf. Today she wore her honey blond hair twisted into a sloppy loop, clipped at the back of her head with a large gold barrette.

He soaked in the sight of her, making note of her long floral dress and flat leather sandals. He'd known Jenna about six months now, ever since he'd moved to Delicious to escape the chaos of Chicago. Thanks to him, her bookstore had become a tourist attraction, not that she gave him any special attention for it.

Jenna treated everyone, young and old, male and female, with a sort of maternal consideration that never failed to frustrate him. He wanted her, but she saw him only as a friend.

In nature and appearance, Jenna was the sweetest thing he'd ever met, caring and protective of one and all. He liked the fact that she was near his age, close to forty. She'd been widowed about three years now, yet she never dated, never gave any guy—especially not him—more than a friendly smile and platonic attention. With just the smallest encouragement from her, he'd make a move.

But she never encouraged him.

When he released the door, the bell chimed, and Jenna glanced up. Dangly earrings moved against her cheek, drawing attention to a dimple that formed when her mouth kicked up on one side. "Hello, Stan. All ready for your interview?"

She straightened, and the dress pulled taut over her sumptuous behind and thighs. Unlike younger women he knew, Jenna had a full figure meant to attract men. Feeling strangely intense, Stan strode toward her and for a moment, only a single moment, he forgot to bar the thoughts bombarding his brain.

Like a clap of thunder, Jenna's nervousness struck him, but at the same time, giddy excitement rippled . . . and clear as a bell, he saw what she saw: him naked, sweaty, fucking—

Staggered, Stan drew up short. Her thoughts were so incredibly vivid that his jaw clenched and his stomach bottomed out on a rage of sexual desire.

Watching him, Jenna licked her lips and smoothed her skirt with visible uneasiness. "Stan? Are you all right?"

Incredible. She looked innocently concerned when Stan knew good and well what she'd been thinking. About *him*.

Why had she never let on?

As he continued to stand there, staring hard, absorbing her wanton musings, she laughed. "What is it? What's wrong?"

Her thoughts were so evident to him, he saw them with the same color and clarity of a moving picture. *Her stomach was quivering, deep inside her, down low* . . . Jesus. Out of self-preservation and to prevent a boner, Stan attempted to block her thoughts. Muscles tight, he took a step back, distancing himself physically as well as mentally.

It didn't help. Sensation continued to roll over him with the effect of a tactile stroke. "Nothing's wrong." Except that he was suddenly turned on and they were in a public place and he had an interview to do any second now.

Her smile faltered. Her gaze skimmed down his body, over his crotch, then jerked upward again. "It's probably the heat, then."

He hadn't suffered an unwanted erection since his teen years!

As casual and natural as ever, pretending she hadn't noticed the bulge in his jeans, she breezed out of the aisle and strode past him. Buttons marched up the front of her dress, from the hem to a scooped neck, and she'd left several undone all the way to her knees. With her long stride, the dress fanned out around her, showing smooth, shapely calves and a sexy ankle bracelet. "Would you like something to drink? I've just made lemonade. Or we have tea, of course."

Lemonade? No, he wanted her. Right now. Maybe on the counter or up against one of the book aisles. Watching the sensual sway of that sweet behind, he almost missed her panicked thought. *Oh, God. Did he see me looking at him?*

He soaked in her response to him—and knew that he'd have to have her. Soon. Tonight if he could manage it. Hell, if she'd shown even the slightest interest, they'd already be intimately involved. But she hadn't. She kept her attraction to him private, so private that if it weren't for the blue moon, the second full moon this hot July, he still wouldn't have a clue.

She glanced over her shoulder, innocence personified. "Stan?"

Oh, she was good. "Tea." He drew a calming breath and said belatedly, "Thanks."

How should he proceed? They weren't teenagers. Hell, at forty, it had been a long time since he'd done any serious flirting. Before leaving Chicago, he'd known several women who wanted no more than he did—a good time with someone safe, and no commitments.

When they wanted him, they let him know. Or vice versa. There was no mind reading, no guessing, no need to use his rather rusty skills at wooing.

But that was before he'd moved to Delicious. Before he'd met Jenna. Before he'd even really known what he wanted.

Now he knew.

Jenna was different from other women, certainly different from the women he'd been with in the past. She was the commitment type. She'd been married, and by what he'd heard from the gossiping denizens of Delicious, her marriage had been a very happy one.

Watching while she poured tea into a tall glass of ice, Stan cautiously approached. Jenna always kept fresh drinks and cookies for the neighbors who visited her store. Book shopping at The Nook was more like visiting a favored relative, one who pampered you and made you feel special.

Everyone spoke to her, spilling out ailments and troubles or sharing news good or bad. And when Jenna listened, you got the feeling she really cared. When she said, "How are you?" she meant it.

Did she care about him?

If he kept listening to her very sexual thoughts, he'd end up climbing over the counter to show her just how hot the reality would be. Knowing she wouldn't like that, he tried distracting himself. "Where's the reporter?"

Jenna drew a deep breath, and no way in hell could he not notice that. Even nearing the big Four-Oh, she still had one of the best racks he'd ever seen. Her breasts were heavy, but suited her sturdy frame. She wasn't a frail woman, but rather one with meat on her bones. Shapely in the extreme, sexy as hell. . . . His gaze zeroed in on her chest and got stuck there.

"He, ah, ran to the drugstore to buy new batteries. He should be here in just a few minutes."

Stan's gaze lifted and locked with hers. Sensation crackled between them. His awareness of her as a sexual woman ratcheted up another notch. Even without hearing her thoughts, what she wanted from him, with him, would be obvious to any red-blooded male. Heat blazed in her eyes and flushed her cheeks. A pulse fluttered in her pale throat. Her lips parted . . .

Amazing. A mom of two, a quiet bookworm, a woman who remained circumspect in every aspect of her life—and she lusted after him with all this wanton creativity.

Not since the skill had first come to him when he was a kid of twelve, twenty-eight years ago, had Stan so appreciated the strange effect the blue moon had on him. It started with the waxing Gibbous, then expanded and increased as the moon became full, and began to abate with the waning Gibbous. But at midnight, when the moon was most full, the ability was so clean, so acute, that it used to scare him.

His parents didn't know. The one time he'd tried to tell them they'd freaked out, thinking he was mental or miserable or having some kind of psychosis. He'd retrenched and never mentioned it to them again.

When he was twenty and away at college, he signed up for a course on parapsychology. One classmate who specialized in the effects of the moon gave him an explanation that made sense. At least in part.

According to his friend, wavelengths of light came from a full moon and that affected his inner pathogens. With further studies, Stan had learned that different colors of lights caused varying emotional reactions in people. It made sense that the light of a full moon, twice in the same month, could cause effects.

In him, it heightened his sixth sense to the level that he could hear other people's tedious inner musings.

Now he could hear, *feel,* Jenna's most private yearnings, and for once he appreciated his gift. Nothing tedious in being wanted sexually. Especially when the level of want bordered on desperate.

She needed a good lay. She needed him.

He wanted to oblige her. Damn, did he want to oblige her.

Casually, Stan moved closer to her until he invaded her space, and her alarm thumped louder with every beat of her heart. He left himself wide open to her, relishing each tingle she felt, absorbing each small shiver of excitement—and letting it excite him in return. He no longer cared that he had a near-lethal erection.

Reaching out, he brushed the side of his thumb along her jawline, up and over her downy cheek, tickling the dangling earrings that suddenly seemed damn sexy. "Maybe you need the iced tea," he murmured, his attention dipping to her naked mouth. Jenna never wore lipstick, and he liked the look of her soft, full lips glistening from the glide of her tongue. Oh, yeah, he liked that a lot. "You feel . . . warm, Jenna."

Her breaths came fast and uneven. "I've been . . . working."

And fantasizing. About him.

Lazily, Stan continued to touch her. "Me, too. Out in the sun all day. It's so damn humid, I know I'm sweaty." His thumb stroked lower, near the corner of her mouth. "But I didn't have time to change."

Her eyelids got heavy, drooping over her green eyes. Shakily, she lifted a hand and closed it over his wrist— but she didn't push him away. "You look . . . fine." *Downright edible*. She cleared her throat. "No reason to change."

Stan's slow smile alarmed her further. "You don't mind my jeans and clumpy boots?" He used both hands now to cup her face, relishing the velvet texture of her skin. "They're such a contrast to you, all soft and pretty and fresh."

Her eyes widened, dark with confusion and curbed excitement, searching his. He leaned forward, wanting her mouth, needing to know her taste—

The bell over the door chimed.

Jenna jerked away so quickly, she left Stan holding air. Face hot, she ducked to the back of the store and into the storage room, closing the door softly behind her.

Well, hell. He'd probably rushed things, Stan realized, aware of her exaggerated embarrassment. But holding back had been impossible. Especially with her desire so clear to him—giving permission to his desire, leaving the way wide open for some mutual satisfaction.

With her in another room and the reporter looming, Stan's focus on Jenna was diluted. He caught the garbled mental intrusion from the reporter and blocked it.

Teeming with frustration, he readjusted himself within the confines of his stiff jeans and then faced the reporter, who luckily had his attention on his recorder as he snapped in batteries. "Sorry I'm late," he called out without looking up. "Batteries died."

The sooner he got the interview over, the sooner he could get back to Jenna. Stan strode forward. "No problem, but let's make it quick, if you don't mind. I have a lot to do today."

From behind her counter, Jenna Rowan watched Stan on the pretense of listening to the interview. Stan might be a renowned landscaper, author of several best-selling gardening books, and an expert businessman now featured on the local radio station every Saturday morning, but it was his colorful past that made him a favorite among the media.

For years, Stan Tucker had wavered in and out of trouble. As a much younger man, he'd narrowly missed spending time in jail. He'd been married and divorced, a celebrated playboy, and now . . . he planted flowers.

Jenna sighed softly. She had no doubt Stan could retire comfortably, but his extreme energy level forced him to always do something, to be active, in the sun, sweating, working his muscles . . .

Oh, she knew what he could do with her—if only he were interested. How he'd use that energy in bed teased at her senses every time he got near. To call Stan hand-some would be very misleading. He was far too raw, too rough, to be termed anything so pretty. He could appear cruel—wow. Like he did now, glancing at her with those fierce eyes as if he knew her thoughts and didn't like them one bit.

Hands shaking, Jenna pretended to straighten the paperwork behind her counter. In truth, she couldn't seem to keep him off her mind. Maybe the idea of turn-ing forty next month had caused her hormones to go on a rampage. Or maybe three years of celibacy was three years too long. Whatever the cause, she wanted sex. Hot, gritty, sweaty sex.

With Stan.

She craved it, aching with the need at night in her lonely bed, unable to sleep. Whenever she daydreamed, which lately seemed to be all the time, it was Stan Tucker she saw. In his prime, he had thick but natural muscles and undeniable strength. His light brown eyes looked almost golden at times. Working in the harsh sunshine had streaked his brown hair that was usually unkempt and so sexy she wanted to touch it.

She wanted to touch him.

All over. Both of them buck naked . . .

With a clatter, Stan suddenly shoved back his chair. Pulled out of her current fantasy, Jenna jumped.

Stan stared at her, all that severe attention startling her while the reporter simply waited in stunned silence.

Stalking toward her, Stan leaned in, close enough that she could feel his breath and smell the rich musky sweat of his skin. God, he was *so* male . . .

Voice rough edged, almost desperate, he whispered, "Jenna, honey, do you think you could find something to do in the back? Or better yet, go take your lunch break."

He wanted rid of her?

Cursing low, Stan ran a big, darkly tanned hand over the back of his neck. His eyes lifted, his gaze boring into her. "I'm going to sound dumb as shit, but you're making me nervous."

"Why?"

"You're listening in."

"Oh." She licked her lips, trying to understand—and got distracted by the way he stared at her mouth. "I . . . I always listen."

"This time it's bothering me." His gaze caught hers again. His voice lowered to a ferocious growl. His eyes narrowed. "I keep thinking of you instead of what I'm saying."

"You do?"

"Yeah." He glanced over her from head to toe. "You look great in that dress."

The reporter cleared his throat. "Is everything okay?"

He likes my dress? Flustered, Jenna pushed off her stool and tried an uncertain smile. "I understand. It's all right. I was getting hungry anyway." She glanced at her watch. "Half an hour okay?"

Stan hesitated, appearing angry, then annoyed. Taking her totally off guard, he caught her around the neck and pulled her forward over the counter while he leaned in. Then, as if he had the right, as if he'd done it a million times, he put his mouth to hers, firm and warm, lingering, one heartbeat, two . . . and he lifted away. "Thanks." No smile, no softness.

Jenna touched her lips, tingling from her mouth to her breasts and down into her womb. "Oh, uh . . ."

Face hard, expression harder, Stan went back to the reporter. "Now, where were we?"

The reporter said, "You were telling me about . . ."

In Jenna's mind, the words trailed off. Who cared what they said? Stan had just kissed her. A brief, almost nonsexual kiss, except that she wanted to melt on the spot.

Knowing she needed a breath of fresh air and a few minutes to figure out what had just happened, she grabbed her purse and made a hasty retreat, pausing only long enough to put her CLOSED sign in the door so Stan and the reporter wouldn't be interrupted.

At a fast clip, she went down the walkway to the Mom and Pop diner next door, on the corner of Jonathan Ave. and Winesap Lane. She darted inside. There were a few customers present, the normal lunch crowd, but no one paid her any attention. And thank God, because she just knew she breathed too fast and looked the fool.

Hand pressed to her heart, Jenna glanced around and located an empty booth in the very back, away from windows and other patrons. Normally reserved for the few smokers who came into the diner, it stayed almost abandoned, and so that's where Jenna headed. She needed the privacy, and the lack of prying eyes would help her get collected.

Legs shaking, she hurried over to the plastic seat and slid in. Her mind in a riot of mayhem, she covered her mouth.

Just *what* had happened? One minute, Stan was merely a friend, then in the next, he'd kissed her. Or had he meant it as a friendly gesture and she, being a widow with desperate clichéd lust, read more into it than she should have? Whatever it meant, wow, what a hot smooch. She'd always known it'd be that way, that with Stan, every sense would be magnified and a simple kiss could never be simple. No two ways about it, the man turned her on, always had.

But being a mother took priority over everything

else, making an affair taboo. No matter what she felt for Stan, all she could indulge were fantasies. Now, if Stan was the type who wanted to settle down and enjoy domestic bliss . . . but he wasn't. She might be half in love already, but Stan Tucker didn't feel the same way.

She'd do well to remember that one small fact.

Ten minutes later, the waitress noticed Jenna buried in the corner and, full of good spirit and sunshine, hustled over to take her order. Jenna finally shook off her daze. She didn't want anyone else to read the carnal hunger on her face. For crying out loud, at her age, with her family responsibilities, she had to be very discreet about her shameful hankering for one very hot landscape and gardening expert.

"Hey, Jenna." Marylou Jasper, an eighteen-year-old working toward college funds, pulled out her white pad and a pen. Because the owner of the diner liked to experiment with new things, they didn't offer a regular menu. On any given day, it was anyone's guess what would be served.

Trying to appear normal, rather than ravaged with lust, Jenna smiled and said, "What do we have today, Marylou?"

"I just made a pot of coffee, the peach pie is still hot, croissants are fresh from the oven, and we have some really awesome chicken salad to go with them. There's also chili, hamburgers, and lunchmeat sandwiches. So what can I getcha today?"

Maybe food would help settle the churning in her stomach. Jenna smiled. "The chicken salad on a croissant, a pickle slice or two, please, and a diet cola."

Marylou rolled her eyes. "Why you always wanna drink that nasty diet stuff, I'll never understand."

Of course she couldn't understand. Being a typical eighteen-year-old with a slender body and not an ounce of fat, Marylou could eat anything she fancied. Her brown hair shone with natural highlights, and her blue eyes were always smiling. Jenna had no doubt the girl could have her pick of beaus. "That's because you're young and shapely, but I'm old and—"

"Very shapely."

Ohmigod. At the sound of that rough male voice, Jenna stiffened. Eyes wide, heart hammering madly, she swiveled around to see Stan stepping past Marylou. Without an invitation, he joined her at the booth, placing his perfect body on the opposite bench, directly in front of her.

Sexual tension, thick as soup, suddenly hung in the air. Marylou just stood there, her mouth gaping, her eyes going back and forth with a ping-pong effect.

Unconcerned, Stan glanced up at her and said, "I'll have whatever Jenna ordered—but make my cola nondiet."

"Oh." Marylou shook herself. "Right." Then with a big fat smile, "I'll get right on the order." And whistling, she took herself off with telling haste, no doubt on her way to the kitchen to relay a whole lot more than a simple order.

Confused, excited, giddy with expectation, Jenna soaked in the sight of Stan. She savored the wild beating of her heart, the dryness in her mouth, and the curl of excitement deep inside her. It had been so long since she'd felt such wonderful things.

Stan smiled with shrewd calculation. "The interview finished early."

Jenna wondered if he'd rushed through it. She cleared her throat. "After that unexpected compliment . . ." She hesitated. What if he hadn't meant it as such? What if instead, he'd been remarking on her weight? She could stand to lose a few pounds—

"A compliment you deserve," Stan interjected, his gaze intent on her face. "Your figure is spectacular."

"Oh." A blush of happiness warmed her from the inside out. "Well, thank you. But you realize Marylou is going to start some ripe gossip."

Reaching across the booth, Stan took her trembling hand, holding her firm. "Gossip implies rumor or hearsay." His rough fingers moved over her palm. "But if what she says is true, how can it be gossip?"

Two

Damn, he liked the way Jenna's cheeks warmed and how her fast breathing shimmied her breasts. And that tiny pulse fluttering in her throat gave everything away, even if he didn't have access to her every emotion and sensation.

Stan brushed his fingertips over her palm again, felt the undulating wave of growing response that rolled through her, and he pushed up from his seat.

At the same time, Jenna pressed her shoulders back in the booth, not out of disinterest, but from utter surprise. That didn't deter Stan at all, not when he knew she wanted him, that her longing was so strong it scared her a little.

Holding her hand so she couldn't completely retreat, he leaned over her, hesitated with his mouth a breath away from hers, building the anticipation, then gave in to the urge.

Jenna made a small sound as his mouth covered hers, and this time he made damn sure she wouldn't mistake his claim as some forward form of friendship. As he deepened the kiss, her mouth softened, her lips parting, and Stan used just the tip of his tongue to taste her, just inside her lips, over her teeth, touching against her own tongue—and retreating.

Jesus. Heart thumping hard, thighs tense, Stan pulled back. He'd meant to tease her, to make her understand what he wanted from her. But while Jenna did look more heated than ever, Stan felt ready to self-combust. Hell, at his age he'd done his fair share of necking. It shouldn't have been any big deal.

But not once could he remember enjoying the feel and taste of a woman's mouth quite so much. He wasn't a sweaty-palmed, hair-triggered kid anymore, not by a long shot, but damn if he didn't want to drag Jenna out of the booth and rush her to the nearest form of privacy they could find.

A simple kiss had him primed, and he knew it was the woman responsible, not the kiss itself.

As he settled back in his seat, a little disconcerted by her effect on him, Jenna touched her lips. Voice faint, gaze searching, she whispered, "What was that?"

Stan made a sound of disgust. Her confusion mirrored his but probably for different reasons. "I thought it was a kiss."

Her gaze dropped, and she looked around the table-top, at her hands, at his. "Yes." Her green eyes lifted. "A kiss, but . . ."

Stan flattened his mouth. "I know. A punch in the gut, huh? Kissing is nice, but kissing you flattens me. It makes me think of a hell of a lot more than mouth on mouth, that's for damn sure."

Her hand went to her stomach, and she nodded. "I don't understand, Stan. What are we doing?"

Marylou reappeared, her expression filled with titil-lated nosiness. "Got your sandwiches and stuff." Wide-eyed, she looked between the two of them, plopping down the plates and glasses without the attention nec-essary to the task.

Stan scooted his plate back a little so it didn't end up in his lap. "Thanks."

Jenna wouldn't look at Marylou, and that bothered him.

Marylou lingered, and that bothered him even more.

"That's all we need for now, Marylou. But save me a piece of pie, okay?"

"Oh."

At least the girl knew a dismissal when she heard one.

Wearing a smile, she nodded. "Yeah, 'kay, sure. No problem, Stan." With a lot of reluctance, she eased herself out of hearing range.

Jenna moaned and put her face in her hands. "It's starting already."

It had started the moment he stepped into her shop and knew she pictured him naked. Over her. With her naked, under him, anxious and ready to come.

It was Stan's turn to groan. "When do you get off today?"

Her head shot up. "Why?"

Rolling his eyes, Stan said, "Honey, something's happening between us. You know that as much as I do. I want to see you. I damn sure intend to kiss you again." He shifted his booted feet under the table until they caged her smaller feet in. "So tell me, when do you get off?"

Her regret bombarded him before she answered. "At five, but I have to get home to Ryan because Rachelle has a date."

Her son Ryan was a rambunctious ten-year-old, and her daughter Rachelle was a beautiful eighteen-year-old young lady. Stan had met them both several times now. Jenna sometimes kept Ryan at the bookstore with her, and with the town so small, you eventually ran into everyone at one time or another. He'd seen them in the grocery, at the fountain in front of the town square, and at the diner.

She had nice kids, polite and happy and healthy.

A family get-together wasn't quite what Stan had in mind, but he knew he'd go nuts wondering about things if he went home alone. "Why don't you let me take you both out on the boat?"

Turbulent puzzlement warred with buoyant desire. Stan's heart wanted to melt. How long had it been since a guy asked her out? Had the fact of her kids been a deterrent? Hell, as a divorced bachelor with no close family, the idea of her children pleased him. He liked kids—always had.

Jenna was a terrific mom, and that appealed to him as much as everything else. It emphasized her loving nature, her sense of responsibility, and the loyalty she had for those she loved. Important qualities. More important than her sexy good looks—which he appreciated, too.

Filled with wariness, she licked her lips and said, "Ryan would love that, I'm sure."

Stan leaned one elbow on the table and cupped her face with his right hand. "I'm glad. But what about you?"

"What about me?"

"You enjoy boating?" His fingertips brushed over her cheek, down to her throat and across the very top of her chest. "You're so fair. You don't get out in the sun much, do you?"

Her eyes sank closed. "Stan, you have to stop touching me."

"But I don't want to stop." And if she'd be truthful, she wanted more touches, not less.

She drew an unsteady breath. "I don't really want you to stop."

Stan stared in amazement.

"But I can't think when you touch me."

Her honesty astounded him. And left him shaken. He thought of his ex-wife, of the lies he'd learned during a blue moon—no, forget that. He'd gotten over her and her deceptions ages ago, and he wouldn't mar his time with Jenna by thinking of that.

"All right." Stan dropped his hand, but said, "I like it that you tell me what you're feeling."

Horrified, she gave a shaky laugh. "Oh, no, never that. Well, maybe some of what I'm thinking, but not all."

A predator's delight curled through him. *Too late, sweetheart,* he could have told her, but she wasn't ready to hear about his whacky relationship with the moon. He didn't want to send her running from him with truths she couldn't handle.

"Why not?" he asked, just to tease her. "What is it you're thinking, Jenna?"

"I'm thinking that this is happening awfully fast."

"We've known each other six months."

"I know. So . . . Why now?"

Deliberately dragging things along, Stan took a bite of his croissant and contemplated her while chewing. Flustered, Jenna nibbled on her own sandwich while she waited.

"Tomorrow night, there'll be a full moon," Stan finally told her, deciding it might be best to ease her into the idea of his lunar-inspired intuition.

"And so you're going to change into a lycanthrope?"

"A werewolf?" He hated that stupid legend. Whenever he researched the moon, he invariably ran into the myths.

She grinned. "I remember the whole wolf transformation really ramped up Jack Nicholson's libido in the movie." She toyed with her sandwich. "Are you telling me you're the same? Should I expect you to sprout hair on your back and start howling at the moon?"

Stan gave her a long look. "I might howl, strictly out of sexual frustration, you understand. But I won't actually turn into an animal." He ran a hand through his shaggy hair. "Hell, I'm hairy enough as it is. Any more would be overkill."

Her gaze went to his chest, then his forearms. Her voice again grew quiet, a sure sign of her mood. "You're just hairy enough. It's sexy. Very manly." Then she shook her head. "So tell me, what does a full moon have to do with you kissing me twice, when in six months, you've never given me a second look?"

Disbelief left him speechless, but he could tell by her expression—as well as her thoughts—that she believed what she said.

"Jenna, honey, there's not a man alive who doesn't give you second looks. And third and fourth looks, for that matter."

"Right," she said in exaggerated tolerance. "I'm almost forty. I've had two kids. I'm hardly a sex symbol."

"Wrong. You're incredibly sexy. Warm, friendly . . . and sweet enough to eat."

He tacked that last on just to prod her, and sure enough, she caught her breath—then got exactly the visual he wanted. Watching her, seeing what she saw, made him feel it almost as if he had her spread out on his bed, completely naked, twisting with pleasure while he showed her his favorite way to make a woman come.

"Damn." He rubbed his face, then gulped down half his coke. He had to stop tormenting himself.

"Stan?" His name emerged as a thread of sound, filled with longing.

Nodding, jaw tight, Stan said, "You see?" He struggled to keep the harshness, the savage need, from his tone. "The moon affects us all, Jenna, did you know that? It's called the Lunar Effect and can be responsible for everything from mental disorders to heightened awareness."

She didn't dispute him, but then, her mind was still on other, more carnal matters, making him nuts.

Stan took her hand again. "Listen to me, Jenna. Studies have proven that more crimes, more births, more conceptions, more animal bites, and more unintentional poisonings all occur during a full moon. The earth and sun and moon are all lined up, causing higher tides, and you have to believe if the moon can do that, it can damn sure work on our glands, our organs, and our moods."

She blinked hard. "So . . . you're interested in me because of the moon?"

"No way." He'd been hooked from the first day he saw her, he just hadn't realized that the feeling was mutual. "Didn't you hear what I said about you being sexy? I've wanted you since day one. Make no mistakes about that. And the more I get to know you, the more I want you. But maybe it's the moon that's bringing us together, that's helping us to admit it."

Stan waited, but she didn't deny wanting him, and something strangely close to anxiety uncoiled and relaxed in his chest.

Yet her lack of a denial wasn't enough. He squeezed her fingers. "Tell me you want me, Jenna," he commanded. "Say it."

Marylou chose that inauspicious moment to come bebopping back to the table. "You guys ready for your pie?" She eyed Jenna's uneaten food and raised an eyebrow. "You don't like the chicken salad?"

"Oh, uh . . ." Flushed, Jenna picked up her croissant. "It's wonderful, I've just . . ."

Swallowing his curse, Stan said, "Give us ten more minutes, Marylou, then bring two slices of pie and two coffees."

Jenna protested. "I'll need to get back to the store soon."

"I locked up." Stan pulled her keys from his pocket and slid them across the table. "The reporter's long gone. The bookstore is safe." He pressed his feet farther under the booth, letting his calves brush hers. "Stay for pie."

Marylou giggled. "Yeah, Jenna. Live a little. Stay for pie."

Giggling got on Stan's nerves, but the girl was a good sort and a hard worker, so Stan winked at her and said, "Maybe seeing it will convince her."

"Right." Again, Marylou hurried off.

Glancing at her watch, Jenna said, "I suppose I can stay a little longer. I haven't even been gone a half hour."

Stan just waited.

With slender fingers, Jenna smoothed her hair, glanced at him and away, and finally drew a deep breath. He could feel her working up her nerve, and it was both endearing and a gigantic turn-on.

"Yes, I want you." Before Stan could recover from that awesome declaration, she added with earnest sincerity and an appalling lack of deception, "I have since the first day I met you."

"You never let on."

"I didn't think there was any reason to." In explanation, she said, "If you think I'm attractive . . . well, it's nothing compared to what I think about you. It's probably safe to say you're the sexiest man I've ever laid eyes on. Of course, every woman in town thinks so, so I'm sure you're used to hearing that."

"No," Stan growled, floored with how her announcement affected him. "I'm damn well not used to it at all. But it wouldn't matter anyway, because you're not every other woman in town. You're special—to me, and to everyone who meets you."

Shrugging that off, she sipped at her drink and nibbled on her sandwich. Again Stan waited, sensing her efforts to sort things out, to decipher both his feelings and her own. Picking up a pickle slice, she whispered, "Are we going to have an affair, Stan?"

For some reason, he didn't like her wording. An affair indicated a noncommittal relationship, and damn it, Jenna was the type of woman a man settled down with. She was every man's fantasy, proper on the outside, torrid on the inside. He wanted to know both sides better.

"I'm going to take you and your son out on the boat tonight. If Ryan wants, he can do some tubing. Or just swim in the cove. We'll talk. Maybe grab dinner somewhere. And later, when Ryan gets ready for bed, I'm going to kiss you again—probably do more than kiss you."

Alarm skittered through her. "Oh, but—"

"Jenna," he said, cutting off her objection, "I understand your privacy is limited. Your kids are a big part of your life, and that's how it should be. Know that I'd never make things awkward with them."

Jenna watched him with longing on her face as well as in her heart. She craved the special bond between a man and a woman, but her kids came first, and Stan appreciated that. Even if he hadn't read it in her head, he'd have said and done the same things. He was sure of it.

How hard would it be for a woman with children to develop any sort of intimacy with a man? Was that why she'd never dated, because it was just too complicated? Well, he wasn't a bastard who'd ever make her choose or pressure her into an uncomfortable situation.

"Later," Stan added, wanting her to have no misunderstandings on his intentions, "when we can find some private time so you can relax and enjoy every single second, I intend to make love to you."

The pickle slice slipped from her lax fingers and landed half on the plate, half on the tabletop.

"You'll like what I do to you, Jenna. I'll make sure of it."

Her head moved in a dazed nod of acknowledgment. "I believe you." But the images in her head weren't of him touching her. Just the opposite.

Her sexual imagination played for him like a porn video, and he was the recipient of every hot, wet kiss, every lick and gentle suck and firm stroke. Jesus, the woman had a great knack for covering the details.

On the ragged edge, glad the booth hid his arousal, Stan leaned forward again. "I'm not a kid, Jenna, after a quick tumble and instant gratification. Should I tell you what I want?"

The word, *"Yes,"* floated out on a breath from between her parted lips.

"I want a woman who isn't shy in the sack. A woman who'll let me make her feel good without hiding under the sheets or turning out the lights." And then, pushing her, he said, "I want a woman who wants me the same way. Who enjoys getting naked and sweaty, fucking, sucking, with no taboos as long as we both enjoy it."

Oh, yeah, Jenna was that woman. Just hearing him say it had her primed and ready and squirming in her seat.

"I want a woman," Stan added, knowing how his words would hit her, "who insists on a screaming orgasm every time."

Out of the corner of his eye, Stan saw Marylou approaching. The girl's timing couldn't be worse, what with Jenna flushed, soft in all the right places, her eyes heavy, her nipples taut against her dress.

"Blow your nose," Stan told her, quickly handing her his paper napkin.

Some of the sensual haze faded from her darkened eyes. "Excuse me?"

"Marylou's on her way, and honey, she'll take one look at you and think I've been getting you off under the table. Take the napkin, lower your face, and blow."

Jenna fumbled to do just that, her hands shaking, her breath coming too fast. She turned awkwardly away and lowered her face just as Marylou set the plates of peach pie on the table.

"You want me to take some of these dishes?" she asked, hoping for a reason to hang around.

"That's all right," Stan told her. "We'll be done shortly, and then you can get it all." He handed her a twenty, which more than covered the bill, and said, "Keep the change."

Stan knew she was saving for college, so he always gave her a huge tip. Marylou saw nothing amiss. "Thanks, Stan. See ya later, Jenna." And off she went.

Jenna's forehead hit the table. "Oh, God," she said, her voice muffled through the napkin still covering her face. "I'll never be able to come in here again."

Stan couldn't resist touching her hair. He glided his fingers over the warm silk, thinking of it loose and drifting over his body—his chest, his abdomen. His thighs.

He lifted her face. "So you're a hot woman with a sexual appetite? It's nobody's business—but mine." He brushed her lips with his thumb. "I'll keep our secret."

Jenna looked at her uneaten croissant and then at the piece of pie. She shook her head. "I can't eat."

"Yes, you can." Stan picked up her sandwich and handed it to her. "I'll help. For the rest of our meal, I'll make sure we talk about something else."

Jenna still struggled to get her breathing in order. "Like what?"

There were times when the nonglamorous job of

gardening came in handy. "A new low-maintenance rose shrub that'd look great in that bare spot at the side of The Nook. It's going to be a big seller, so you need to order it now."

Bemused, Jenna listened as he detailed the finer points of the flower, and within minutes, she'd consumed her lunch. Lust, Stan knew, worked up an appetite, so he enjoyed watching Jenna eat.

After he gave her an evening of mind-blowing sex, he'd feed her a four-course meal. She'd forget about her diet colas and aversion to pie and learn to appreciate her curves as much as he did.

But for now, he had to get back to work before he forgot his good intentions. He walked Jenna back to the bookstore, gave her a brief kiss on her delicious mouth, and told her he'd see her at five-thirty, at her house.

Hopefully the lake water would be cold. Because he had a feeling Jenna's more sumptuous thoughts were going to be hell on his libido, and on his control. Out on the boat, at least he'd be able to dunk himself in the water as necessary.

Three

When Jenna got home, rushing so she'd have time to refresh her hair and make-up before Stan showed up, she discovered her daughter still in the bathroom, primping for her date.

When she knocked, Rachelle said, "I'll be out in a few minutes."

Jenna sighed. "Hello to you, too, honey."

The door opened. "Hey, Mom. I thought you were Ryan."

They exchanged a quick hug, and Jenna asked, "Where is your brother?"

Wrinkling her nose, Rachelle said, "Out back, digging up worms in the hopes you'll take him fishing."

Because Rachelle still had hot rollers in her long blond hair and only half her make-up on, Jenna knew she'd be busy longer than the predicated "few minutes." Sharing one bathroom with an eighteen-year-old daughter wasn't easy.

But at the same time, Jenna knew she was going to miss her something awful when college started. "I'll let him know I'm home." Then she hesitated. "Where are you going tonight?"

"To the movies, and then the Old Orchard Inn for dinner."

Jenna frowned. The theater was located just outside of town, and that was bad enough, but the Old Orchard Inn was also a B&B—meaning there were beds right upstairs. At eighteen, Rachelle was on the verge of being a woman, but she was still Jenna's little girl. She didn't want to be smothering, but neither could she be cavalier. "You're going to be late?"

Rachelle shrugged. "Maybe midnight or so. Is that okay?"

"I suppose so." But as usual, Jenna felt the need to lecture. "Please just remember that as nice as Terrance seems, it's *you* I trust, not him. If he tries to buy you alcohol or if anything happens—"

Rachelle rolled her eyes and headed back into the bathroom. "I know, I know. I'll call a cab, or call you, or I'll hit him over the head. Don't worry, Mom. It's just dinner and a movie. I promise."

Don't worry? Dear God, Jenna well remembered the raging hormones of youth, how she and her husband had found plenty of inconspicuous places to explore their sexuality. They'd married young and had a wonderful marriage that had lasted until his death three years ago.

But Jenna wanted so much more for her daughter. . . .

"Mom!" Ryan came thundering into the house with all the delicacy of a herd of elephants. His untied, dirty sneakers brought him to a skidding halt on the hardwood floor right in front of Jenna. "I've dug up a bunch of night crawlers." He lifted a paper cup filled with dirt and wiggling worms. "Let's go fishing."

Hiding her revulsion, Jenna peered into the cup. "Wow, you do have a bunch. And they're so . . ." She swallowed hard. "Big."

"They're juicy," Ryan said. "The fish'll love 'em."

Jenna mentally prepared herself and said a quick prayer that her son would be happy with the change of plans. "I'm sure there'll be time for some fishing, but guess what? Stan Tucker offered to take us out on his boat."

Ryan's eyes widened. A heartbeat later, the bathroom door opened and Rachelle stuck her head out, her eyebrows raised in comical wonder.

Dear God, Jenna thought, she'd rendered both kids mute.

Forging on, she cleared her throat and tried to be casual when she felt nearly frantic instead. "I don't know what type of boat he has, but he said you could go tubing or swim in the cove. We can take the fishing gear along. Stan might like to fish, too."

Still, both children just stared at her. A deep breath, then another, and a bright smile. "You remember Stan, don't you?"

They each nodded. Ryan fought a grin. "For real? He'll take me tubing?"

"That's what he said."

Rachelle sent Jenna a sly look—and began teasing. In a soft, singsong voice, she said, "Mom's got a boyfriend, Mom's got a boyfriend . . ."

"Rachelle! Of course I don't. Stan is a—"

"Stud," Rachelle said. "And if he's not a boyfriend, then why are you turning bright red?" Laughing, Rachelle threw her arms around Jenna and squeezed. "I think it's cool."

"Me, too." Ryan was suddenly beside himself, jiggling, hopping, and antsy with anticipation. "When's he gettin' here?"

Jenna glanced at her watch and gulped. Time slipped by far too fast. "In about ten minutes."

"*Mom.*" Rachelle pulled her into the bathroom. "For heaven's sake. Why didn't you say something! It's all

yours. I'll finish up in my room." Hands flying, she un-
plugged her rollers, grabbed no less than three hair-
brushes and her assortment of make-up, and said, "Don't
just stand there, Mom. Do something with yourself.
Change into your bathing suit and that really cute cover-
up you have. And let your hair loose. The wind from
the boat will tear it out of the clip anyway."

Rachelle closed the door before Jenna could think
of a single thing to say, but she heard her daughter give
rapid orders to Ryan. "Now, behave yourself, squirt.
Don't be a toad, okay? Show Mr. Tucker your best side.
Don't embarrass Mom—"

Their voices faded as Rachelle dragged Ryan and
his worms down the hall, listing off all the things he
shouldn't do.

Jenna stared at herself in the mirror. Oh, God, she
was still red-faced. But not for the reason Rachelle assumed. She didn't suffer embarrassment so much as
unbridled eagerness. She'd turn forty soon. She was a
middle-aged widow, a mother of two children, one a
grown daughter. She owned her own business.

But at the moment, she felt like a giddy teenager on
her first date.

Jenna put her hands to her warm cheeks and sur-
veyed her appearance. Yes, definitely a mess. No way
would she wear a bathing suit—the very idea of showing so much skin to Stan left her mortified. The years,
and two births, had not been kind to her body. Any man
who hadn't seen her before she lost her figure sure
wasn't going to see her now, at least, not so soon.

If, as Stan said, they eventually made love . . . yes.
She craved his description of unrestrained, bold lovemaking. Jenna sighed. Then, and only then, she'd let
him look all he wanted. After all, if he was looking,
she'd get to look, too. And Stan Tucker was a definite
feast for the eyes.

* * *

Stan arrived five minutes early. The hazy sun and low ninety-degree temps had him wearing reflective sunglasses and casual khaki shorts with a mostly un-buttoned white cotton shirt. He'd showered, shaved, slapped on a spicy fragrance, brushed his teeth, combed his hair—and generally spiffed up as much as a gardener in the midst of a small town during a heat wave could.

He parked his sporty red SUV in Jenna's drive and got out, peering at her tidy ranch-style home with a critical eye. Updated landscaping would improve the looks of the house a lot, not to mention the trim could use a fresh coat of paint.

He was considering that when he saw the small, compact body bounce off the porch swing and stand at the top step, hands on hips, eyes squinted from the sun-shine. He seemed to be restraining himself with great effort.

Stan couldn't quite tell if Jenna's son wanted to challenge him or welcome him with berserk joy.

Joy won out. He leaped off the steps and came dash-ing across the lawn, bubbling over with enthusiasm. "Mom said you were coming."

Stan smiled, amused at the boundless energy vibrat-ing from the boy. He opened his mind to him and then wished he hadn't. Ryan still missed his father terribly, and a giant void existed inside him. He was so hungry for a father figure that Stan put a hand to his chest, rub-bing at the ache of a broken heart.

"That's right," Stan said. "Boating alone is no fun, so I'm hoping you're game."

"You bet I am!" Ryan leaned around him to see his SUV. "Where's yer boat?"

"I keep it docked at the lake."

"We used to have a boat. But Mom sold it." His face scrunched up. "Cuz of my dad dying and everything."

"You haven't been boating since?"

Skinny shoulders lifted in a shrug. "I go with friends sometimes. But Mom likes to worry, and sometimes she doesn't let me go."

A smile tugged at Stan's mouth. He touched the boy's head and started him toward the house. "It's a mother's sacred job to worry, and I bet your mother is good at anything she does—including worrying."

"Yeah, she's real good at it."

His long face got Stan to chuckling. "Speaking of your mom, is she ready?"

"I dunno. She was runnin' around, grabbin' clothes and changin' clothes and complainin' about her hair and—"

"Ryan." That stern admonishment came from a younger version of Jenna poised in the doorway. Rachelle pasted on a friendly smile. "Hello, Mr. Tucker."

Stan looked her over and knew poor Jenna must do most of her worrying about her daughter. The girl was a real looker and, from what he remembered, smart to boot. The little dress she wore would make any lad with hormones go nuts. It was stylish, but it also accented her figure a bit more than any protective, father-aged man would like.

"Rachelle." If she were his daughter, he'd dress her in a potato sack—but he hid that thought with a cordial smile. "Call me Stan."

"All right, Stan." Her return smile was pretty and welcoming and made Stan want to protect her from the world. "Mom's almost ready. You want to come in for iced tea? I just made it fresh."

"Hey! I was gonna show him where I dug up most of my worms," Ryan protested.

Rachelle's face tightened. "Stan might not want to look at worms, Ryan." She bestowed another beatific smile on Stan. "Come on in out of that heat. It's much cooler inside."

It didn't require a mind reader to know that Rachelle wanted to make a good impression. She sensed that her mother wasn't completely happy on her own and maybe saw him as a step in the right direction. Yet it was so much more than that. Both Rachelle's and Ryan's neediness clawed at him, destroying his composure. The love they felt for Jenna was overpowering, but with that love was an almost desperate craving for a return of things lost—a happy home with two parents, a more flexible budget, family vacations.

Jenna tried to fill the gap in their lives, but she could only do so much. Ryan missed the male camaraderie that only another guy could supply. And Rachelle missed her father's teasing protectiveness and the smell of his aftershave, the way he lifted her off her feet when he hugged her. She missed knowing her daddy was there, the backbone to their home, ready and able to defend them all.

Stan tried prodding her thoughts a little, to see if there were particular concerns on money, but he wasn't skilled enough to separate the many emotions swirling between the two kids. And truthfully, his own emotions were getting in the way now, because he cared—about both of them, and about their mom.

Wanting to please both kids, he pulled off his sunglasses and gave his most charming smile to Rachelle. "If you could pour me the tea—with plenty of ice, please—both Ryan and I'll be right in. Just give me two minutes to see this worm farm he's discovered. Okay?"

Rachelle shot her brother a look of disgust, but accepted the compromise. "I'll be in the kitchen. Just come in the back door."

Ryan grabbed Stan's hand and tugged. "It's this way. C'mon. I found about a gazillion of them under one rock. My cup wasn't big enough for them all, so I left some so that next time I fish, I can get 'em. Mom said you might let me fish off your boat. Can I bring my rod and reel?"

Ryan didn't wait for an answer. He didn't even draw a breath.

"It's one my dad bought me and it's really cool, like for an expert fisherman or something. Dad said I had all the makings of a professional. But that was three years ago, so I'm rusty now. Me and Dad used to fish in the mornin's, when the fish were really bitin' and you could fill the boat up with enough bass for dinner."

The rambling monologue brought them through the backyard and all the way to the perimeter where the woods bordered. Jenna had a spacious lot with plenty of room for kids to play. He liked it.

"Of course you can fish," Stan told Ryan. "We'll go back in the cove where the big ones hang out."

"Seriously?"

Stan laughed. "You haven't fished in three years?"

"Sure I have. Mom takes me sometimes when she doesn't have to work. But she works lots, and she doesn't know much about fishing anyway, so she doesn't like for me to cast the rod." In a stage whisper, Ryan said, "I got a lure caught in her hair once. So now we just take reg'lar poles. She'll hand me worms, but she won't put them on a hook or nothing like that. I can tell she don't really like fishing too much."

"You're obviously an astute young man."

"What's astute?"

"It means you're already good at reading women. Trust me, it'll come in handy someday." Stan crouched down with interest when Ryan used all his meager strength to lift a heavy rock.

"You see 'em?" Ryan asked, his voice strained as he struggled with the stone.

"I sure do. You were smart to leave some here. They'll probably just get bigger, so next time you fish, imagine what they'll look like."

"Wow." Ryan dropped the rock to the side, leaving the worms exposed. "I hadn't thought of that."

"They'll have nothing to do but eat and grow."

"They don't have mouths. How can they eat?"

Stan turned to Ryan. "You're kidding, right? Of course they have mouths. Look at this one. He's grinning at you."

Ryan chuckled. "Is not."

Stan lifted one long, squirming worm and explained. "These first few segments hold the brain, hearts, and breathing organs. Did you know that a worm has five pairs of hearts?"

"Wow."

Stan nodded. "The rest of the inside of an earthworm is filled with the intestines, which digest its food."

"So all of that is belly?"

"Close enough. Earthworms eat soil and the organic material in it—like insect parts and bacteria."

"Gross."

"Right here's the mouth, but it's covered by a flap called the prostomium, which helps the earthworm sense light and vibrations, so it can find its way around. Tiny bristles, called setae, are on most of the earthworm's body."

Ryan gave him a skeptical look. "How do you know that's the mouth end and not the butt end?"

"Simple. This is the end he led with when he was crawling. Now, wouldn't you crawl head first, instead of butt first?"

Ryan grinned. "Yeah, I would."

"All these worms mean you have good earth here.

They aerate it and make the soil richer with their castings."

"What are castings?"

Grinning, thoroughly enjoying himself, Stan said in a whisper, "Poo."

Ryan started laughing—and suddenly Stan felt it, simple happiness, gratitude, and overwhelming tenderness. So much tenderness he felt wrapped in it, lending him a peace he hadn't experienced in years. He turned his head and smiled at Jenna, standing behind him.

She wore a beige tank top and matching capris, with an oversized mesh tunic over the top. A floppy-brimmed straw hat shielded her face from the sun. Her long hair hung free to her shoulders. She looked . . . fabulous. Comfortable. Casual. *Sexy.*

And she had her heart in her eyes.

Stan narrowed his gaze on her face. "Have you been eavesdropping on our worm lessons?"

Her mouth curled, and more tenderness blanketed around Stan. "Fascinating stuff," she teased. "How could I resist?"

Stan's heart wanted to crumble. Witnessing her son's happiness had given her great joy and had shifted her emotions for him from purely sexual to so much more.

Such a simple thing—sharing laughter with her son. And now she was soft and emotional, even tearful.

He stood, stepped closer to her, and whispered, "Hi," then kissed her on the cheek.

Ryan stared wide-eyed.

So she'd understand, he said, "Ryan was entertaining me while you finished getting ready." Without really thinking about it, he sought out the little boy, his palm to the top of Ryan's sun-warmed hair. "If it's okay with you, I'd like to ask Ryan to go fishing with me some morning. He tells me that's how it's done, and being he's an expert, I'm sure I could learn a thing or two."

With Ryan's loud squeal of excitement, Jenna's lips quivered. "He'd love that," she whispered with tearful gratitude that cut Stan like a sharp knife.

Damn, he wanted this woman to be happy, all the time, every second of the day. She deserved that, and by God, he'd see to it. Somehow.

He brushed her cheek with his thumb. "Me, too."

Blinking away the tears, she said, "Ryan, let's go get washed up and let Stan drink his tea, so we can get to the lake before it gets any later."

Stan put his right arm around Jenna's waist and his left hand on Ryan's bony shoulder. Together, like a family, they crossed the grassy lawn to the back door of her house.

Rachelle waited in the doorway, watching them all with a sort of earnest serenity. Stan wanted to close them all out, just to regain his balance, but he couldn't. It seemed intrusive, knowing what was in their hearts, but at the same time, he felt compelled to know even more, to understand them so he could get a toehold into their lives.

A flicker of concern struck him, and he found himself asking Rachelle about her plans for college as they entered the kitchen. Tea waited on the table, but he and Ryan washed their hands first. Over his shoulder, Stan glanced at Rachelle.

She didn't quite meet his gaze. "I'm going to a state school here."

The way she said that told him volumes. "What do you want to study?" He took a seat next to Jenna and sipped his tea. "This is good, Rachelle, thanks."

"You're welcome." She laced her fingers together over her middle. "Don't laugh, but I'll be an art major."

"Now, why would I laugh at that?" Her self-conscious shrug prompted him to dig further. "What type of art?"

"Graphic design. I want to do ad layouts."

Lori Foster

Ryan said, "Like on cereal boxes."

Rolling her eyes, Rachelle said, "Maybe some cereal boxes."

Stan settled back in his seat. He had a feeling he already knew the answer, but he asked it anyway. "You doing the state school because you want to be close to home, or did you decide it was the best choice?"

Rachelle darted a glance at her mother. "I want to be close to home."

Jenna reached for Rachelle's hand and gave it a squeeze. "Actually, since she was fourteen, she's had her heart set on SCAD—Savannah College of Art and Design. Now, we just can't afford it."

"And she don't wanna leave me," Ryan boasted.

Half laughing, Rachelle mussed his hair. "You would be missed, rat."

True enough, Stan realized. Rachelle wanted to be close at hand to help her mother out with Ryan. A little awed, he acknowledged what an amazing young lady she was. "I have a feeling that whatever college you choose, you'll do great." But in his heart, Stan wanted her to have the college of her choice, not be limited by funds and responsibilities.

He wondered if he could manage that somehow. God knew he had more money than his simple lifestyle required. One look at Jenna, and he knew she was far too proud to take a handout.

Ryan guzzled his tea, fed up with idle chitchat when swimming, boating and fishing awaited. Nothing more was said on colleges. Stan assured Jenna he had everything on the boat that they'd need—life preservers, a tube and ski rope, sunscreen and towels.

Rachelle's date showed up the same time they were ready to leave. Stan took one look at the young man and wanted to forbid the date. Dumb. But damn it, he knew exactly what both kids were planning, and he felt like a peeping Tom. Quickly, he blocked the intimate thoughts, but he couldn't remove the warning scowl from his face when he looked at Terrance.

Before they drove off, Jenna again cautioned her daughter to be careful and made her promise she'd call if she was later than midnight.

On the way to the lake, Jenna was quiet, but then Ryan talked nonstop, leaving little room for adult conversation. Stan didn't mind. He enjoyed Ryan's chatter, and he sensed the peacefulness of Jenna's mood. She simply enjoyed the ride and her son's giddiness.

Ryan loved Stan's SUV and asked permission to touch every single button and knob. Stan figured if he liked the car, he'd go bonkers over his Stingray 220DR deck boat that looked a lot like a pontoon on steroids. When Ryan spotted the boat, Stan wasn't disappointed with his reaction.

He'd nearly run to the dock when Jenna caught him and hauled him back. Her rules required a life preserver before Ryan got anywhere near the murky lake water.

Golden Lake had one small station to gas up your boat and a goodie shack that sold everything from ice cream to beer to bait. Stan loaded up on snacks, premade sandwiches, and bought plenty of colas to stow in the ice chest beneath the fresh water sink in the cabin.

The rest of the evening went by in a blur for Stan. He'd never dated a woman with kids, and his ex-wife hadn't wanted any. Ryan on water was a revelation. He went tubing for what seemed like forever, never tiring, loving the big waves and the sun and the cold spray of water from the boat. Since Jenna enjoyed it, too, and he enjoyed watching her, Stan had no complaints.

Afterward, he dropped anchor in the mossy cove. Jenna and Ryan had put on sunscreen earlier, but they needed a fresh application. When she finished with her son, Stan took the bottle from her hands.

"Let me."

She glanced at Ryan, who sat on the back of the boat, his feet braced on the ladder, his rod cast out near the shore. When her gaze came back to Stan, it was hotter than the evening sun. "All right."

She had already removed her tunic, and Stan eyed her golden shoulders and collarbone, and the way the tank top hugged her breasts. Unless he missed his guess, she wasn't wearing a bra. With the summer heat, it made sense to wear as little as possible, but he'd never seen her without a bra. His palms itched to hold her, to feel the shape and weight of her breasts, to explore her nipples . . .

Swallowing a groan, he poured a small amount of sunscreen into his palms and said, "Lift your hair."

She did so slowly, and it was such a provocative pose that Stan couldn't help but think of sexual things. As he smoothed the sunscreen onto her neck, shoulders, and upper chest, she dropped her hair, and her eyes closed.

If her son weren't sitting a few feet away, singing off key to the Beach Boys in the CD player, he'd show Jenna just how close to reality her imagination had gotten.

But her son was near, and that meant Stan had to behave himself, no matter how hard behaving might be.

Hard being the operative word.

With an apologetic smile, Stan kissed the tip of her nose and went over the side of the boat into the icy water.

The splash drew Ryan's attention, and he quickly reeled in his line so he could swim, too. The water cooled Stan's ardor, but nothing could appease the growing ache in his heart—except having Jenna for his own.

Permanently.

Four

After a long swim, Ryan took turns eating and fishing, which meant Jenna had her work cut out for her trying to keep worm slime off his hands and out of the pretzel bag. The sink got more use in one day than it ever had in the rest of the time Stan had owned the boat. Ryan claimed they had everything they needed, so they never had to go back.

Jenna told him they at least had to be home when Rachelle returned from her date. She kept her cell phone out and available so she wouldn't miss a call, and Stan wondered if she wasn't maybe more aware of Terrance's intentions than he'd first assumed.

After catching several fish that he threw back for being too small, Stan put away his rod and folded out the backseats. When opened, they supplied the space equivalent to a bed. Shirtless, wearing only his still damp shorts, he settled into the corner with an icy cola and stretched out his legs to watch Jenna play mom.

By the time Ryan began to wind down, the sun had sunk low in the sky, turning everything around it crimson red. Wearing trunks, a life preserver, and a towel, Ryan half lounged in the bow seats, his hair tangled from sun, wind, and water, his hands limp on the fishing rod.

The CD player sent music over the surface of the lake. Somewhere off in the distance, a cow lowed. Along the shore, frogs croaked. Back in the cove, away from the power boats and jet skis, it was peaceful. And . . . comforting.

As Ryan nodded off, Jenna slid the pole from his hand and reeled it in. She rolled up a towel to use for a pillow and eased Ryan to his side. He didn't awaken.

"Amazing." Stan watched the boy sleep and shook his head. The rocking of the boat lulled him, too, but he couldn't remember a time when he'd ever, not even as a kid, fallen asleep so easily.

"He sleeps like a baby," Jenna told him, taking the seat facing Stan, her bare feet curled under her, her hair dancing in the breeze. She closed her eyes and sighed. "Thank you, Stan. This has been wonderful. I'd forgotten just how relaxing the water can be, how all your worries just seem to disappear."

His gaze trained on her serene features, Stan asked, "What worries do you have, Jenna?"

"The same as any other mother, I suppose." Her eyes stayed closed, and her voice whispered past her smiling mouth. "Luckily, I've been blessed with really terrific kids."

Stan figured that had more to do with her than anything else. "You're a terrific mom."

"I try." The smile faded and she sighed again. "I only want them to be happy. It's not always easy. But Stan?" Her lashes lifted and she looked directly at him, inadvertently sharing with him everything she felt, everything that was near and dear in her heart. "Thank you for today. It's the most fun Ryan's had in ages."

A lump the size of a grapefruit lodged in Stan's throat. "For me, too."

She didn't believe him. She thought he wanted to get laid and was doing what he thought necessary to make it happen. Not a nice opinion of him, but given his colorful past and even his more current public lifestyle, Stan couldn't really blame her.

But he could convince her otherwise. Stan patted the seat beside him. "Come here, woman, and let me kiss you."

Rather than refuse him, she glanced at Ryan. "He's still sleeping."

Stan nodded. "Yeah, I know."

Her bottom lip got caught in her teeth. Feeling guilty, then determined, she glanced again at Ryan before sliding out of the seat and over next to Stan. He put his arm around her and tugged her into his side. Even with the setting sun, the temperatures still hung in the upper eighties, but a soft breeze stirred the air.

Eyes searching, Jenna peered up into his face—and Stan was lost.

He cupped her cheek and gently touched his mouth to hers. Her dewy skin held the fragrance of the wind and the lake—and woman, an aphrodisiac so powerful that Stan had to struggle to keep himself in check. He wanted to absorb her, to nuzzle into all her dark, damp places and fill himself with the luscious scent of her.

Instead, he contented himself with tasting her mouth, keeping things easy and gentle, when inside, his blood raged and his heart thundered. He wanted her, more than he'd ever wanted any other woman.

Maybe more than he'd ever wanted anything else in his life.

He had to start sharing some truths.

Against her lips, he murmured, "Even two days from a full moon, the moon can be ninety-seven percent illuminated. Did you know that?"

Confused, laughing a little, Jenna pulled back. "No, I

had no idea." She leaned into him again, trying to deepen the kiss.

Stan accepted the invitation of her parted lips, dipping his tongue inside, still gentle, exploring with a leisureliness that belied the bulge in his shorts and the tightness of his muscles.

When her breath grew choppy and her hands clutched at him, Stan ended the kiss and glanced at Ryan. The boy snored, affording him more opportunity to ease her into the idea of his gift.

With his fingertips exploring the delicate texture of her cheekbone, Stan whispered, "Although Full Moon happens every month at a specific date and time, it seems full for several nights in a row. If the sky's clear, the effect can be the same."

"What effect?"

He touched his mouth to her bottom lip, licked, sucked carefully. "Any that might occur," he explained. "Some people feel unsettled, some get heightened emotions. There are suicides and, on the opposite scale, a lot of lovemaking."

"I hope you're thinking more of the latter."

Smiling, Stan continued to educate her. The more she knew, the easier it'd be for her to accept when he told her everything. And he would tell her. She had a right to know that he could read her thoughts. It was the worst invasion of privacy, but it was also something he couldn't always control.

His ex-wife had hated it, but then, she'd had secrets better left concealed. He already knew Jenna would never cheat. She was as loyal, as moral, as any person he'd ever met. If she took a vow, she'd mean it—till death do us part.

The thought excited him more, because he wanted her as his own, now and forever. He wanted more days like today, with better nights to follow. He wanted it all.

"The percentage of the moon's disk that's illuminated changes slowly around the time of Full Moon, so most people won't notice the difference. Even two days from Full Moon, people can still be suffering the Lunar Effect."

Her small hand came up to his jaw, her brow drawn in a slight frown. "Stan, I don't know what you're talking about."

"You've been thinking about me a lot lately. Sexually explicit thoughts."

She ducked her face and touched her fingertips to his chest hair. "Yes."

"Have you always?"

One shoulder lifted. "I've always been aware of you. I've always been attracted to you. And, yes, I've thought of you that way plenty of times."

He felt her thoughts skittering this way and that, and said, "But?"

"But lately, I don't know. It's been different. Stronger. Even . . . powerful. I thought maybe it was because I'm turning forty soon." Her smile went crooked, creating that small dimple he adored. "Maybe old age is catching up with me, turning me into a lech."

The admission made her uneasy, leaving her embarrassed and uncertain. Stan didn't want her to ever be ashamed of her sexuality. He slid his hand under her hair, kneading her nape, turning her face up to his. "There's nothing wrong with wanting me, Jenna." And with grave sincerity, "For a night, or for more than a night."

He posed it as a statement—but waited to see how she'd react, where her personal thoughts would take her.

His chest expanded on a deep breath, and relief filled him. Yeah, Jenna wanted him forever, never mind that she considered that a farfetched fantasy. He could get around that, but he didn't want to pressure her for things she didn't want.

She wanted him, and he'd show her just how possible that could be.

To better his odds of winning her over, Stan absorbed every nuance of her feelings for him. Her logical mind shied away from the idea of pinning him down, because she didn't think he could be satisfied with one woman. She'd had fidelity and loyalty and commitment from her first husband, and that's what she wanted again.

She would never settle for less—but then, neither would he.

Stan didn't like it that she saw him as a playboy, a mature man with too much money, too much recognition, and too many women at his disposal. True, he'd spent a few years wallowing in the celebrity status of his newfound popularity. And women had come easy over the years. But that didn't mean he wanted to remain a bachelor forever.

His healthy bank account could be an asset to her, a way to send Rachelle to the college of her choice, enough money to reinstate the missed family vacations, the boat, the comfort of financial security.

But Jenna wouldn't care about the benefits he could bring if she thought she couldn't trust him. Stan cursed softly, making Jenna press back in puzzlement. "What is it?" she asked.

"Can we talk seriously for a few minutes?"

She stared at him, looked at her hand on his chest, then at his mouth. She blinked. "Sure, Stan. Talking is just what I had in mind."

Laughing, he pulled her closer so that her cheek nestled on his shoulder. It felt good to hold her. Almost as nice as kissing her. "Don't be a tease, woman. You know damn good and well you weren't going to do anything with Ryan so close."

"Of course I wouldn't. But a few more kisses would have been nice."

His hand opened on her waist, and he squeezed. She was rounded in all the right places, full of curves and soft like a woman should be. He couldn't wait to feel her under him, all that softness cushioning his harder frame.

Stan swallowed a growl, knowing he had to keep on track. "I'll kiss you silly tonight," he promised in a raw, dark whisper, "after you tuck Ryan into bed."

Her thoughts were too naked, too vulnerable and anxious, and Stan felt like a bastard for being privy to them. But he had to make her understand that he wasn't a cheat, that ten easy women meant nothing compared to a woman he could love.

Nothing meant more to him than Jenna did.

She was close, wanting him, confused by her feelings but determined to do what was right for her children and for herself. She didn't want her kids hurt, and she feared that involving him in their lives, only to say goodbye when he grew bored and left, would leave her kids unhappy.

Stan listened to the knocking of his heart, but that became a primal beat, urging him on, heightening his awareness of her as a gentle woman, sexy as hell and damp in all the right places. Her thoughts veered, picturing him naked, her hands all over him, her mouth following . . .

Abruptly, Stan pushed away from her. Bending forward, his elbows on his knees, he tapped his fisted hands against his chin. She tortured him without even knowing it.

Not looking at Jenna, determined to get her mind off sex so he could think straight, he asked, "How much do you know about my past?"

Her confusion warred with her instinctive need to offer comfort. "I know what the press has shared." Her hand touched his back, resting on his shoulder blade. "I know that you got in trouble a few times when you were younger."

Feeling dangerous, Stan twisted to face her. "I've been convicted of assault and battery."

Her fingers stilled. "You beat someone up?"

"The creep was going to jump a guy we worked with. He and his girlfriend had broken up, and she'd chosen this other guy . . ." Stan ran a hand through his hair. "He was going to wait for him by his car one night and use a tire iron on him. So I stopped him."

Her comforting fingers again drifted over his back. "And they convicted you for that?"

Stan could understand her astonishment. Under normal circumstances, he'd be considered a hero.

Only there was nothing normal about the way he got his information.

"I got a year's suspended sentence."

"But . . ."

"No one knew what he intended, Jenna, and I couldn't prove it." Stan turned completely to face her until their knees touched. He clasped her wrist. "My wife cheated on me. That's why I divorced her."

His jump in topic left her floundering, but her concern and caring remained a live thing, drowning out her puzzlement at his current mood. "Stan, I'm so sorry. I didn't know that."

"I wanted what you had, Jenna. Trust, love, fidelity. That's not what I got. Within a month, she'd gone bed hopping."

Her heart was soft and open to him, and that left her exposed. But she was the type of woman who always cared deeply about others, too much to protect herself. "How did you find out?"

She thought he'd walked in on the sordid scene and she hurt for him. The truth was worse. Stan pulled away from her and looked up at the sky. This was harder than he'd ever imagined. "The moon will be out soon."

More confusion, then impatience. "I don't understand this fixation you have about the moon. It's like you're trying to tell me something—or maybe several things—but you're not being clear."

"I know." He felt like a damn coward but decided to take her home before telling her. Ryan could awaken any minute, interrupting them. But once she had him tucked into bed, Stan would be in a better position.

If his truths shocked her too much, he could always take advantage of her sexual attraction to bring her back to him. No, he wouldn't make love to her with her kids in range, but he could kiss her silly, heat her up with a touch, make whispered, sensual promises that would leave her desperate to accept him, on any level.

"It's getting late. We should be heading back."

Her pride kept her from pushing him. Back going straight, chin lifting, Jenna said, "All right. Fine. If that's what you want."

He'd hurt her, when that was the last thing he wanted to do. But he'd make it up to her. After he talked her around her disbelief, he'd prove to her that he could be everything she wanted in a man, and more.

Turning on the boat lights both stern and aft lent a mellow glow to the cabin. The sun had long since sunk behind the hills, leaving the sky dark with shades of deep lavender and gray. A few stars appeared, surrounding the moon that hung like a fat crystal ball, taunting him.

Jenna remained oblivious to it all as she struggled to understand what had happened. Stan finished lifting the anchor, then glanced at her and cursed softly. She thought he'd led her on. She thought he'd changed his mind about wanting her.

He pulled her resisting body close, until her breasts were against his chest and their heartbeats mingled.

"Jenna," he said, and pressed a kiss to her forehead, to her chin, and finally on her pursed mouth. "It's a lot to ask, but do you think you could trust me just a little longer?"

"What does trust have to do with it?"

He kneaded her shoulders and put his forehead to hers. "Everything. It has everything to do with it. We'll talk when you've got Ryan in bed. Okay?"

"I won't sleep with you at my house."

She sounded so prudish, Stan smiled. "I already know that, but for the record, I wouldn't ask you to." He smoothed his thumb over her chin. "I have scruples, too, you know. And I like your kids. I wouldn't do anything to upset them."

She only half believed him. "Well . . . all right, then."

"Good." Half was better than not at all. "Let's get home." The sooner he got this over with, the sooner he could have her in his bed. He glanced at Ryan. "Want me to move him back here?"

Curled on the padded bow seats, Ryan looked comfortable and down for the count. He didn't awaken even when the engine roared to life.

"I'll keep an eye on him." Jenna pulled on her overtunic, settled in the passenger seat beside Stan, and looked over the calm surface of the lake. "Rachelle was always a light sleeper, like me. But Ryan is like his dad. A herd of stampeding buffalo wouldn't wake him. He'll probably sleep straight through the night."

And with a little luck, Stan thought, Jenna would accept his odd relationship with the moon. Because one way or another, she'd have to accept him. Now that he knew so much about her, he knew she was meant to be his.

Convincing her would be the trick.

Five

Rachelle pulled up about the same time that Stan parked his SUV in the drive. Dividing her attention between Stan's strange behavior, her sleeping son, and the fact that her daughter just left Terrance's car with the slamming of his car door and without a farewell kiss, Jenna automatically prioritized.

She opened her car door and stepped out. The full moon filled the yard with light, making the porch lamp unnecessary. "Rachelle? Is everything okay?"

Already on her way toward them, Rachelle ignored how Terrance sped away. "I'm great," she said, with the false brightness Jenna recognized as anger. "Fine, perfect, peachy-keen."

Jenna had a very bad feeling about this. "What happened?"

Suddenly Stan was beside her. His hands landed on her shoulders and he pulled her back into his chest. "Nothing that Rachelle couldn't handle, isn't that right, Rachelle?"

Jenna saw her daughter's mouth twist in a wry smile. "If you call bashing the little weasel over the head handling it, then yeah, I handled it." Rachelle lifted her wrist and checked out the illuminated face of her watch. "Hey, it's only ten-thirty. I thought you guys would hang out longer."

An obvious attempt to change the subject, but Jenna wasn't ready to let it go. "Rachelle . . ."

Again, Stan squeezed her shoulders, almost as if to convince her to put off her questions. She didn't want to, but perhaps Stan felt uncomfortable being privy to their family business.

He leaned down and whispered in her ear, "She'll talk when she's ready, honey. Give her a little time."

Indeed, Rachelle seemed determined to change the subject. She peered at the SUV and grinned. "The squirt's asleep?"

Stan said, "He snores like a trucker."

Laughing, Rachelle hefted her purse strap up to her shoulder and headed for the vehicle. "I'll take him in so you two can . . . visit more." After a wink to Stan that had Jenna blushing, Rachelle got Ryan on his feet, but his eyes remained closed.

"Want me to carry him in?" Stan offered.

"Thanks, but I've got it covered." Ryan was more a sleepwalker than a willing participant as Rachelle guided him up the porch and inside.

After one more quick smile and a suspiciously scheming look, she closed the door and the porch light went out. A little embarrassed, Jenna shook her head. Her daughter could use an ounce or so of subtlety.

"Don't worry about it," Stan said. "She's just showing that she likes me."

Of course she did, Jenna thought. Everything about Stan was likable, from his easy nature to his charming smile. But she sensed it was more than that for Rachelle, almost as if she felt something had been missing from their lives, and Stan could fix that.

It made her feel like a bad mother, as if she hadn't done the best she could for her kids.

In her own grief, had she neglected a portion of her children's needs? The last three years hadn't been easy for any of them, but she'd thought her kids were now happy and well adjusted. As a single parent, there were too many times when she couldn't be somewhere, couldn't do something . . .

"You're tense," Stan said. "Let's sit on the porch swing and talk."

Jenna nodded agreement, but at the same time, she worried over how quickly her kids had accepted Stan. What would they do when Stan stopped coming over? They'd be hurt for sure. Maybe she'd be smarter to end things now, before she slept with him . . .

"Come on." His tone grim, Stan slid his arm around her waist and urged her along the walkway.

Absently, her thoughts still jumbled, Jenna told him, "Today was wonderful, Stan. I haven't seen Ryan so excited in a very long time. Thank you."

"No thanks necessary. I enjoyed myself."

They reached the porch swing, and Jenna shook off her odd distraction. "I'm sorry. Maybe I should go in." If she sat down, he'd kiss her, and she'd forget everything else.

"Why?" He didn't look disappointed by her suggestion, so much as patient.

"I know my daughter," Jenna explained, "and something happened tonight. She might need to talk with me."

"Not yet." Stan pressed her into the swing and then crowded in close beside her. With one big foot, he gave the swing a push.

Under the porch roof, the moon's illumination couldn't quite penetrate, leaving them in heavy shadows. A sense of intimacy enveloped them, crowding out other, more restless thoughts.

Then Stan said, "Rachelle fancied herself in love with Terrance. Earlier, before she left, she considered sleeping with him."

Jenna jerked around to face him. "She *told* you that?"

"No." Stan's voice remained calm and even despite her disbelief. "She'd even had thoughts about marrying him some day. But tonight he moved too fast, pushing her, not being very nice."

Lost, Jenna stared at Stan, her gaze seeking in the darkness.

"The good news is that her eyes were opened to the type of guy he really is. The bad news is, she's hurt." He squeezed her shoulder. "But your daughter is smart, Jenna. She won't be seeing him anymore."

Everything inside Jenna went still. Stan acted as though he knew it all for fact, when that couldn't be. "What are you talking about, Stan? You can't possibly know what my daughter is thinking or feeling."

"I know." Stan stared down at his lap, then abruptly turned and pointed at the moon. "You see that, honey? A big, fat full moon, just hanging up there in the sky, lighting the yard like midday. And not just any full moon. This is the second full moon this month. A rarity. A blue moon."

A little spooked, Jenna turned her head and glanced up at the sky. The yard did seem unusually bright, and suddenly, the air settled, not even a leaf rustling.

A chill of alarm went up her spine.

"Don't get spooked," Stan told her. "But this is what I've been trying to tell you."

Jenna had nothing to say to that, so she remained quiet, waiting.

As if he knew her every thought, Stan smiled. "For some people, maybe for you, a full moon heightens emotions. It's not turning forty that made you think more about me. It's the moon. Obviously, for a blue moon, the effect would be exaggerated. It definitely is for me."

Jenna frowned. "Exaggerated how?"

His jaw worked. With his arm around her, her side pressed into his, Jenna felt his muscles tightening. "I was in trouble with juvy—juvenile hall—three times. All three times, I did things people couldn't understand. I jumped one kid, put myself in front of another, refused to let a girl ride her bike home . . ."

Awareness dawning, though it didn't make much sense, Jenna asked, "This all happened during a full moon?"

He gave one quick nod. "The guy I jumped was going to buy dope from some creeps, just to impress his girlfriend. After they tossed me in juvy, he did it anyway. And got in a shitload of trouble—just as I knew he would."

"Buying dope is never a good idea, Stan."

Rather than look at her, he stared straight ahead. "The guy I got in front of was going to challenge a bully who would have beat him up and humiliated him in front of everyone. That kid had enough troubles without adding more to his list."

Idly, almost as if he didn't realize it, Stan's fingertips teased over her shoulder, caressing, stroking—keeping her close.

In a faint voice, somehow tortured by memories, he whispered, "The girl had lost her mother. She was feeling suicidal. I know, because . . . I felt what she felt. I couldn't let her leave, knowing what she'd do. I caught hell for detaining her, but as a result, she got caught up in the same chaos that surrounded me. She got attention." He shrugged. "It helped." And with insistence, "At least she didn't kill herself."

The knocking of Jenna's heart made her tremble. She didn't move, not to pull away from Stan and not to move closer. "I think you need to just spell it out, Stan, whatever it is you want to tell me."

"You're right." After a deep breath, he faced her. His glittering gaze pierced the darkness, holding her captive. "From the time I was a kid, the moon heightened my ability to read other people's thoughts. When there's a blue moon, the thoughts are as clear as written text."

Jenna barely had time to assimilate what he'd said, to consider the ramifications of what he believed, when he cupped her face in his big hands.

"Jenna." He bent and kissed her forehead. "Don't be afraid of me, honey. And don't try to placate me. I know it's farfetched. Hell, my own parents thought I was mental. I can only tell you from experience that it's true."

"Stan." Jenna eased herself away—and he let her go. On her feet, she backed up one step, then two.

He watched her. "Think something, Jenna, other than the obvious." He didn't leave the swing. "I know you're worried about me, and about your kids. You want to help me even as you're wondering if I might be dangerous." He half laughed. "But then, anyone would know that just by the look on your face. Think of something else. Anything."

Dear God, Jenna mused. *For him, it's some warped game.*

"No game." He leaned forward, elbows on his knees. "Warped or otherwise. It's just the truth."

Her eyes widened. *Could he have . . . no.*

"Yes."

Her breath caught in her throat, strangling her.

Hands fisted, Jenna tried to think of something totally off the wall, but instead, she remembered the way he'd kissed her, how much she'd wanted him—

"I hope you still do," Stan whispered, pushing slowly to his feet. "Because I want you like hell."

"Oh, God," she said out loud.

"I'm sorry, baby. I don't mean to intrude on your privacy. It just happens. Sometimes I can block it out, but with you . . . the things you think just work their way in." With a cautious stride, he moved toward her. "Do you have any idea how hard today was on me? I knew every single time you thought about me."

"No."

"You pictured me naked. You thought about kissing me all over, and me doing the same to you. You thought about sex in a dozen different ways. Your visuals of my naked body are off a little. Hell, Jenna, I'm forty, not twenty-five."

Her mouth went dry.

"But I won't disappoint you." Another step brought him closer. "I'll fuck you as hard and fast as you want. I'll make love to you slow and easy. I'll kiss you from your eyebrows down to your knees—and I'll damn sure linger at all the best places in between."

"Stan, stop it."

"Like hell I will. Do you know what it's like for me, wanting you, already in love with you, and knowing you consider me incapable of commitment? To you, I'm a free-wheeling runaround. I'm a guy who'd be ideal for a fling, a stud to fuck a few times, but not good for much more."

"That's not true."

"No? You're willing to have an affair, but you don't want to love me."

Jenna gasped. Her stomach knotted and her chest hurt. Love him? She didn't want to, but—

As if sensing an advantage, he pressed forward. "Your kids like me, Jenna. They've both missed having a dad around. There's this huge empty hole left in their lives, a hole you've tried your best to fill, and God knows you've done an incredible job. But you're their mother and that's role enough."

Defiance became her only defense. "You're saying you want to play Dad?"

"No playing to it. You've got great kids, and they'd be easy to love."

"I need time to think." Never in a million years had Jenna expected so much to be dumped on her at once. Stan didn't want an affair. Did he mean he wanted forever?

"Damn right." He stood only a breath away, invading her space, heightening her awareness of him. "Tonight, tomorrow, and every day after. I want your kids. I want to make a home with you. I want family vacations and budgets and grocery shopping and trips to the school. Forget my damn past and the trumped-up reputation and the stupid borderline celebrity status. Just concentrate on how you feel with me."

Jenna shook her head. "Stan, this is . . . too much. Too over the top."

"You think I don't know that? Do you think it was easy reading my wife's mind and knowing she'd slept with other men? You think it's easy knowing how badly you want me, but also knowing you don't trust me?" He moved against her, pulling her close. His gaze searched hers, his dark eyes mysterious in the moonlight, then filled with awareness. "You're not afraid of me, Jenna. What I've told you . . . it doesn't scare you."

"No, of course not." Jenna realized it couldn't have been easy for him to share such a personal experience. He'd said his parents thought him mental. How hard must that have been on him?

"It made my life hell," he admitted. "After their re-action, I kept it to myself until I met my college room-mate. He was totally into the moon and luna effects, and after he swore secrecy, I shared with him. He helped me understand how it works."

"You've never told anyone else?"

"Not till you." His fingertips smoothed away a long tendril of her hair, tucking it behind her ear. "I had to tell you."

Jenna stared up at him, her heart full. "Why, Stan?"

He kissed her, long and hard and deep, lifting her to her tiptoes, letting his hands cup her hips and bringing her body into stark contact with his erection. "Because I want to make love to you," he rasped. "I want it so bad, it's eating me up. But I couldn't sleep with you until you understood. You have a right to know what you might be getting into."

His sense of fair play astounded her. Most men would have used their ability to take advantage of a woman—

"I want you forever. Not just for a quick lay. Believe that. Years from now, I'll still know your thoughts. At least once a month you'll have no privacy at all. Whenever there's a blue moon I'll be a part of you, in your head, absorbing your every thought like it was my own."

Again he kissed her, gentler this time, as if in apol-ogy. A bubble of renewed desire swelled inside her. Re-gardless of their uncertain future she had to reassure him. "You're a good man, Stan."

Of course, he read her every thought, and his eyes narrowed. "Right. Good at knowing things I have no right knowing."

"You said you can block the thoughts . . ."

Stan shrugged. "With most people, sure. I don't give a damn what they think anyway. After getting that suspended sentence for battery, I knew it'd be safer for me to ignore trouble, rather than try to help. The voices were still there, like birds in the trees, making background noise. But I was able to focus on other stuff so that it didn't register. With you . . . I can't block you, Jenna. Your feelings hit me like a sledgehammer."

She blushed. "It's embarrassing, knowing you were aware of my fantasies." As things became clear, she groaned. "That's why you asked me to go to lunch today, isn't it? You *knew* what I was imagining . . ."

"Yeah, I knew." He cuddled her closer, rocking side to side, his hands low on her hips. "But don't be embarrassed. Hell, woman, you turned me on until I had a damn boner all through the interview. I haven't come in my pants since I was a green kid, but you had me there, close to totally losing control." He nuzzled against her cheek, and Jenna could feel his smile. "Can you imagine how the interview would have turned out?"

She covered her face, chuckling, but also vividly aware of him as a man and how his honesty brought out more fantasies—of making him lose control, of watching him . . .

"Jenna," he groaned, "we'll be good together, I swear it." Only a whisper separated them, so Jenna could feel the faint trembling in his hard frame. "Your kids would love to have me around. Your daughter could go to Savannah, and I'd take Ryan fishing every weekend until he got sick of worms."

Jenna pressed a finger to his mouth. There were a few things she had to make perfectly clear. "I want my kids happy, Stan. But I'd never use a man to make that happen."

"I know that, damn it. That's not what I meant." His fingers tightened on her, then abruptly loosened so that he caressed her, stroking from her hips to her waist and finally up to her breasts. He palmed her and growled in satisfaction when her low moan filled the quiet night.

"*Stan.*"

"Think about us in bed together, Jenna. Every night. Sometimes during the day." His mouth kissed a damp path from her lips to her cheek and up to her ear. "Anything and everything you want, I want, too. There's nothing you can imagine that I'm not willing to do." His fingertips moved over her, finding her stiffened nipples, moving back and forth, back and forth—then tugging, rolling.

Her nails dug into his biceps where she held him. Her breath became choppy. God, she'd wanted him for so long.

"Think about just the two of us, honey. Have you wanted any other man like this?"

"No." This wanting was almost awful, so strong that she felt lost in its grip. Helpless.

His mouth ravaged hers, his tongue stroking, claiming. He continued to toy with one nipple while his other hand went to her waist, then her belly—and below.

It wasn't easy, but Jenna caught his hand, stopping him.

Breathing in harsh pants, Stan said, "Sorry. I know. Not here. You make me forget myself." He held her tight a moment more, then released her and took a step back.

She forgot herself, too. And she was almost tempted . . .

"No," he said. "We'd both regret it."

Jenna put her hands in her hair. "Stan, even if you know my thoughts, quit spitting them back at me. It's disconcerting."

His dark eyes glittered. "Sorry."

Back-stepping, Jenna removed herself from temptation. When she stood several feet away from him, she met his gaze squarely. "I need tonight to think."

"There's nothing to think about." His face was hard, his expression hurt. "You either want me or you don't."

"I do, you know I do." He had to understand that much. "But I've been thinking in the short term, and now you're talking about so much more. You can't rush me, Stan. I can't rush me, because there's not just me."

"You're a package deal." His hand slashed through the air. "I know that. And I already told you, I like your kids. They like me. No problem."

It took an effort, but Jenna held herself still and kept her voice firm. "I have to think about how this will affect them. The fact that you could read their thoughts, too, has to be considered. Can't you see that? It's not just my privacy you'd invade, but theirs as well."

"I could try to block their thoughts, but . . . I don't know if I can. Not every time. I care about them. That seems to make a difference. If Rachelle looked upset and it was in my power to understand why—" He stopped, propped his hands on his hips, and glared out at the moon.

Voice strained, he rasped, "It's only once a month at the most. And I can't pick up every little thought. Just the glaring ones."

"Unless there's a blue moon," she reminded him, "like tonight. Then you'd be in our heads every minute of every hour."

He cursed low, looking hurt and needy—that thought made him scowl.

Before he could protest, Jenna took the few large strides she needed to reach him. "Give me tonight, Stan." She went on tiptoe and kissed him, a quick goodbye peck. "I'll talk with you tomorrow, okay?"

And then she turned and hurried inside.

Stan stood there, watching the door close, hearing

the lock turn. Fuck it, he thought, but at the same time, he listened to Jenna, hearing her loud and clear even through the door. Her indecision scraped over his already raw nerves. He felt her sadness, her warring confusion, and he jerked around to leave.

He didn't have a gift. He had a curse. And in the end, it just might cost him the thing he wanted most—marriage to Jenna.

Wearing only jeans, Stan stood on his covered deck, coffee in hand, showered but not shaved. He stared out at the wet, gloomy morning and wished he wasn't alone. A lingering rain, accompanied by the occasional low rumble of thunder and distant lightning, obliterated plans for landscaping work.

After a sleepless night, he'd shoved out of his rumpled bed at five A.M. and started drowning his problems in caffeine. Because his house sat next to his garden center, and both backed up to the lake, he could see the turbulent waves rolling to the shore with a splash.

Usually he loved days like this—perfect for lingering in bed, making love all day long, slow and languorous, letting the pleasure build and peak while the wind whistled and the rain beat against the windowpanes.

Stan cursed. Today he hated the damn weather.

He needed the distraction of his work, sweating in the hot sun, digging and planting until his muscles ached. But all he could do was wait—and think about Jenna.

He considered calling her, but knew he shouldn't. She wanted time to herself, and even though he figured too much thinking would bring her to conclusions he wouldn't favor, he had to respect her wishes.

Working on his next book, *Season by Season Gardening*, was out. He doubted he could hold a thought

long enough to get anything down on paper. He de-
tested early morning television. He wasn't hungry.

And so he stood there, his skin chilled from the early
morning rain-cooled air, his gaze directed blindly at
the lake, his muscles twitchy and his soul in turmoil.

When his doorbell rang, Stan didn't at first move.
Seconds ticked by while he held himself immobile . . .
and then Jenna's thoughts sank into him, alerting him to
her presence. They were too jumbled to decipher. Or
maybe he was too jumbled, too filled with satisfaction
and surging lust and possessiveness.

She'd come to him.

He left the sliding doors to the deck open as he
strode inside. Even before he went down the hall and
opened the locks, he knew what he'd find—Jenna standing there with her crooked smile and her dimple and
her gentle green eyes. She wanted to make love, but
did she want him forever?

He jerked the door open.

She blinked up at him, and he was afraid to hope, to
open his mind to her for fear she'd come to tell him
things he didn't want to hear.

Holding the coffee mug in one hand, Stan used the
other to brace on the doorknob. How long they stood
there staring at each other, he wasn't sure. With no expression at all, he whispered, "Hi."

Her smile wobbled. "Morning." Then her gaze dipped
to his naked chest—and stayed there.

Lust. That's what he felt from her. Desire. Need.
Nervousness and urgency and determination—

"Come in." Stan pushed the door wide and stood
back while she crept over the threshold. And she did
creep. As though she had reservations, or was afraid . . .

It hit him, a storm of sensation, exploding inside his
brain like a migraine. Jenna badly wanted to talk to him,
to clear the air by her own choice before he read her

thoughts. Stan struggled to abide by her wishes. He tried thinking of things the total opposite of Jenna—his mother, grub worms . . . It didn't work.

Singing to himself to drown out her feelings, Stan took her arm and trotted her down the hall and into the family room that opened out to the deck. The open sliders had let in the humidity, leaving the room damp and cool and as turbulent as the storm itself.

He led her to a soft striped couch, pushed her down onto the cushions, set his coffee on the end table and crouched in front of her. His heart hammered and a sudden erection made his old faded jeans uncomfortable. "Talk to me quick, sweetheart. I'll do my best to hear only what you say, not what you think."

Jenna's lips trembled. She touched his face with one small, cool hand. "Stan." Her hair was loose, and very little make-up colored her face. She wore an old, soft sweatshirt with a pair of drawstring shorts and flip-flop sandals. Her knees pressed into his chest and she licked her lips, bringing her thoughts together. "I spoke with Rachelle."

He hadn't expected that. A dozen other possibilities had occurred to him, but not that. "Yeah? And?"

She licked her lips again. If she didn't quit doing that, he wouldn't be responsible for a delay in conversation. Already he wanted to push her flat on the couch, to open her thighs and settle between them and strip off her sweatshirt—

"I told her everything."

Stan had been studying her taut nipples beneath the soft cotton sweatshirt with interest, but at her confession, his gaze shot to her face. *"Everything?"*

Scooting forward to the edge of the sofa, earnest in the extreme, Jenna tunneled her fingers through his hair and launched into explanation. "I had to, Stan. I couldn't sleep and I was up all night pacing and trying to sort things out, and finally at five this morning, I gave up."

Stan stared at her. "I got up at five, too. Same reason. Couldn't sleep."

Her expression softened. "I'm sorry," she whispered. "I know this isn't easy for you."

Damn, she made him feel like a wimp. "I'm fine," he said, his voice gruff. "What the hell did you tell Rachelle?"

"She was concerned. She wanted to know if you'd done something mean to me, something to upset me. She told me about Terrance—you were right, by the way. He is an ass. He made my daughter cry."

"If he was a little older, I'd stomp him for her."

Jenna smiled, and she had her heart in her eyes. "I told Rachelle you weren't like that, but then she kept prodding, telling me how perfect you are. She thinks you're smart and nice and sexy—"

"Sexy?" he croaked.

Her smile widened. "Yes. But she said it in an attempt to convince me, not out of personal interest."

Burning heat came into his face. "Damn it, I know that."

"I told her I thought you were wonderful, and she wanted to know why I was up moping and pacing instead of in bed dreaming about you. So . . . I told her."

"She knows I can read her thoughts?"

"Yes. We talked through an entire pot of coffee."

Shit, shit, shit. Stan's shoulders slumped a little. "She thinks I'm a wacko."

With a quiet chuckle, Jenna leaned forward and wrapped her arms around his neck, hugging him tight. Stan could feel her breasts on his bare chest, her warm breath on his shoulder.

He closed his eyes and whispered, "You're killing me, babe," and then he pulled her closer still.

Jenna pressed a small kiss to his throat, another to his shoulder. "Rachelle said, in a rather admonishing tone, that most men never have a clue what a woman thinks or feels, and they're even more lost as to what a woman wants."

"True." But given the female psyche, how could you blame them?

"She told me that I should grab you with both hands and never let you go."

Stan's heart almost stopped. "Is that right? And what did you say?"

"I reminded her that it wouldn't only be my thoughts you could listen to. But Rachelle says she has no secrets, and when she does, she won't be around during full moons."

Some of Stan's tension started to ease. He stroked his hands over Jenna's back, down to the swell of her hips.

"I thought about that," Jenna admitted. "About how it'd be between us, how you'll know what I want, even before I realize it."

"You mean in bed."

When she nodded, her hair teased his cheek. "I've waited long enough, Stan." Her teeth closed on the muscle of his shoulder, sending a rush of sensation through his veins. "I don't want to wait anymore."

"Neither do I." Jenna hadn't said anything about love or the future, but in that particular moment, Stan needed her too much to care.

In one smooth movement, he pushed up from his knees to sit on the sofa, cradling Jenna on his lap. She curled against him, right at home, her rounded tush pressing against his boner, her arms around him, her big cushy breasts smooshed against the hard wall of his chest.

He struggled to catch his breath, but her thoughts

penetrated. It had been an effort, letting her talk without reading her feelings, her mind. Now he couldn't stop the tide and it flattened him. Like an inferno, she burned from the inside out. Stan knew that her breasts were throbbing, that between her thighs she was wet and aching, trembling all over.

He caught her face and kissed her hard, giving her his tongue and accepting hers in return. Her urgency became his own, and he shoved up her sweatshirt, desperate for the feel of her body, her soft breasts and stiffened nipples.

As his rough thumb stroked over her nipple, pressing, circling, Jenna jerked her mouth free and cried out.

Raising the sweatshirt higher, Stan lowered his head to kiss her. Jenna struggled, trying to free herself of the shirt while squirming under him. When his mouth closed over her nipple, she arched her body and gave a long, ragged groan.

Jesus, she was on the ragged edge, and he knew, *knew* that she wanted his hand on her now, his fingers inside her, stroking and working her. Without a word, Stan levered himself up and off her, stripped her shirt away and went to work on the drawstring of her shorts. Jenna helped, kicking off her sandals, but once Stan prepared to remove her shorts, she froze.

He felt her lack of confidence and paused long enough to cup her face. "Listen to me, Jenna. You're beautiful. Every inch of you."

"I'm forty."

"You're stacked."

Pleasure at his compliment warred with uncertainty. "I've . . . I've had two kids."

Stan continued to look into her eyes while he slipped his hand over her rounded belly, circled once, relishing her softness, then pushed into her shorts. Her lips parted on a sudden breath.

He found her pubic curls and fingered them briefly before pressing lower, into damp, hot flesh, swollen and ready. His chest labored.

Her eyes grew unfocused—but she didn't break the connection of their gazes.

For a time he just petted her, lightly prodding, exploring. Then he found her clitoris, already turgid, and using his middle finger, touched her gently.

Her shattered moan filled the air. "Oh, God, Stan."

She needed release more than foreplay, Stan realized. It had been a very long time for her. Jenna wasn't a woman to indulge in one-night stands, and in a small community where everyone had known her husband, there'd be no such thing as privacy. She'd been in a position of all or nothing, and so, putting her kids first, she'd chosen nothing.

But now she had him.

Stan looked at her breasts, and his lust kicked up another notch. They were big and soft, very pale with rosy nipples drawn tight. Slowly, deliberately building the anticipation, he closed his mouth over her, suckling softly, tonguing her—and all the while, he teased her clitoris, lightly abrading, moving his finger back and forth.

Her hips lifted and her thighs opened. Stan paused long enough to tug her shorts over and off her hips, then threw them aside. Without haste he looked at her, lying naked on his couch, her belly trembling, her chest heaving, her face flushed.

All his.

Every muscle in his body strained with the savage need to take her. Her timidity wasn't strong enough to overpower her sexual yearning. She wanted him and, at least for that moment, didn't care if her body lacked perfection. Stan shook his head. To him, she was better than perfect, everything he'd ever wanted, more than he thought he'd ever get.

"Stan . . . please."

He shifted his position at the side of the couch so that he faced her feet, then levered himself over her. He slid his arms under her thighs and pulled them farther apart. With his fingertips, he explored her, opening her swollen lips, tracing along her opening, up and over her clitoris.

Her small moans and soft gasps urged him on. He kissed her belly before pressing his mouth lower.

Yeah, she wanted this, had dreamed about it, fantasized for long, endless nights about how it'd feel to have his mouth on her, tonguing her. Sucking. Making her come.

Her excitement was a live thing, invading his head, obliterating his concentration.

Harsh, trembly sounds of anticipation mingled with her fast breaths. Her heels pressed into the sofa cushions. She groaned, and her fingers curled over the waistband of his jeans at the small of his back.

Stan inhaled the hot scent of her sex, gave his own groan of excitement and closed his mouth over her. Being very gentle with her, he circled her clitoris with his tongue, finding a rhythm that made her wild. The weight of his body held her still, but she jerked hard when he pushed one finger into her.

With each new pulse, each throb and shiver that coursed through her, his own pleasure expanded. She tasted so good, he could have eaten her for hours, but only a few minutes later, with two fingers buried deep inside her, pressing hard, alternately sucking and licking her, she came.

Stan was so wrapped up in her pleasure, so into the

moment and so turned on, that he forgot about reading her thoughts. Everything he did was out of love for her, because he wanted her pleasure and enjoyed kissing and touching her—as much as he'd enjoy her touch in return.

Attuned to her every sigh and moan and movement, he knew just when to increase the pressure to give her the most explosive orgasm. He knew when to ease back, when to slide his fingers free, when to gentle her.

Because he was a man in love, not because of the twice cursed moon. It astounded him that during her climax, her thoughts hadn't been clear to him at all. He hadn't needed them to be. Jenna was an open, giving lover.

She was all his.

He had his cheek on her belly, his fingers idly tracing circles on her thigh when her soft sobs reached him. Still, without delving into her thoughts, Stan smiled with pure male satisfaction. Jenna's tears weren't from sadness, upset, or disappointment. She cried out of an excess of emotion, because she knew that what they'd just shared was special.

Enjoying her femaleness, this sign of her caring, Stan kissed her pelvic bone. "Shhh, sweetheart," he whispered, feeling very indulgent. "Don't cry."

She made an endearing little hiccupping noise, then stammered, "I'm sorry. I don't know why I am."

Carefully, Stan eased his arms out from under her thighs and began kissing his way up her body. "You," he said with his lips on her belly, "enjoyed"—he lingered on her breasts—"what I just did to you."

Her eyes were liquid with tears, sated and filled with love. "You already know I did."

"Yeah." Using one fingertip, he brushed away a tear clinging to her lashes. "Because I'm not unfamiliar with a woman's body or her response." Uncaring if she understood his statement, Stan stood, then unzipped his jeans. "You'll enjoy me inside you even more."

As he shoved his jeans down and off, she caught her breath. "God, Stan, you are so gorgeous." She quickly sat up, tucking one leg beneath her bottom, reaching out with both hands to touch his abdomen, lower, over the trail of hair that thickened at his crotch. Fully erect, his cock throbbed as her soft fingers wrapped around him.

Tipping his head back, Stan locked his knees and let her explore him at her leisure.

In an absent voice, she asked, "Do you have a condom, Stan?"

"Yeah." He dropped one onto the coffee table. "I stuck three in my jeans pocket as soon as I knew you wanted me."

Using both hands, she squeezed, slid up his length, then slowly back down again. "Three, huh?"

Stan swallowed his groan. "Yeah." Talking wasn't easy. "You never know when opportunity might knock, and I believe in being prepared."

"That's because you're such a great guy." The last whispered word no sooner left her mouth than her lips brushed the head of his penis, and Stan growled out a low curse.

"Jenna."

"You already know how often I've thought about doing this." The hot interior of her mouth closed around him and he felt her wet, velvet tongue moving, sliding . . .

He couldn't wait any longer. Not with Jenna.

He caught her shoulders to pull her away, then tipped her to her back on the sofa cushions.

Rumbling thunder nearly drowned out her laugh as Stan stretched out over her. The lights flickered and a strong wind brought the storm into the room. "Why such a hurry, Stan?" Jenna teased.

He kissed the smile right off her mouth, then kept on

kissing her until she clutched him again, until her skin heated and she moaned and writhed under him. Again, he pushed his fingers into her, and he felt her muscles clamp down, squeezing him, making him desperate to feel her on his cock.

When she again made those sweet female sounds he adored, Stan sat up long enough to roll on the condom.

"Look at me, Jenna."

Her heavy eyes opened, but grew dazed as he guided himself into her. Straightening his arms, Stan stayed above her so he could see her every reaction as he became a part of her. "Christ, you feel good, Jenna."

Her neck arched and she sank her teeth into her bottom lip, whimpering. The tension grew, until finally she gasped. "Stan, I'm sorry."

And before he'd seated himself fully inside her, she groaned long and low, rocking out another climax. Her heels pressed into the backs of his thighs and her fingers dug deep into his shoulders. Stan took great pleasure in just watching her, feeling her contractions rhythmically squeezing him, knowing that he had the power to satisfy the woman he loved.

When she quieted, her forearm over her eyes, her body damp with sweat, he began thrusting, shallow, easy, slow deep thrusts.

"Oh, God, Stan," she whispered.

With his right hand, he gripped the cushion beside her head and with his left, he braced on the arm of the sofa. He clenched his jaw, driving into her with more force, shaking the couch, feeling the power of the storm in his blood.

Restless, Jenna turned her face away from him, but she came right back, eyes barely open, lips red and swollen. "Unbelievable," she moaned, and then her hands slid up and over his shoulders, her fingers delving into his hair.

Stan bent to take her mouth, ravaging her, eating at her soft lips and sucking at her tongue, and then he exploded, great waves of pressure shuddering through him again and again. He lowered himself to hold Jenna tight until finally it all began to ease away. He felt replete.

He felt whole.

Jenna stirred as goose bumps rose on the naked flesh of her waist and hip and upper thigh. Idly, Stan stroked her with his open palm, warming her skin. "You are so soft." He kept his voice low now that the storm had moved past them, leaving only a steady rain. "I love touching you."

She sighed and curled into him. "You didn't close your sliding doors. Your floor is going to be wet."

"Storms turn me on." Stan loved her so much, it hurt. But so far, she hadn't said a word about love. She'd screamed out her pleasure, hugged him with her thighs, begged him and praised him and been as open and giving as a woman could be during hot grinding sex. But she hadn't said a single word about the future.

She was so lethargic, her body, her thoughts. Stan felt her smiles inside his heart. He felt her satisfaction and her contentment. He felt . . . a lot of things. But he didn't know if they equaled love.

"So," she whispered, twining her fingers in his chest hair. "I need to wait for another rainstorm during a full moon to get a repeat of today?"

He swatted her hip, smiled as she yelped, then went back to smoothing her skin. "I was edgy as a junkyard dog when you showed up, and I knew even before I opened the door that you were here to get laid."

Her lips curled. "I was here for you, Stan. If all I wanted was sex, I probably could have found another willing guy."

Shoving up to one elbow, Stan almost toppled Jenna to the floor. His hand gripping her ass stopped her from falling off the sofa. "Who? Where?"

This time she laughed outright. Slumberous, sated eyes mocked him. "I don't know, Stan. I've never offered before. But I figure *someone* would be willing if I started giving it away. I mean, I know Delicious can be a little backward, and there aren't that many single guys my age, but—"

In one swift movement, Stan pinned her beneath him. Catching her wrists in a fist, he stretched her arms up and over her head. "Tell me you love me."

Those green eyes widened, no longer teasing. At the same time, Stan felt the response of her body, the accelerated beating of her heart, the shifting of her thighs, the warming of her skin.

She liked being in a submissive position—and her turn-ons became his own.

Distracted, Stan trailed the fingers of his free hand along the underside of her arm, down, down, until he cupped her breast. Staring into her eyes, he caught her nipple between his fingertips, lightly pinched and tugged.

Jenna's gasp sounded of surprise and excitement and encouragement.

"Tell me, sweetheart," he insisted. "Tell me that you love me and want to marry me."

She turned her face away—but shifted back quickly when he increased the pressure on her nipple. Stan smiled at the wild beating of her heart, the excited flush of her skin. "Yeah, keep looking at me, Jenna."

"Okay."

Such a soft, needy voice. Stan leaned down to lick her bottom lip, then her throat. "Tell me, Jenna." He closed his mouth over her nipple and sucked hard.

"*Stan.*"

The way she said his name did him in. "Damn it."

He quickly grew hard again, and this time he knew he'd last at least an hour. Hell, he hadn't come twice so soon in years. "Don't move."

She watched him with the same fascination she might give a snake. "What are you going to do?"

"Grab another condom."

That earned him a groan—but she didn't move.

The second Stan had the protection rolled on, he settled over her again. "Open your legs, Jenna. Now."

Slowly, her thighs shifted apart, and he thrust in with a long, ragged groan. She was wet and swollen and so hot. "Fuck yeah. Squeeze me. Tighter."

Her muscles clamped down, and Stan ground his teeth. "God, yeah. You feel good, Jenna. So damn good."

"I love you, Stan."

He froze. His gaze locked on to hers.

Smiling, she slipped her hands out of his slack hold to twine her arms around his neck. "I thought you were reading my mind, so you'd already know that I love you."

Shaking his head, his whole body throbbing, Stan swallowed hard. "You were naked, Jenna, here, with me and ready. What you thought didn't seem as important as what you did. What we did together."

"So you couldn't read my mind?"

Stan thought about it, easily picked up her suspicion, and grinned. "I could. I guess your naked body was enough of a distraction. I was too busy feeling you, the texture of your skin and hair. And your scent makes me nuts. And the sight of you when you come . . ."

"Stan, stop."

He took her mouth in a long, tongue-twining kiss. "There's just so much of you to enjoy, it's like sensory overload. I forgot about hearing your thoughts."

Relief had her laughing. "Stan, that's . . . wonderful." Then her brow drew down in a frown. "But if you weren't reading my mind, how did you know to—"

He moved against her and caught her gasp. "Jenna, sweetheart, your body language is very easy to read."

She lifted into him. "Is that so?"

On a groan, Stan muttered, "Damn right." Holding still took gigantic effort.

Her small hands moved up his arms to his biceps. "I love you, Stan, so much that it almost consumes me. I never thought to meet a man like you."

They were intimately joined, their bodies sealed together by the humidity and sexual heat and their own sweat, as close as any two people could get.

Stan didn't want her influenced by sex. "You're sure?" He narrowed his eyes, very aware of his own vulnerability. "Be sure, Jenna."

"Stan Tucker, I love you." Her voice was firm but scratchy with emotion. "I want to marry you and be with you forever."

Staring into her eyes, Stan withdrew, but sank back in. "Say it again."

"I love you."

His guts knotted. His heart pounded. He shifted to wedge a hand beneath her hips, tilting her up, giving him deeper penetration. Through clenched teeth, he ordered, "Again."

"*Stan.*" Her head fell back and her pale throat worked.

Deliberately, Stan opened himself to her, to the physical sensation and the emotional bombardment, to her thoughts and her love and her pleasure. He greeted the churning of a building climax, savored every nuance of sensation burning through her, shivering through her thighs, her breasts, her belly . . . around his cock as her orgasm broke.

He squeezed his eyes shut and kept his rhythm steady, delighting in each high, female sound of excitement that burst from her throat.

When she sank back into the cushions, her breathing still choppy and her face damp, Stan kissed her throat, tasting the salt of her skin, rubbing his nose over her, inhaling her scent. "I love you, too," he told her. "Enough to last three lifetimes."

Jenna put one limp hand to his cheek and managed a sleepy smile. "I know."

Too tired to lift his head, Stan grunted. "So you're a mind reader now, too?"

Her gentle fingers stroked over him. "No, I'm just a woman who feels very loved. And I don't mean the sex, which is . . . well, there aren't words. But the way you look at me, how you touch me . . . I didn't think I could ever be this happy again. And I owe it all to a full moon."

Finally, Stan found the strength to raise himself up, to look at her cherished face and smile with her. "I always figured the Lunar Effect to be a pain in the ass. But every once in a blue moon, things really do work out."

Jenna gave him a coy look. "No way am I waiting for blue moons to have my way with you, Stan, so forget that. Once we're married, I expect you to love me each and every night."

Stan let the smile take him, let his heart fill with love. Then he tipped back his head and howled, and when Jenna laughed, he knew he'd never again resent the effect of the full moon.

MOON
MAGNETISM

Lucy Monroe

One

"Holy crap!" Ivy Kendall stared at the innocent-looking pink memo slip and crossed herself. Not being Catholic, she wasn't sure what good it would do. Did God have issues with that kind of thing?

Oh, man, she didn't have time for a one-sided theological discussion with herself. Not when she needed to book tickets to Alaska, or maybe Zimbabwe, or how about the North Pole? Did they have computers at the North Pole? Sure as certain they didn't have Blake Hawthorne—gorgeous, sexy, business mogul who just happened to run the hotel conglomerate she worked for.

A man who wasn't content to use a mere Palm Pilot, his Rolex watch had been custom-made with alarm and messaging functions. His cell phone had a built-in GPS device as well as Internet capability. She'd seen him use it, but one minute in Ivy's company would have every last personal technology device malfunctioning.

"Poop sticks."

She frowned. Her twelve-year-old niece uttered the phrase with a lot more relish, knowing her mom couldn't get her for swearing, but it didn't satisfy Ivy's sense of the moment at all.

Besides, *her* mother was in Florida living it up with Dad. *She* didn't have to worry about this time of month anymore. *She* could walk into a computer lab and not worry about erasing a single hard drive. Ivy wasn't so lucky, and Blake Hawthorne, king of techno-toys, was on his way this very minute.

It was a darn good thing Mom was far enough away not to hear the words bubbling up inside Ivy, ready to spew forth any second.

"Shit. Damn. Umm . . . never mind the f-word . . . Hell. Mary, Mother of Joseph . . . " Was that even a curse if you weren't Catholic? *"Crap,"* she said again for good measure, but none of her admittedly limited vocabulary of swear words did the least bit to relieve her panic.

Pretty soon, she was going to break out in hives, and wouldn't that be just what she needed?

Her boss was coming. *Today.* In less than an hour if the memo had gotten the time correct.

She banged her head against her desk and groaned. How could she have missed the memo?

It had been sitting in her in-box under a message to call Ed, that's how she could miss it. She'd rather have her teeth cleaned than go on another date with the man, but she was lousy at saying no to fragile people. Ed was more boring than a rerun of the Bob Hope Chrysler Golf Tournament, but he was also sensitive.

She'd convinced herself that if she didn't actually pick up the message, she hadn't really gotten it, and she didn't have to call him back. She'd been very careful not to read it once she got past the "from" line.

Unfortunately, she hadn't thought to check if there was anything under it . . . until five minutes ago. Way too late to get on the next outbound flight for a remote village in Botswana. Even if she *could* get the flight, she couldn't take it. She'd never be able to complete the drive between Delicious and Cleveland, the closest city with a major airport.

She'd stopped driving during this time of month after her last fender-bender. Admittedly they didn't happen every full moon, but she wasn't taking any more chances. After all, the last one had been how she'd met Ed.

"Is that a new pose for meditation?"

Her heart stopped beating. She was sure of it.

The message had been wrong, or he was early; either way, she was screwed.

Desperately sucking air in an attempt not to hyperventilate, she lifted her head. After a moment of shoring up her mental fortitude, she opened her eyes, too. One look had her mentally cursing her inability to have the hi-tech phone system her staff could have used to warn her of her boss's arrival.

She didn't get up. Her legs were shaky, her body reacting predictably to the sight of the gorgeous blond man standing so relaxed in her doorway. And why shouldn't he be? He had nothing to fear . . . or at least didn't realize he did. If he came much closer, thousands of dollars' worth of personal technical gadgets were going to stop working.

Heck, maybe they already had. It was a blue moon coming up after all.

Nevertheless, she had to try to stave off disaster. Didn't she? *"Stay back."*

His brows rose in question, and his blue eyes pierced her with curiosity. "Not finished meditating?" he asked sardonically.

"I don't meditate."

"I didn't really think you did."

Right. "Then why . . . never mind. Uh, I . . . um . . . I think I've got a bug, and I'm pretty sure it's contagious. You should leave. Now."

He smiled, even white teeth reminding her of a tiger drawing back its lips to reveal the deadly fangs of a hunter. "I never get sick." Then he stepped into the room.

"I guess germs are too intimidated by you to take up residence," she muttered, her self-preservation instincts buried under stress.

His mouth quirked, but he kept coming, across the room, around her desk, and finally, she had to swivel in her old-fashioned wooden office chair to face him.

He stood over her, his big body giving off messages she had to be misinterpreting. Sexy, sensual, in her face with his masculinity messages. "Do I intimidate you, Ivy? Is that why you do everything short of quit your job in order to avoid the management training seminars?"

She swallowed, trying to wet a suddenly dry throat. "I don't avoid the seminars."

"You weren't at the last one."

"Something unavoidable came up."

A full moon. No way was she going to New York City to stay in a hotel with thirty-eight floors of rooms (all of them with their own computer-operated climate control systems) when that big white nemesis hung so brightly in the sky.

"Something unavoidable has come up every seminar except two in the last three years."

What could she say? The coordinator's timing stank worse than a skunk's after-trail. But maybe her boss had gotten tired of her excuses.

"I only missed two seminars."

"Which means you're at fifty percent; that's a failing grade in anyone's book." Why did he have to look so incredibly yummy while telling her off?

And he smelled nice, too.

"I'm sorry."

His blue gaze pierced her. "I was, too. I couldn't help wondering if I had something to do with you avoiding the management training."

"You?" she squeaked and cleared her throat, trying for a look of insouciance she didn't feel.

He leaned against her desk and crossed his arms. "You said I intimidate you."

Standing this close he did a lot more than intimidate her. He turned her on. Big time. Why couldn't Ed have this effect on her? *He* wanted to marry her. Heck, he probably even wanted her to have his babies, and then the whole women in her family's curse-slash-gift it-depends-on-how-you-look-at-it thing would be solved. Did it matter that she would probably die of terminal boredom in the first year of her marriage?

Yeah, it probably did. She'd rather deal with a full moon and all its consequences.

"Ivy?"

"Huh?" Great. Now she sounded like an idiot times six, or something. This man was her boss. He ran a huge conglomerate of hotels and resorts. He was used to intelligent conversation from his employees, probably even expected it considering the type of testing you had to go through to get a job with HGA, Inc.

He sure wasn't getting intelligent coherence right now. She tried really hard to remember what he'd said. Oh, yeah. "Not attending the management seminars had nothing to do with you. It was entirely personal."

"Hmmm . . ." He rubbed his chin with fingers she'd really rather have on her. "I suppose I have to believe you. After all, if I really did intimidate you, you would hardly turn down every *request* I've made for you to modernize the inn."

"Not every request. I was thrilled about the new carpeting, and you must have noticed that we're redoing the woodwork as well."

"Redecorating is not modernization." His eyes flicked to the open ledger on her neatly ordered desk. "Most recently, you've resisted implementing a computer reservation and guest check-in system."

She scooted her chair back, unable to deal with his intense presence so close to her for one more second. "Old Orchard Inn is quaint. People who come to stay here like the old-fashioned atmosphere, including signing into a guestbook. It's not one of HGA, Inc.'s big properties. We don't need a fancy computer to keep track of eight guest rooms."

Blake had to agree. They didn't *need* it, but why the hell was she so against having one?

Was she a technophobe? She was smart, and quick to pick up new things; he had a hard time believing she was intimidated by technology. But what other explanation was there?

Blake bit back a sigh and an impatient retort in the same moment of frustration. He'd bought the property three years ago with the intention of building the business and selling. It was too small for a company like HGA, Inc., to take seriously, and he'd known that going in. He'd seen the Old Orchard Inn strictly in terms of short range ROI.

Then he'd met the inn's manager. Ivy had passed the corporate employment tests and been offered a job with HGA, Inc., continuing in her current position before he'd met her face to face. He'd regretted that sequence of events many times over the last three years.

Ivy Kendall made his dick hard and his head feel like exploding within sixty seconds of coming into a room. Her slight body and heart-shaped face weren't exactly centerfold material, but she'd starred in more than one dream that left him hard and aching when he woke up.

He wanted her, and *he could not have her*.

He never dated HGA, Inc., employees. It was too damn messy. Not only was there the whole potential sexual harassment thing, but there were a host of other complications that could arise as well. None of which he'd ever been willing to risk, but his rock-solid commitment to that stance was wearing away as his need for the tiny technophobe grew.

That need was driving him crazier than her unwillingness to upgrade even to the minimum of putting in computer-controlled central air and heating. He hadn't pushed too hard, knowing that once the inn was upgraded, it would have to be sold. He got the impression Ivy had no interest in working for HGA, Inc. at another property. If the inn was sold, he would probably never see her again. The thought bothered him more than it should. It had certainly made him more accommodating with her than he was with any of his other property managers.

That accommodation was coming to an end. "The inn has the lowest percentage of customer complaints of any of our properties."

She smiled tentatively, her brown eyes wary. "That's good, right?"

"Yes, except every single complaint says the same thing."

She chewed on her bottom lip, an expression of resigned understanding stealing over her sweet features. "The guests want central air-conditioning."

"Yes."

"We can give them that without giving up the old world ambience of the inn and getting rid of the radiator heaters."

"What would be the point? If we have to run duct work, it might as well be for the whole shebang." There was such a thing as taking the whole ambience thing too far.

"But do eight rooms really need separate, computer-controlled climate controls?"

"Yes, and if you had attended the last management seminar, you'd know why."

"Seventy percent of our business is repeat customers." She sounded almost desperate.

"Who are also paying only about seventy percent of the room rates they would be paying in a more modernized facility."

"I don't like the idea of modernizing just so we can gouge our customers."

"Your resume says you have a degree in business." It was only a two-year degree from a correspondence school, but even so, she should have gotten some idea of normal business practices.

Her brow pleated in a way he found too cute to be even remotely professional. "Yes."

"Raising rates to accepted industry levels is not gouging your customers."

She winced. "I guess not."

"So, are we agreed that the inn will have to be upgraded?"

Her eyes filled with a sadness he did not understand. "Even if I don't agree, you're going to go ahead with it anyway, aren't you?"

Right in that moment, he wished he could say no. She looked so damn forlorn. "Corporate's made the decision."

"I thought you were corporate."

"I am responsible to a board of directors." Which he could have bucked, but what would have been the point? He agreed with the consensus.

The inn needed to be upgraded and then sold.

"Ivy, Ed's at the front desk. He asked if you were in?" The desk clerk made what should have been a sentence sound like a question. Younger than Ivy, her eyes were alight with both interest and some sort of female telepathic understanding.

Ivy groaned and stood up. "That's all this day needs. Um . . . Trudy, I don't suppose you could tell him I'm busy with my boss?" She turned to Blake. "I am busy, aren't I?" she asked with a tone that implied his interruption into her otherwise neatly ordered existence should count for something.

"Yes, and you will be busy in consultations with me for the next several days." Where the possessiveness came from, he didn't know, or care to analyze, but he did not want Ivy going out with another man while he was in Delicious, Ohio.

Trudy's eyes widened and then narrowed on Blake in obvious appraisal, but she only said, "I'll tell him," and left.

Ivy stood up and pushed her chair into place at her desk with precise movements, then stepped back two paces and faced him. The smooth lines of her small face were tight with determination. "So, will two weeks' notice be sufficient, or do you require a month?"

The words were still reeling in his brain when Trudy came back, her expression pure female commiseration this time. "He asked, what about dinner?"

Blake turned smartly on his heel and walked out to the front desk counter. He would deal with Ed while his usually super efficient brain grappled with the implication that Ivy was willing to quit her job over the proposed improvements to the inn. The sound of a gasp and his name being called in confused appeal from behind him did not slow him down.

Ed was encroaching on his territory, and like millions of the male species before him, Blake had every intention of pushing back. If his behavior could be construed as pissing a circle around Ivy Kendall, that was too bad. She worked for him, and for the next few days she was his.

That the territory of boss and boyfriend should be mutually exclusive did not deter his purpose.

Ed did not belong here at the inn with Ivy, not when Blake wanted her undivided attention. Not when she was threatening to quit over central air-conditioning.

Blake stopped when he reached the front desk. A tall man with brown hair and an impatient glint in his narrowed gray eyes stood on the other side. He was dressed like a businessman without even a hint of country hick about him. In Delicious, Ohio? Who was this guy?

A female guest walked through the lobby toward the inn's small restaurant and gave Ed the once-over on her way. Right. Definitely no trouble attracting women. So why did he have to pester Ivy when she so clearly wasn't interested? Or had Blake misread her and Trudy's silent communication? He wouldn't be the first man misled by that kind of thing.

Maybe her consternation had not been at Ed's arrival, but the fact it coincided with her boss's. The thought pissed him off so bad he scowled at the other man.

Ed didn't even blink, but his eyes narrowed further, and his jaw took on rocklike solidity.

Blake figured they matched in that. His back teeth ground together. "Ivy will be having dinner with me. I am only in town for a few days and expect my property manager to give me her undivided attention."

His words came out clipped, surly even, and shock at his own behavior warred with anger that this man wanted *his* Ivy.

Ed blinked then, his eyes going from angry to speculative. "Isn't that a little presumptuous? She's your employee, not your slave."

The image of Ivy's sweetly feminine form trussed up to play love slave flashed in Blake's mind, and his semiaroused flesh went fireman pole status in three seconds flat. Thank whatever architect had designed the sturdy, concealing guest check-in counter that hid the lower half of his body from the other man's view.

"Expecting my manager to be available to discuss business when I am in town is hardly an indication I see her in a subservient capacity." *But maybe I wouldn't mind it*, a certain very dark part of his mind suggested . . . *just once.*

"Ed, what's the matter with you? You can't go around insulting my boss." Ivy had arrived.

"I'm not insulted. His accusation is too ludicrous for the serious consideration it would take to be offended." Blake didn't dare turn to face her with the raging hard-on pushing against the confines of his custom-tailored slacks. So, he said the words with his focus fixed squarely on the other man.

The intruder.

Ed frowned, his body shifting into a stance any other man would recognize. It was a challenge, plain and simple.

Ivy gasped. Apparently, she recognized it, too. "What's gotten into you, Ed?"

"You haven't returned my calls, Ivy. I want to talk to you."

That did have Blake turning his head at least to see her.

Her cheeks stained a guilty pink. "I didn't read your message until today."

Was that what her head banging on the desk had been about? She'd missed her boyfriend's message?

"Have dinner with me tonight. We need to talk about the direction our relationship is headed."

Cripes. He was one of those new men, the sensitive ones, who discussed his feelings *willingly*, without even being prodded. Blake snorted, and Ed glared at him, his jaw jutting pugnaciously.

"You are not helping things, Mr. Hawthorne," Ivy muttered from behind him.

"I'm sorry, I can't," she said to Ed before stepping around the counter and moving closer to him—too damn close—in an obvious bid to keep her conversation private.

Both Blake and Trudy eavesdropped shamelessly.

"Look," she said quietly, "he's my boss, and if he wants to have dinner with me, that's what I've got to do."

Would she be that submissive about other things? Would she let her big, bad boss dictate sexual preferences to her vulnerable, sweetly nervous, but definitely amorous self? It was his favorite fantasy where she was concerned.

Not one he'd ever get to play out and not just because she worked for him. Some of the sensual desires that rode him around her were definitely the antithesis of politically correct or even socially acceptable. He doubted the innocent Ivy would consent to them, much less be the enthusiastic partner she was in his dreams.

He wanted to tie her to a bed and make love to her until she screamed.

Did that make him a deviant, or just creative?

He didn't know. He'd never had these kinds of fantasies about other women.

Ed was saying something low, but then his voice rose. "You don't have to put up with this. You know I want to marry you. You don't have to work at all."

What the hell?

"She's working right now, and you're doing this little scene on my time. I don't appreciate it." The words were out of his mouth before he realized he even meant to say them. "Take a hike, Ed."

Ivy's head snapped around, her silky reddish brown hair floating in a whirl around her face and her pretty brown eyes round with surprise. "Mr. Hawthorne, I assure you, there is no need for you to get involved."

"It's Blake, Ivy, and has been since the first time we met."

She rolled her eyes at his nitpicking. "Blake, then. Stay out of this. It's not company business."

To hell with that. "You planning to marry this guy?" he asked in another uncontrollable burst of male aggressiveness.

"I . . . uh . . ." She looked back at Ed, and her body went tense, her cheeks stained with embarrassed color.

If Blake couldn't read that sign, he'd turn in his Eagle Scout badge. She didn't want the poor schmuck, but didn't have the heart to tell him.

"I'll give you ten minutes." Now that he knew the lay of the land, Blake felt a lot more charitable toward the other man.

He turned and went back into Ivy's office, passing Trudy, whose mouth hung open in pure, unadulterated astonishment.

Two

She was going to boil Blake Hawthorne in oil and serve him up as the deep-fried turkey for Thanksgiving.

"He'd better have his life insurance paid up," she muttered.

"What?"

Ed . . . darn it. Ed had to be dealt with before she could turn her arrogant jerk of a boss into fricassee.

She met his rainwater gaze straight on. "I can't marry you, Ed. I'm sorry."

"I kind of figured that out when Hawthorne came out snorting fire and belching brimstone."

"What has that got to do with anything?"

Ed shook his head. "I'm not as boring as you think I am, but when you're in love with someone else, any other man is just going to be a poor substitute."

She stared at him, her heart twisting in her chest, her breath coming in shallow, desperate pants. "I'm not in love with someone else."

She couldn't be. Loving Blake Hawthorne would be criminally stupid. She could get ten years in Sing Sing for that kind of thing.

"But you do find me boring."

"You're an actuary . . . I don't get numbers the way you do," she said lamely in an attempt not to hurt him or have to lie.

"I hope he knows what an incredible woman he's getting." Ed leaned down and kissed her temple before moving to cover her lips with his own.

He drew the kiss out, even teasing her lips with his tongue, and if she hadn't been so shocked by the move, she would have jerked back. His mouth on hers did not feel right. It didn't belong there. Though he wasn't a bad kisser, she had to admit.

When he lifted his head, there was an unholy gleam in his eye, and he nodded at something . . . or someone . . . over her shoulder. "Goodbye, sweetheart."

A strange noise from behind her said the kiss Ed had just given her had definitely been for *someone* else's benefit.

A strong hand landed on her shoulder a second after Ed walked out the door. Blake spun her to face him.

"You're quitting?" he gritted.

"Yes." She had no choice.

His mouth slammed down on hers with the power of a conquering army, and her brain short-circuited in a blaze of sparks and hissing nerve endings.

Firm, warm lips devoured hers, and she devoured them right back, tangling with his tongue and savoring the taste of a mouth that had been created for kissing. She wrapped her arms around his neck and pressed her body against hot, hard muscles not even remotely disguised by his conservative business attire.

Superman lived.

A growl emanated from his throat, a sound so primitive, it sent shivers down her spine and her thighs. Maybe not Superman. Blake Hawthorne was more like Conan the Barbarian.

His hands cupped her bottom and lifted, pressing her into the awe-inspiring proof of his desire.

Heat radiated between her thighs, making her aware of dampness there as well.

"Um . . . Mr. Hawthorne . . . " from somewhere behind them.

He squeezed her butt, and she groaned, sucking on his tongue.

"Ivy!" A high-pitched, woman's voice near her ear, but it still didn't register as something she had to respond to.

Blake broke his mouth from hers, and she buried her face against his neck, licking and sucking salty, utterly deliciously masculine tasting skin.

"What?" rumbled up from his chest.

Was he talking to her? She lifted her head to look, dazed and needy in a way she'd never been before.

"Mr. Hawthorne, there's a call for you." Trudy's voice saying something that didn't make sense to Ivy's sensually drugged brain.

"Damn it." Blake dropped her and pushed her away.

Ivy tottered on legs wobbly from her brush with a wild barbarian and looked around her.

Horror was clawing at her insides before her gaze even reached Trudy's shocked and clearly appalled countenance. Ivy, Trudy's boss and manager of this inn, had stood necking like a horny teenager right in front of the reception desk. Anyone could have seen her. Probably lots of people had.

Close to lunchtime, the restaurant was filling up, and Ivy could not help wondering in appalled fascination how many patrons had walked past the passion-locked couple in the lobby.

"I'll take the call in Ivy's office," Blake said, sounding entirely too self-controlled and unaffected for the man who had been squeezing her bottom and pressing her against his erection only moments before.

"Okay," Trudy said, her eyes still fixed on Ivy as if she'd sprouted tentacles and a third eyeball.

Ivy didn't even try for unaffected detachment. She turned tail and ran. Right up the stairs, both flights to the top floor where she slammed into her small apartment with less relief than a sense of desperation.

The small window air conditioner was on maximum cool, but her living-slash-dining room was still uncomfortably warm. Darn it. Blake was right. The inn needed central air, and of course it made sense to cater to the guests' needs by installing individually controlled systems.

She flopped down glumly on her white wicker sofa, and it creaked alarmingly. She shifted, and a twang between her thighs reminded her that though she was doing her best to block the memory of the past fifteen minutes, they had indeed happened.

How could she have lost all decorum and her sense of self-preservation in one go like that?

No way was she in the big city business mogul's league, but now he had to know she wanted to be. And why the heck had he kissed her? He'd been acting possessive and territorial since Trudy announced Ed was there. Ivy had thought at first it was all about her being a good corporate employee, but she didn't think bosses usually used kissing to keep their employees in line. Wasn't that sexual harassment or something? She certainly felt harassed, but as hot as that kiss had been, she didn't feel threatened by Blake. After all, she was the one who had told him she planned to quit.

The kiss had been no threat. To her career anyway. Her heart was another matter.

Ed had accused her of loving Blake Hawthorne.

Remembering the way she had responded to him the first time they met, and every time since—the fantasies she'd had about him, the way she felt in his company—she feared Ed might be right.

Blake was smart, and funny, too, when he wanted to be. He could also be a shark, and that gave her an atavistic thrill she didn't want to admit to, but was there all the same.

Oh, gosh . . . *was* she in love? Forget criminal stupidity, she was right on her way to total insanity.

Bam. Bam. Bam.

Her door shook with the powerful knocking, and that was saying something. The Old Orchard Inn was over a hundred years old and built with the solid construction of that century.

"Open the door, Ivy. I know you're in there."

Like it took a genius to figure out she'd be hiding after what had happened in the lobby.

The knocking resumed, and she stifled an urge to laugh, afraid if she gave in to it, she'd slip into mindless hysteria. The door wasn't even locked.

"Ivy. Damn it." Another bang on the door and then more cursing.

He had a much more expanded vocabulary of colorful words than she did.

"Ouch. Shit . . . a splinter . . . " Silence. "Do you have any tweezers?" through the door.

He was hurt? She flew off the couch and yanked the door open. He stood on the other side, sucking on his forefinger, the expression in his blue eyes scary.

She shivered even as she stepped back to let him in. "The door wasn't locked."

He glared at her.

"I'll just get the tweezers. Have a seat." She waved her hand toward one of the dinette chairs.

The light was better above the table, and she would have a better chance of seeing the sliver and getting it out.

It took Ivy only a second to get what she needed from the bathroom and then come back to Blake. He watched her walk toward him, his temper on a shorter leash than it had been in years. This woman got under his skin and stayed there.

But she had run from him.

He'd expected her to join him in her office and talk about the kiss like two mature, consenting adults . . . She had been consenting, hadn't she? With her tongue practically down his throat he was guessing yes, but no question—he'd initiated the kiss, and he hadn't given her a lot of choice in the matter.

She squatted in front of him and put her hand out. "Let me see."

He didn't even consider telling her he'd do it himself. Even though the last time he'd let a woman fuss over him, he'd been ten years old and it had been his grandmother.

Ivy winced when she saw the splinter embedded in his skin.

"This is going to hurt," she whispered.

"Don't worry about it. Just get the damn thing out."

She didn't respond to his brusque tone. She was too busy torturing him with her small fingers against his skin. Okay, she was trying to get the sliver out, but having her touch him for any reason affected his already overactive libido in dangerous ways.

He figured they needed to deal with the kiss before anything else. "It was mutually consenting." Her silence was not reassuring. "You didn't say no."

She sighed. "I know. You don't have to worry I'm going to file a sexual harassment complaint or something."

Did she really think that after a kiss like that, he was worried about federal regulations? He was a heck of a lot more worried about the possibility she didn't want to follow through on the passionate promise of her body.

She pulled out the splinter, and he sucked in air at the sting. It wasn't bad, but you couldn't tell that by the way she was blowing on his finger and moaning in sympathy.

When her lips pressed against the small drop of blood welling, he lost it.

He yanked her into his lap without a second thought and kissed her again. She gasped against his lips, and he took the sound into his mouth and gave her back his tongue.

Ambrosia.

She was so sweet, he'd get a sugar overload just tasting her lips.

She broke her mouth away, turning her head and panting. "We can't do this, Blake."

"Why not?"

"You're my boss."

"You said you were going to quit." Which reminded him. "What the hell is up with that anyway? Do you have a moral objection to central air-conditioning or something?"

She laughed shortly. "No, but I can't work here once the computerized controls have been implemented."

"Why not?"

She tried to pull away, and his arms tightened around her instinctively.

"I want to get up."

Consenting. That was key. Right. He let her go.

She stood up, and he had to fight the urge to pull her back into his lap.

"I'd rather not talk about the whys and wherefores of

my decision, Blake. I assume you brought a plan for implementation with you. It makes a lot more sense to focus on that right now."

"Not to me. I want to know why HGA, Inc. is about to lose one of its best property managers, and we are going to lose you, aren't we? You aren't interested in training to work on one of the other properties."

She shuddered. As though the thought was more than repugnant, like it was chilling. "No."

"Tell me why." His gut clenched. "It's not that Ed guy, is it? You aren't going to marry him, are you?"

"No. It's not Ed."

"Then what?"

She bit her lip and looked at him for several tense seconds. Her heart-shaped face was flushed, her lips swollen from his kisses, and her perfectly pressed general manager uniform was rumpled. She looked delectable and edible and everything in between, but her soft brown eyes were dark with wariness, and that stopped him from acting on his baser impulses.

"Why?" he practically begged.

Her full lips thinned in a line of determination. "Would you mind telling me what time it is?"

He frowned, but looked down at his watch obediently. What the hell? "It's stopped. My Rolex quit."

He sounded as stunned as he felt. He'd paid enough money for this watch to work into the next century.

She didn't look surprised, though. She looked resigned. "Maybe you could check your Palm Pilot?"

Feeling like something was going on here he didn't get, he pulled the slim case from his inner breast pocket and flipped it open. He pressed the power button and swore. None of his usual icons showed up. In fact, the only things on the screen were the basic operating system links. He tried clicking into setup, and a message came on screen offering to initialize the unit.

"My entire database and all my programs are gone. The memory had to have corrupted." That was going to be a pain in the ass. He could sync with his laptop, but anything he'd put in since the last sync was gone.

She sighed. "What about your mobile phone?"

That's right. His cell phone had a time function. He never used it because he always wore his watch. He pulled it off the clip on his belt, and this time the words that came out of his throat were vicious.

It had that little message on it that said it could only be used for emergency calls.

"What is going on?"

"I'm sorry," she said at the same time.

He pinned her with his gaze. "Why?"

"It's my fault."

"Crappy engineering is your fault?"

"It isn't bad engineering. It's me, well, me and the full moon."

"What, you're a werewolf?" he asked, laughing at the very thought of such a delicate woman getting hairy and growing fangs.

"That would be easier to live with," she grumbled.

Now, this had to be good.

"You'd rather be a werewolf?"

"Than get so magnetic I erase hard drives once a month . . . yes."

"Magnetic?" This was too bizarre to deal with on a muggy head. He stood up and walked into her small kitchenette. "You got anything up here to make coffee?"

"Sure." She started putting together an old-fashioned glass percolator pot.

"You don't have a microwave."

"There would be no point. After the first full moon, it would be broken."

He let that slide and filled the glass pot with water.

                                * * *

They took their coffee into the living room, and if
the sofa creaked when she sat on it, it positively groaned
when Blake lowered his over six-foot frame onto it.
"So, what, a regular sofa would give you problems, too?"

She would have glared at the irritating question if he
didn't sound so aggrieved. As it was, she had to bite back
a smile she was sure he wouldn't appreciate. He looked
so funny with his big body sprawled on her tiny sofa—
if you could even call it that. Even she had to curl her
legs up to lie down on it and read.

"I liked the way the wicker furniture looked in the
showroom, and I figured it would be easy to get up to
my apartment," she admitted.

"The unit wasn't furnished?"

"No. I took over management when the last family
member that owned the inn decided she wanted to travel
the world. The pieces up here were heirlooms, and her
nieces and nephews laid claim to them before her first
cruise ship sailed."

"I suppose wicker was cheaper than a regular living
room set as well."

She was surprised a guy with his money would recognize such a consideration and said so.

His blue eyes mocked her. "I didn't get this far in
business ignoring expenditure issues."

"Working for the family company didn't hurt." She
said it teasingly, but he didn't smile.

"My dad owned three properties when I joined HGA,
Inc. He didn't want to diversify into resort properties,
but now that's the bulk of what we own."

"In other words, it wasn't nepotism that got you this
job, but sound business acumen."

Burnished red accented his cheekbones. "I sounded
pretty defensive, didn't I?"

"A little."

"I guess I didn't want you thinking of me as the kind of man who rode through life on his dad's coattails."

"Like it matters to you what I think."

"Obviously it does. I'm not real sure why that should surprise you after me practically inhaling you with my lips twice in less than an hour."

"Has anyone ever told you that you're—"

"Bold?"

"Blunt."

His lips twitched. "Yes. Does it bother you?"

"I just don't know how to take it. I work for you; I don't think you're supposed to kiss me senseless. It isn't businesslike."

"You told me you were going to quit."

"Is that why?"

"I'd like to think knowing you wanted to quit made the difference, but I'm not sure it would have mattered if you hadn't said anything about leaving HGA, Inc. I didn't like seeing Ed lock lips with you."

"I don't know why."

Blake shrugged. "Around you a lot of primitive feelings come out. I get possessive. I want you, Ivy."

She choked on her coffee and had to stand up to stop coughing. "Forget blunt," she wheezed, "you're certifiable."

He stood up and patted her back, the feel of his hands on her anything but soothing. "Come on, honey, it can't be that big of a surprise."

"It is." She had never known another man as uninhibited in declaring his desire for her.

Heck, she'd never known a man who wanted her with the possessive hunger Blake had exhibited since arriving earlier.

She stepped away from him. "I'm fine now."

He searched her face, as if looking for signs that she needed further ministrations, and then nodded.

They returned to their seats, but she found herself sitting next to him on the narrow sofa instead of in the chair she'd occupied earlier.

She tried to move, but his hand locked onto her knee, and she froze as sensations she wished she could ignore washed over her.

"Tell me about the moon thing."

"Are you sure you want to hear?" she couldn't help asking.

"Yes."

She marshaled her thoughts, trying to decide where to begin. She'd spent so many of her adult years trying to pretend that she was as normal as everyone else. Now that the time had come to actually admit to her gift-slash-curse it-depends-on-how-you-look-at-it thing, her heart started hammering against her ribs.

Her fingers curled into fists against clammy palms. "I've only talked about it with one person outside my family since I told my best friend, Linda Baker, in the seventh grade."

"That's a long time."

"She didn't believe me. She said a lot of stuff that hurt."

"I'm not an adolescent girl."

"In other words, you might not believe me either, but you won't call me a lunatic and tell me you'd rather be best friends with Angela Potter?"

"Linda was the idiot to choose another girl over you for friendship. I was never that stupid. Not even when I was a kid."

She smiled. Years later and totally irrelevant, his encouragement still warmed her through. "Thank you."

"My pleasure." His fingers squeezed her knee, and

jolts of sensation zinged along nerve endings that traveled a path straight to the core of her.

She had to start talking, or she was going to lose her ability to do so. "For as long as anyone in my family can remember, puberty has caused the advent of more than a menstrual cycle for the females. It's also when the moon magnetism starts."

"What is moon magnetism? I've never heard of it."

"It's not scientifically documented, but refers to the phenomenon that happens to the women in my family every full moon."

"You get magnetic?"

"Right, only it's not totally consistent. Sometimes things happen I don't expect." Like the car accidents. "And then things I least expect to be immune to me are."

He looked skeptical.

"I'm sure there is a scientific explanation for that part, but I don't know what it is. Probably something to do with the material surrounding technology I expect to be affected, or maybe a dip in my magnetism during that time."

"Give me an example."

"Of the exceptions?"

"No, of what happens when you get *magnetic.*"

"Well, you've already seen what happened to your watch, your Palm Pilot, and your cell phone." What more did he want?

"All of which can be explained by technical malfunctioning."

"All three at once?" Did he really believe that? Maybe it was easier to take than the bizarre truth about her messed-up body chemistry.

"It could happen."

"I'm the malfunction, or at least I cause it."

"That's pretty conceited of you, or paranoid, depending on how you look at it," he said, his humor close to the surface.

"Do you seriously think I would make this stuff up?"

His expression turned serious. "No. I'm sure you believe what you are saying, but a few broken gadgets does not mean you're a walking magnet every full moon."

"It would be a lot more than a few if I didn't stay away from hi-tech areas during that time of month."

"Have you ever tested that theory?"

"No, but, Blake, I'm not the first woman in my family to experience it. I don't need to test the theory. I know what would happen."

"Family folklore is often based in fact, but it isn't always accurately interpretive of events."

She should have known Blake would be this way. He and Ed had one thing in common. They were both better at dealing with concrete realities than inexplicable phenomena.

"I've had four car accidents in my life, and they all happened during a full moon. Not one of them has been my fault either. It's like the other driver couldn't avoid hitting my car. They were drawn to me in some very strange way."

"If it were really a matter of you drawing the other cars, you would have had a lot more accidents than four in your lifetime."

He thought she'd come up with this as a way of excusing poor driving habits. "You have no idea how careful I've been."

He shook his head, a small smile playing around his lips. "I've been in a couple of accidents myself, and I can guarantee you the moon had nothing to do with them."

He didn't believe her. He wasn't even pretending to

give her a fair hearing. His skepticism was as palpable as his desire for her. She shouldn't be surprised, but somehow she had thought he would at least try to understand, if not believe.

"It doesn't matter what I say to you; you're going to explain it away as something else."

"Not if you don't want me to."

"But you'll be thinking it."

"I can't deny that."

"At least you're honest."

"I'm sorry."

She shrugged off his apology and his disbelief. Neither of them mattered. She wouldn't let them matter. "Okay, fine. I've explained my need to leave your employment, and whether or not you accept it won't change the outcome. I *am* quitting."

A speculative gleam entered his narrowed blue eyes. "If I can convince you that your family tradition is nothing more than an excuse for technophobia, will you stay on with HGA, Inc.?"

"I am *not* a technophobe."

"Right."

Oooh . . . he was lucky steam wasn't coming out of her ears. "Trust me when I say that you have even less chance of convincing me than I had of convincing you. And I'm not a bullheaded male too stubborn to see what's right in front of his face."

He smiled at her insult. Actually smiled. "Honey, I'm not ashamed to admit that in some ways a bull and I have a lot in common."

"I'm talking about the head between your ears, oh, master of crude innuendo."

He laughed and leaned forward until his lips hovered right above hers. "I like it when you get feisty, Ivy."

She could taste his lips on the air between them, and

that kind of thing was way too dangerous. Without giving him a chance to stop her, she slipped off the sofa and around the matching wicker coffee table.

"Stop trying to seduce me."

He leaned back, and the wicker groaned again. "Why?"

"*Why?*"

"Uh-huh."

"Because you . . . because I . . . It's a bad idea!"

He crossed his arms over his chest, his sleeve raising to reveal his dead Rolex. "Come to Cleveland with me tomorrow. There's an appliance store there that specializes in guest properties. They've got some air-conditioning and heating units I want you to look at with me."

This was way worse than Linda Baker's refusal to believe. He was not only dismissing her concerns, but he was asking her to fly in the face of them. "That would be insane."

"I take full responsibility for anything that happens while we are there connected to your supposed magnetism."

"So, if we walk into a store and all the electronic units stop working, you'll what . . . hire a repairman?"

"Something like that."

She had spent her entire life since puberty avoiding just such a situation. "No way."

"Give it a chance, Ivy. Look at it this way. Either I convince you that your fears are groundless, or you convince me they aren't. Either way, the trip isn't wasted."

"You're assuming I care whether or not you believe me."

"I know you care. The question is, do you have enough courage to do something about it?"

"I'm not a coward."

"Prove it."

"I don't have anything to prove to you."

"Then prove it to yourself."

"You don't know when to give up."

"Sure, I do. When it's hopeless. You are not a hopeless cause."

"I can only agree on one condition." Even as she uttered the words, her mind shrieked in shock at them.

Three

"Name it."

"We don't go anywhere my magnetism could cause lasting or irretrievable damage."

"I won't take you into any data entry offices."

She rolled her eyes. "For a techno-geek, you sure have a limited understanding of what can be messed up by a magnetic field."

"You think I'm a geek?" he asked, sounding really offended.

"If the pocket protector fits, wear it."

"I don't use a pocket protector," he growled, sounding more like an angry wolf than a techno-geek, but she wasn't about to tell him that.

"You use a Palm Pilot, you don't need a pocket protector, but I bet you've got an attachment to carry it on your belt."

"So what if I have? That doesn't make me a geek."

"Just because I don't own one doesn't make me a technophobe either."

His eyes narrowed. "Touché."

"We'll have to take my car."

"Why?"

"It doesn't have an onboard computer, and if you want to get farther than the entrance to the parking lot, it will have to be in a car that runs on old-fashioned mechanical ingenuity."

"What do you drive?"

"A '66 Mustang."

He smiled. "I was afraid you were going to say a Model T."

"I'm not a twenty-first century anachronism, Blake. The way I live my life isn't always my choice."

He nodded, looking pained. "I'm sorry. I didn't mean to make fun of you."

"No offense taken."

"Are you sure?" His gaze pierced her as if he was trying to read her mind. "It doesn't bother you that I think your curse is more in the realm of family folklore than reality?"

Put like that . . . She sighed. "Maybe a little, but I'm not mad at you."

"I'm glad."

He was getting that look in his eyes again, the one that said he was thinking about kissing her. She leaned back where she was kneeling on the other side of the coffee table. As if two more inches of distance would help. "Do you mind doing the driving?"

"You don't mind me driving your car?"

"I've never been in an accident when I was the passenger."

"And you're positive that has nothing to do with your driving . . . ," he teased.

She laughed, realizing he really meant no disparagement of her character. The guy had a sense of humor that needed a leash.

"I'll drive," he said with a smile.

"Okay, then. It's a date. I mean an appointment." He

just smiled at her slip, and she stood up. "Let me take you on a tour so you can see the inn's improvements."

He stood as well. "That sounds great. Are any of the rooms currently empty?"

"Actually, we're full for the next few nights. I was even on the verge of putting the executive quarters available to rent before you showed up."

"If it means saving space, I could room with you."

"Nice try, but I'm sure the inn can handle the loss of income."

"Especially at the nightly rates we're charging."

"Let's not start in on that again."

They were doing an inspection of the kitchen when Blake mentioned HGA, Inc.'s plans to sell the inn once they had improved its profitability margin.

Ivy went rigid with shock, her brown gaze narrowing in clear consternation. *"You're doing all of these updates just to turn around and sell?"*

"Yes." He didn't understand why she sounded so horrified. "The property was an investment purchase, not a long-term acquisition."

"Then, why not sell it now, before investing more money?"

"The kind of money we want to invest, combined with the inn's reputation for occupancy, should net a significant ROI."

She was silent for several minutes after that, letting Blake ask the chef questions about his special line of menu items that included apples as a key ingredient. Blake had found the practice a bit corny at first, seeing as how the Old Orchard Inn was located in Delicious, Ohio. That in itself was pretty quaint, but he'd had the baked apples the last time he visited and now thought the chef bordered on brilliant.

Ivy didn't say anything as she led him out of the kitchen and to the front lobby.

"Is something wrong?" he asked his suddenly silent companion.

"No."

Silence. Again.

"Did you want to save going over reservation procedures until later?"

She didn't look at him. "That might be best. I've got some work to catch up on."

"Me, too." He hadn't checked his e-mail since leaving Cleveland early that morning. "I don't suppose there's anywhere nearby I can get a high-speed Internet connection?"

"In Delicious? I don't think so."

He remembered the last time he had visited, he'd resorted to driving a half an hour south so he could use the wireless connection at a Starbucks. Apparently, nothing had changed since then. "What time do you want to do dinner?"

She shrugged. "Whatever works for you. You're the boss."

The words didn't give him the sensual thrill they had earlier. She said them with too much resignation.

He grabbed her shoulders and forced her to face him, recognizing somewhere deep inside that he was acting like a Neanderthal and unable to alter that reality. "What is the matter?"

She bit her lip and then frowned. "Don't you find it the least bit ironic that you're going to update the inn and force me to quit my job, just so you can sell it?"

"Honey, I—"

She shook her head, her expression pained, cutting his words off as effectively as if she'd covered his mouth. "I shouldn't have said that. This isn't about me. It's about making money for HGA, Inc."

An unfamiliar sense of guilt washed over him like a poisonous red tide. "I'm sorry."

She jerked her shoulders from his loosened grasp. "There's no need for you to be. I'll see you for dinner." She spun on her heel and left, disappearing behind the counter and into her office before he could unstick his usually eloquent tongue from the roof of his mouth.

Blake knocked on Ivy's door ten minutes before they were due in the restaurant. She'd been expecting him to be early, so she was ready.

His blue gaze traveled over her as though he was memorizing each dip and valley of her feminine form. His eyes said he liked what he saw, even if the terrain was somewhat modest. "You're not on duty anymore, Ivy. I wouldn't have minded seeing you in something besides an HGA, Inc. uniform."

She looked down at her crisply ironed blouse, no-nonsense blazer, and straight skirt she habitually wore when in her office and then back at him. "We can't have what we want all of the time, and I'm having dinner with my boss. That means I'm on duty. Ask Ed. He wanted to have dinner with me, too, but business came first."

"You didn't want to eat with him." Blake sounded so sure of himself that she almost lied just to take him down a peg.

"No, I didn't."

"You're not going to marry him." Another statement of incontrovertible fact.

She shrugged.

"You won't be seeing him anymore." This time, he sounded slightly uncertain, and she couldn't help playing out his tension.

"Maybe."

"Damn it, Ivy. Is it over between the two of you, or not?"

As quickly as the desire to tease had come, it left. He was way too intense for her to treat his question lightly. "It's over. I doubt I'll see him again."

"Good."

"Why does it matter? You're in town for what, two, maybe three days? Then you'll be gone. Who I see then is none of your concern."

"Wear something besides a uniform tomorrow for our trip into Cleveland," he said, ignoring her assertion of independence in her social life.

"Do you think that as my boss you have the right to dictate what I wear?"

"If I told you to wear your uniform, would you?" he asked instead of answering.

She thought about it. "Probably."

"So, I'm telling you not to wear it. I'm not telling you what you should wear instead."

He was being entirely too reasonable considering the aura of masculine intent emanating off of him.

"Fine, I'll wear something else." A burlap sack. Wouldn't he just love that? "Now, can we go to dinner?"

"Sure."

She stepped into the hall and closed her door, locking it before turning to head for the stairs.

"Is there a reason why we can't take the elevator?"

She stopped short. "Uh . . . no. I'm so used to taking the stairs, I never think of it."

They stepped into the elevator, and he pulled the gate closed before turning the key toward the down position. The elevator started its slow descent. "I've always loved this elevator."

She smiled. "Me, too."

"You could do very interesting things in this space."

She looked around them at the rich mahogany walls and the temporary privacy afforded by the slowly passing wall between floors. "Um, I guess so."

He stepped closer until his body hemmed hers in with his heat and solid bulk. "For instance, it moves so slowly, there's plenty of time for a stolen kiss between floors."

She got a mumbled "mm-mmm" out before his lips claimed hers. Unlike their previous kisses, this one was soft and gentle. Although, it felt just as much of a claim staking as his more aggressive behavior had earlier.

The elevator jolted to a stop as he stepped away from her. "You may look like a buttoned-down, all-business property manager, but you kiss like a woman I want to possess."

Her mouth opened, but nothing came out. She'd gotten the message he wanted her, but to have him state it so blatantly in a public place was unnerving.

It was also exciting, and the throb between her legs testified to that fact.

He opened the gate and then slipped his hand under her blazer in an intimate and proprietary move that could not be mistaken. His hand settled against her waist, and he led her from the elevator.

Trudy had left an hour ago. However, the evening desk clerk, an older gentleman who had retired from the Apple County Savings and Loan the year before, gave her and Blake the same blank-eyed stare of shock Trudy had had on her face earlier. And it was no wonder. Blake was acting like her lover, not her boss.

His hand branded her with its heat through the crisp cotton of her blouse, forcing her body to accept what her mind was still fighting. This man was going to be her lover.

They were seated at a table on the far side of the big

fireplace. It was the one place in the restaurant that afforded a modicum of privacy from the other patrons, and she couldn't help wondering if Blake had requested it.

She straightened her already perfectly placed cutlery. "Did you ask for this table earlier?"

His feet settled on either side of her left leg, and then his calves came together, pressing her leg between his and making the air hiss out of her lungs in a startled gasp. "I wanted to be able to focus on you, not the other diners."

"I thought you were here to check out the inn."

"I already know you are doing an excellent job managing it. I came to get you to agree to the upgrades I wanted."

"You could have done that over the phone."

"Then I guess I really came to see you."

"Oh," she said on another gasp of sensual delight as his leg moved against hers.

"Can you doubt it?"

Her sensible navy blue pump slipped off against his calf, and she shivered as her nylon-clad foot rubbed along the tense muscles of his lower leg. He smiled and leaned forward. Suddenly her foot was locked in strong fingers and then lifted to his lap. He pressed her arch against a truly impressive bulge in his pants.

"*Blake.*"

"Don't you want to feel what you do to me?"

"I . . ." She couldn't say no. It excited her unbearably to know she had this effect on a man she found so amazing and delectable. "This is not the place."

"Yes, it is."

Her eyes widened and then narrowed. "You're awfully bossy."

"I'm your boss. Being bossy is part of my job description."

"Are you trying to say that my employment with

your company somehow depends on me letting you do this sort of thing?"

"And if I am?" he asked in a voice that made her insides shiver.

"I would remind you that I've already given my notice."

"So, I guess you know you've got a choice. Are you going to *choose* to let me tell you what to do?" The dark promise and obvious desire in his voice sent frissons of sensation up and down the backs of her thighs.

"You want to order me around?" she asked, never having considered the possibility a turn-on, but inexplicably excited by the prospect now.

"In the bedroom? Oh, yeah."

Oh, man. She was going to melt into a puddle of need right there on her chair.

"You want to play some kind of dominant/submissive game with me?" she asked just to clarify.

His hand held her foot against him as she tried to wriggle away. "And if I do?"

"I . . ."

"Maybe I want to take you back to my room and play sexy games with you until you can't stand because your legs are so rubbery from exertion and you can barely talk from screaming your throat raw."

Heat pooled low in her belly, and heaviness settled in her womb. "I'd say I'm glad no one is close enough to hear us talking and that it's a good thing the walls are so thick in this place." She tried to say it lightly, but her voice came out seductive and rasping instead.

Molten desire flared in his eyes, and every trace of humor left his face. "How thick?"

She could barely breathe. "The kind of walls married couples wish they had between them and their kids so they could make love without Little Johnny asking what all the ruckus was the next morning."

"Sounds perfect."

"For what?" she croaked out.

He didn't answer immediately, and all sorts of scenarios ran through her mind. Some totally implausible . . . or were they?

"Are you ready to order?" The chirpy voice from over her left shoulder made Ivy's body jerk in reaction, but Blake kept her foot firmly in his lap.

"We'll both have the chef's special tonight."

"*We will?*" she asked, not even remembering what it was, and she'd approved the menu for the week.

Blake had no right to look so disgustingly in control and unaffected while she could feel her face flame with embarrassment, even though there was no way Bonnie could see what was going on under the long white table cloth they used to cover the tables for dinner.

He nodded and smiled at Bonnie as if *she* were the one who had asked the question. He also ordered a bottle of wine and appetizers of Waldorf salad. Bonnie took the order, a look of bemusement crossing her perky, youthful features.

"I'm perfectly capable of ordering for myself," Ivy said as the waitress walked away.

Blue eyes challenged her with serious regard under blond brows drawn just slightly together. "Hawthorne."

"What?"

"If you want to stop playing anytime tonight, all you have to do is say my last name."

She'd read about that kind of thing. It was called a safe word, and it gave the submissive partner the power to actually control the intimacy by being able to stop it anytime. However, she couldn't quite see why she would need one with Blake, unless he had some very different ideas about lovemaking than she did.

"I'm not into pain."

His mouth twisted with instant revulsion. "I'm not either, not giving it or receiving it."

"Then why Hawthorne?"

He leaned across the table, his gaze mesmerizing with its intensity. "I want to push you past your comfort zone, Ivy. I want to make love to you like no other man has or ever will. I want everything you have to give and then some."

"You sound like an army recruiter. *Be all you can be.*"

His lips quirked at one corner. "We can play drill sergeant and new recruit another night, sweetheart."

"I didn't say I wanted to play at all."

"Then say my last name. I'll stop."

"You mean you'll stop trying to seduce me?" No doubt the man had been working on her desire to succumb since that first powerful kiss in the lobby.

"Is that what you want?"

All she had to do was say yes, and he would stop. She could see it in his eyes.

She opened her mouth, but she couldn't make the word come out. She wanted to make love to Blake Hawthorne, had wanted to since the first day they met. He wanted her, too, and that knowledge served only to fuel the fire of her own desire until it was a river of unstoppable lava flowing through her veins.

In one day, maybe two, he would leave Delicious, and she would never see him again. He was right about her not wanting to continue working for HGA, Inc. She couldn't. She would have to find another job not impacted by her monthly magnetic pull.

A job that would not include phone calls, memos, and the infrequent on-site visit from the compelling man sitting across from her.

She closed her mouth and licked her lips nervously.

He caressed her foot under the table, doing things with his thumb against her instep that sent sensual thrills straight to her womb. "Are you going to let me love you tonight, Ivy?"

"Do you play games in the bedroom often?" she asked, trying to hedge around a direct answer.

His thumb moved to a spot between two of her toes and pressed. Oh, jeeze, that felt good. She barely stifled a gasp, but her shallow breathing had to be giving her away.

His eyes darkened to the color of the night sky. "I've never played this game before. I've never wanted to, but I feel things with you I don't feel with anyone else."

He didn't mean what her heart wanted him to mean, that he was maybe falling in love, too. However, knowing that she was unique to him on a sexual level was pretty heady stuff. Blake was the kind of man who drew women to him like hungry bees to honey. He was one of the beautiful people with a sense of personal power that never wavered.

She wasn't his type, not with her small-town lifestyle and quirky full-moon magnetism. Only he didn't seem to see things that way. In fact, he was saying she was exactly his type in a special and unique way. She wanted that to be true. Badly.

He massaged each of her individual toes with strong, steady fingers that knew exactly what to do to make her quiver between her thighs. His hard-on still pressed intimately against the bottom of her foot, and if she wasn't mistaken, it was growing. Oh, wow. *It got bigger?*

More sexy images flashed through her brain, making her hotter than she'd ever been in her life, and he wasn't even touching her intimately. Her eyes slid shut, and it was all she could do to stay on her chair.

Bonnie chose that moment to return to the table with the wine.

Ivy jerked upright and almost fell sideways when her leg didn't move with the rest of her. She made a startled sound and grabbed the table to maintain her balance.

"Are you all right, Ivy?"

"I'm fine, Bonnie." But her cheeks were blazing, and the look she gave Blake let him know it wasn't only excitement she was feeling. "Why don't you have Mr. *Hawthorne* taste the wine?"

Her foot was released immediately, and she lowered it to the floor, searching desperately for her pump. She found it and pushed her foot inside, finding it harder than it should have been because she was trembling.

Blake went through the ritual of sniffing and tasting the wine before approving it.

Did anyone ever say, *No, thank you, this Riesling is just too fruity for my palate?* she wondered whimsically and then laughed at her own joke. Both Blake and Bonnie looked at her questioningly.

She shrugged. "Uh . . . nothing. Just something I was thinking about." She was losing her mind, and it was all Blake Hawthorne's fault.

So, say his last name again and end the game, her mind taunted. But she knew she wouldn't do it. She *wanted* to lose her sanity in a haze of desire and charged emotion at least once in her life, and this would probably be her only chance. No other man had ever impacted her like her soon-to-be ex-boss.

Not even Danny, the only man she'd ever shared her body with.

Bonnie poured them both a glass of the duly approved wine, put the bottle in a standing ice bucket beside the table, and left.

Blake looked at her with an enigmatic expression and took a sip of his wine. "You used the safe word."

"I almost fell off my chair."

"Was that why?"

Had he thought she meant to end the game entirely? "Yes."

"Does that mean you want to play?"

The sense of recklessness that had been growing since she realized she would soon be out of his life forever drowned her inner caution under a tsunami wave that left room for no other answer than a positive one. She nodded.

"I need the words, Ivy. I want your verbal surrender."

"This isn't a war."

"No, but it is a campaign, and I want it clearly understood that I have your permission to invade your territory."

Considering the type of lovemaking he wanted, the level of personal sexual submission he was asking for, she could understand completely his desire for absolute clarity on what she was willing to do and participate in. It just went to show that no matter how dominant he wanted to play in the bedroom, he didn't want to take anything she wasn't prepared to give.

She liked that. She liked it a lot, and it gave her the courage to give him the verbal confirmation he needed.

"Yes, I want you to love me." She meant that quite literally, but she would settle for the physical variety. She didn't have any choice.

The prospect of never knowing anything of his love for her entire life was too depressing to even consider.

"Any way you want," she added for good measure.

Passion and approval flared in his eyes. "You don't know how much that pleases me, sweetheart."

The rich satisfaction in his voice was hard to mistake.

"I think I do."

He smiled. "Maybe you do."

He didn't try to play footsie with her again, or say anything even borderline embarrassing as their meal was served and they began to eat. They discussed his proposal for upgrading the inn, and she had to admit his ideas were sound. Neither of them mentioned the fact those ideas would put her out of a job.

He probably thought she was overreacting and didn't see that as the actual outcome. She knew better, but had no desire to diminish the rapport with a negative reminder.

They were halfway through the main course, and she had just finished telling him a humorous story about one of the guests, when he got that look in his eyes again. The sexy-pirate-I'm-going-to-ravish-you look.

Her breath caught in her throat, and she stared at him with the feeling she'd just been caught in the hunter's sights and no matter how fast or far she ran, it wouldn't be enough to get away.

"I want you to go to the ladies' rest room and remove your panties, then come back to the table."

"*What?*" she demanded in shock.

"You heard me."

"But, Blake!" She'd never done anything like that in her life.

"You know what to do if you have a problem with that." There wasn't the least amount of give in his expression, and the tone of his voice challenged her.

"I'm not wearing panties," she said, blurting out the first thing that came to her mind, just managing to keep it to a staccato whisper so other diners did not hear.

If he'd looked dangerous before, he now looked pos-

itively feral. "Hose or thigh-highs?" he asked in a gut-
tural voice.

"Hose."

"Go to the ladies' and remove them."

Ivy stared at him. All she had to do was say his last
name, and he wouldn't ask her to do it again. She was
tempted. It would be safer. It would also establish limits she wasn't willing to go beyond—limits she'd never
gone past before—but he'd said he wanted to push her
past those limits, and the thing was . . . she wanted to
be pushed.

She took a sip of her wine, wetting a suddenly dry
mouth.

"Ivy?" The look of concern mixed with sexual hunger
in his eyes wrapped itself around her heart and squeezed.

This man was so incredible.

She pushed her chair back and stood. "I'll be right
back."

Blake couldn't believe she'd done it. He couldn't believe he'd asked. Hell, he'd always been an aggressive
lover, but he'd never felt this need to obliterate a woman's
sexual boundaries. Except that was exactly what he
wanted to do with Ivy Kendall.

She was so controlled. So buttoned up and proper.
Giving control to him in the bedroom would be hard
for her, but ultimately rewarding. He knew it. They both
knew it, or she wouldn't be on her way to the rest room
right now, her hips shifting in a subtle rhythm that
made his arousal pulse painfully against his fly.

Ivy walked back to the table, feeling free, just a little
naughty, and very, very excited. She wondered if he'd
taken into consideration the fact that without her hose,
the moisture between her legs might get uncomfortable. Not that she felt uncomfortable. She felt sexy,

feminine, and daring. It was incredible, the way the air brushed her most sensitive flesh.

She slipped into her seat, amazed at how the silk of her skirt's lining sliding against her bottom could be such an erotic experience. Her panties never made her feel like this.

Blake looked at her with one eyebrow quirked in question.

"Yes, I did it."

Four

His smile was pure sexy male bent on dominating his mate, but tinged with surprised pleasure, as if he'd been waiting to hear she would chicken out at the last minute. Once again she considered how the submissive partner actually had a lot of power in this particular game.

She ate very little of the remainder of her dinner and nothing at all of dessert. With so many butterflies doing loops and dives in her stomach, she was too charged to eat.

When he finished his dessert, he complimented the wait staff and the chef before leading her back to the elevator. Once again he had a proprietary hand on her waist, but this time the night clerk was too busy with a customer to notice.

She peeled away from Blake as soon as they entered the small enclosure, her senses overwhelmed by his nearness. The past half an hour had been an exercise in self-control for her. Every movement she made reminded her of her less than fully dressed state, and she'd had to stifle more than one moan as pleasure jolted from one synapsis to another in a never-ending domino effect.

She stood against the far wall while he closed the gate and started the elevator's ascent with the key.

"You're good with the employees," she commented, unnerved by the silence between them as the elevator slowly rose.

"Am I?" he asked, turning to face her.

The look of untamed desire in his eyes made her legs weak, and she leaned back against the wall. "Yes," she said breathlessly. "They were all thrilled by your praise."

"You've got a well-run operation here, Ivy. Your employees know their jobs and do them well."

"Thank you."

"However," he said, his voice lowering to a seductive rumble, "their boss is not so cooperative about doing her job."

The dark menace in his voice sent a perverse thrill of delight spearing through her.

"I'm very cooperative," she argued, wondering where this game was going.

He reached behind him, and the elevator stopped moving. They were between floors, which meant no one could see them and they could see nothing but the wall through the brass gate.

She was locked in total privacy with him in a space that left no room to run. She didn't want to run, but an atavistic chill made her shiver all the same.

He shook his head, looking regretful. "No, Ivy, you've been a very bad employee."

"I haven't," she gasped.

"But you have. You've fought every suggestion I've made for improvement. You've missed important training meetings. That sort of insubordination has to be dealt with."

"Um . . ." She didn't have an answer for him, but sweat trickled down her back. If this was leading where she thought it was leading, she might have to stop the game.

"Come here, Ivy."

Incredibly, legs she thought too weak to move took her the steps across the elevator until she stood directly in front of him. She hadn't consciously decided to obey him; she simply had. She was forced to tip her head back to see his face.

"I think you need a lesson in cooperation, don't you?"

"Uh . . . what kind of lesson?" She wasn't sure she *hated* the idea of being spanked in love play, but she wasn't sure she *liked* it either.

He cupped her face with one hand and leaned down until he was speaking against her lips. "Are you worried?"

"A little."

His hand reached around and caressed her backside. "You need some discipline, sweetheart, and I'm just the man to give it to you."

Her breath seized in her chest, and it was all she could do not to choke on her own nervousness. "D-discipline?"

He cupped her bottom, kneading the resilient flesh with a gentle touch belied by the ruthless expression in his eyes. "Not all discipline is punishment, Ivy."

"Oh."

"Do you know what the word *discipline* means?"

She should, but right now remembering her own name was a little difficult. "No."

"It means *to teach*. I'm going to teach you how to cooperate."

"H-how?"

"By demanding complete and unreserved cooperation from you from this point forward."

Her immediate relief that he hadn't been talking about a sexy spanking was mitigated quickly by one question: what would he ask her cooperation in doing?

"Are you ready to take your discipline like a big girl?"

The condescending question set her back up, and she glared at him. She could take whatever he wanted to dish out. "Yes."

"Good. Kiss me."

Now, that was no hardship. She'd wanted his lips back on hers since cutting off their kiss earlier. The gentle kiss in the elevator had been too short to come anywhere near assuaging that need. She pressed her mouth against the one he had so obligingly brought down to her level. At the feel of his warm lips against hers, a rush of pleasure whooshed through her body. She clasped his head with both her hands and deepened the kiss, darting her tongue between his willingly parted lips.

She tasted him, loving the warm, wet texture inside his mouth, the yummy essence that was his alone, and the feel of their lips locked in a battle as old as the first man and woman.

Her already peaked nipples tightened and ached for his touch. She pressed her breasts against him and rubbed like a cat. It felt wonderful, but it wasn't enough. There were too many layers of clothing between the two of them.

She whimpered.

He broke his mouth from hers. "What do you want?"

"I . . ." She couldn't say it.

"Tell me what you want."

The direct order reminded her that this was supposed to be an exercise in cooperation on her part, and she'd already decided she could take whatever he threw at her.

Then his blue gaze warmed, and he brushed the backs of his fingers against her temple. "Come on, honey, you can do it. Tell me what you want, and I'll give it to you. Whatever it is."

"You know what it is," she said breathlessly.

"Maybe. I want to be sure." He played with the skin exposed at the neck of her blouse, making her shiver in response. "Tell me."

How could one man be so caring and yet so relentless at the same time?

She forced her lips to form words they'd never formed before when speaking to a man. "I want your hand on my breast . . . on my nipple," she said on a rush of brutal honesty.

"I want that, too." His hand slid down her chest, under her jacket and cupped her small breast.

He upbraided the aching nipple with his thumb.

She groaned.

"You like that?"

"Yessss . . . "

"I like it, too. Your body turns me on." He pressed against her, giving concrete evidence to his claim.

"You excite me, too."

"Do I?" he asked, his voice a sensual caress to her ears.

"Yes."

"Are you wet for me?" he asked.

She buried her face against his chest, the bluntness of the conversation getting to her. "Yes."

"I want to feel."

Her head jerked up. "What?"

His eyes were set on her with serious intent, his mouth a firm line of uncompromising strength. "I want to see how cooperative your body is right now. Lift your skirt."

"But I'm not wearing any underwear."

His lips twitched. "I know."

His amusement mixed with the cool challenge in his devilish blue eyes decided her before she even considered whether or not she wanted to use the safe word.

She reached down and grabbed her skirt by the hem on either side of her hips. She inched it up until it barely covered the apex of her thighs.

"All the way, sweetheart."

If he'd been watching while she did it, she probably wouldn't have been able to, but he was looking into her eyes, his gaze compelling her to acquiesce. She didn't even know how he knew she hadn't uncovered herself completely. Nevertheless, she brought the skirt up the last couple of inches. Air tickled her damp curls and caressed her bare bottom.

He moved back slightly, reaching down between them. His fingertips played gently over the top of her mound and upper vulva. It felt so good, she closed her eyes and savored each small movement.

"Spread your legs."

Without opening her eyes, she shifted until her thighs were far enough apart for his hand to slip between them, but he didn't trespass her outer lips. His fingertips barely touched the sensitive hairs covering her sex, making her yearn for more and whimper with that need.

"Do you want me to touch you?"

"Please . . ."

One finger slipped between her slick folds and probed her entrance. "Yes, you are wet for me, aren't you? That's a very good sign of your cooperation. In fact, that kind of cooperation deserves a reward, don't you think?"

She couldn't think, couldn't make sense of his words in order to make a response. She could only react to her body's needs, rocking her hips, seeking deeper penetration with his finger. But then the heel of his hand was pressing against her clitoris.

And it felt so good. "Oh, Blake . . . oh, oh, oh . . ."

"Keep your skirt up, Ivy, do you hear me?"

What? Oh . . . "Yes."

She tightened her grip on the skirt's hem until her fingers ached from the pressure.

His mouth claimed hers again, the kiss hot and hungry.

He slipped another finger between her thighs and then used them to tease up and down the sides of her labia, the heel of his hand continuing its teasing stimulation of her swollen sweet spot. Tension like she'd never experienced spiraled inside her until she was shaking with preorgasmic muscular rigidity.

She moaned against his lips, the sound shocking in its carnality. She needed more, but couldn't make herself break the kiss and tell him. She moved her body against him, riding those fingers in a wanton abandon she would never have considered herself capable of.

He added a third finger, using his middle one to caress her clitoris directly while his others continued the massage of her vulva, and then he pinched the nipple he had been teasing with his thumb. She detonated, pleasure exploding inside her with the power of an atomic split.

Blake swallowed Ivy's scream, his own body perilously close to going off.

She was so damn responsive.

A rush of hot moisture covered his fingers as she jerked against him in spasmodic convulsions in the longest climax he had ever witnessed in a lover. He kissed her through it, gentling her with his fingers and his mouth until her quaking had been reduced to a mere quiver.

Finally, she sagged against him as if she'd lost the ability to stand on her own. Hell, she probably had. This was not your average cop a feel in the elevator.

He slid his mouth from hers, placing calming kisses against the corner of her lips and against her temple. "You are amazing, sweetheart."

Her head fell against his chest, and a sigh shuddered out of her. "You're the amazing one. That was incredible."

He removed his hand, and then he tilted her head back so she could watch him as he cleaned his fingers with the only thing handy, his mouth.

Her eyes widened. "Oh . . ." But she kept watching him, an expression of fascination coming over her features.

He popped the last finger out of his mouth. "You taste good."

"Do I?" she asked in a voice barely above a whisper.

"Want to taste?" he asked, pressing his fingertip against her lip.

Several emotions swirled in her soft brown eyes. Confusion. Alarm. Curiosity. *Desire*. "I don't think—"

He pushed his finger between her open lips. "Taste."

She closed her lips around him and sucked tentatively.

His dick pressed against his pants like a tidal wave trying to break over a dam. It hurt in a very good way. "Use your tongue, baby, taste it."

She obediently swirled her tongue around him, and his body jerked and shuddered against her as his sex pulsed in a short beat that left the tip wet and the shaft ready to finish.

His control was hanging by a thread, and her hot mouth clinging to his finger was going to be the scissors that snipped it.

But he didn't want to take her for the first time in the elevator. He wanted her in his bed and under him. He wanted to do more than join their bodies; he wanted to stake a claim.

He reached behind him with a hand that trembled and turned the key. The elevator started its ponderous ascent upward.

The movement jolted her, and she catapulted from his arms, landing against the back wall with an audible thump. She still had a grip on her skirt, and the sight of her glistening red curls almost did him in.

"I can't . . . I can't . . ." She closed her eyes and swallowed. "I can't believe we're doing this."

"What's the matter? You liked it, Ivy. Don't try to pretend now you didn't."

"Of course I liked it. I'm not insane, but someone *could see us.*"

And if they saw her now, they'd get an eyeful. "Honey, your skirt is still up around your belly button."

She looked down, her expression horrified. "Oh, my gosh!" She yanked it down. "I can't believe I forgot."

"You were preoccupied."

She covered her face with both hands. "I'm going to die of embarrassment right now."

The old-fashioned elevator got very little use, and being at the back of the inn, it wasn't a glaringly public place either despite the open grillwork of the gate that left its occupants exposed through the matching grill-work gate in the doorway of each floor. "Don't worry about it."

"That's easy for you to say. You're not the one who looks mussed," she mumbled through her hands, spreading her fingers so she could peek at him.

He grinned. Her hair was a little messier than its usual silky smooth flip, but the biggest giveaway to what they had been doing was in her eyes. She looked dev-astated.

Good, because touching her devastated him.

"No one is going to know what you've been doing by the state of your dress."

"Anyone who has been waiting for the elevator is going to speculate." Her voice came out trembly.

He liked knowing that despite her embarrassment, she was still reeling from his effect on her.

They were passing the second floor. The area in front of the gate was empty. "No one is around on this floor, and the only rooms on the third floor are your apartment and corporate quarters."

Her stance did not relax appreciably, but she lowered her hands so she could look at him fully. "Blake?"

"Hmm?"

"Why did you stop?"

The question surprised him. "You wanted to make love in the elevator?" he asked, his voice raspy from desire that had had no outlet.

"A minute ago, I wouldn't have cared if we were in the lobby."

The admission did things to him that weren't related entirely to how tight his pants had become in the crotch area. "I like your honesty."

"I'm not sophisticated enough for sexual games."

"Aren't you?"

Incredibly, she blushed. "I meant head games, pretending I don't want you when I do, that sort of thing."

He grinned. "I'm glad. I hate *that sort of thing*, and for the record, I want you, too."

"I got that impression, only why . . ."

"I want you fully naked and under me the first time I come inside of you."

Her eyes widened until she resembled a shock victim. "You're so blunt."

"So you've said." He stalked her to the other side of the elevator, stopping when she was pressed tightly against the back wall and his body barely touched hers. "That makes us a good couple. Blunt is just another way of being honest."

The air vibrated between them, and her breath came in shallow pants. She licked her lips and gasped when he followed suit, tasting her while placing his hands on either side of her head against the wall.

He pushed his tongue inside her mouth, unable to resist deepening the kiss, even though one part of his brain was telling him what a stupid choice that was. If he was going to make it out of the elevator without dropping his pants and impaling her against the wall, he had to keep his raging libido under control.

Tasting the sweet warmth of her mouth was not going to help him do that.

The elevator stopped with a gentle jolt, and he managed to pull his mouth from hers and step back. "We're here."

The only sound that came out of her mouth was a low whimper. Her eyes were shut again, and her lips were parted as if inviting further kisses. He would take that invitation, just as soon as they made it into his room.

He swept her up into his arms and pivoted on his heel. "You'll have to pull the gates open."

She did, her fingers fumbling with the locking mechanism, but finally managing to get both gates pulled open and then shut after they stepped from the elevator.

It was only a few feet down the hall to his door, but it felt like a mile, each step excruciating. Not because she was heavy, but because holding her excited him. To his already overstimulated nervous system, the feel of her body against his was enticement it took every ounce of his self-control to ignore.

Once inside his room, he let her stand, but kept an arm around her. She was wobbly.

"I want you naked, Ivy."

She stared at him, her expression uncomprehending.

He stepped back. "I. Want. You. To. Take. Your. Clothes. Off."

The glazed desire in her eyes faded a little. "Just me?"

"Yes."

She crossed her arms over her chest in a defensive gesture that intensified his desire to push her farther than any lover had ever pushed her before. "Can't we undress together?"

"Are you refusing to cooperate?" he asked silkily, knowing that would prick her pride, push her toward proving her mettle.

She saw his attempt at dominance as a personal challenge. It also excited her. He liked knowing that. It told him they were on the same wavelength in every way.

Her eyes narrowed. "I'm not refusing; I just want it to be more mutual."

"It is mutual." He cupped her face and kissed her, branding her lips with his barely restrained passion. "It will give me a lot of pleasure to see you undress." He kissed her again. "And you will enjoy undressing for me."

"That's not what I meant." But she didn't deny she would enjoy him watching her.

She'd loved revealing herself to him in the elevator. Her arousal had been strong and blatant. Remembering the way she'd climaxed in his arms sent arrows of awareness straight to his dick. He stepped back.

"Are you having a problem with our game?"

"Um . . ." She licked her lips.

He reached out and ran his fingertip down her cheek, letting it settle against the rapid pulse at the base of her neck. "If you don't want to do it, all you have to say is my last name."

She glared. "I'm not giving in."

"This isn't a contest."

"Isn't it?"

Maybe it was, but it was more about exploring feelings and needs that had never surfaced with another woman.

She covered his hand against her neck with her own. "I want to undress, but I want you to undress, too. You've already seen me half naked, but you haven't even taken off your tie, for goodness sake. Please, Blake."

Please was not the safe word. Please was part of the game. "Does the thought of you standing there naked while I'm dressed make you feel vulnerable?" he asked, knowing the answer and ready for her to admit it.

"Yes."

"I *want* you vulnerable. I don't want any barriers between you and me."

"My clothes aren't a barrier, not in the way you mean."

"Yes, they are. You've used your uniform and professional image as a defense mechanism with me. Tonight that ends."

She flinched as if his words had struck deeply. "That's not fair. I dress this way as part of my employment with *your* company. How can you hold that against me?"

"You dressed for work to go to dinner with me. You were trying to keep me at arm's length tonight, and I intend to be as close to you as your skin."

He waited, to see if she would deny it, or if her innate honesty would carry over even when it made her uncomfortable.

"I was . . ." She sighed, her face averting. "I was trying to keep a barrier between us, but I'm not anymore." She looked at him again, her eyes filled with compelling brown warmth. "That's got to be obvious."

"I want the barrier gone."

"It is gone."

"Get naked and it will be gone."

"Why are you being so stubborn about this? Why

does it matter?" she implored, the very tension in her voice telling him she knew damn well why it mattered.

"You tell me."

"I don't want to be that vulnerable."

"If you trust me not to hurt you, not to take advantage of your femininity no matter what the circumstances are, it won't be a problem for you."

"But—"

"There are no buts. Either you trust me, or you don't." Suddenly this need, this compulsion to push her, to dominate her as his sexual mate, made sense. Ivy Kendall kept herself separate from other people; she'd been doing it since the first time they met. She had emotional barriers that protected her from getting involved, and he wanted her involved with him.

He wanted everything, and everything included her unwavering trust. Each time he pushed her and she complied, it knocked another chink out of the wall around her and put another piece in the bridge between them. He wanted that bridge rock solid.

"Do it." His hand fell away from her, and he took another step back, challenging her with his eyes. *"Do it, or say the safe word."*

Her eyes snapped dark fire at him. "Fine." She yanked her jacket off, the thin cotton of her blouse not enough to hide nipples still hard from their time in the elevator.

She started unbuttoning it. "If you need the juvenile thrill of having me naked while you are dressed, I'll take my darn clothes off."

"You're pretty mouthy for a woman who is supposed to be learning how to cooperate more fully with her boss."

"I am cooperating," she practically growled. "Can't you tell?" She ripped the shirt off and tossed it on the floor.

He didn't watch to see where it landed; his focus

was too fixed on the beauty of her creamy breasts revealed in the stretchy lace cups of her bra. "That's a scandalous piece of underwear."

She shrugged. "No one can see it under the blouse and jacket."

"I'm seeing it now."

She reached behind her to unfasten it. "For a second longer anyway."

"Stop."

She froze with her hands behind her back, a question in her eyes. Her delicate curves pressed forward in an intensely erotic display, the blush of arousal unmistakable on her fair skin.

"Peel it away slowly."

Her breath hitched, and she did as he said, revealing the flawlessness of her form one delicious centimeter at a time, until she finally let the bra fall to the floor.

He sucked in air, but he felt like all the oxygen had gone missing from his immediate vicinity. "You're perfect."

"I don't feel as vulnerable as I thought I would."

"Why should you? I'm the one ready to have a heart attack."

She laughed, the sound soft and ultrafeminine. Was she amused by him?

He couldn't drag his gaze from her gorgeous breasts to tell. They were small, but deliciously round and firm with tip-tilted nipples that were turgid points, colored a deep red from the blood rushing through them.

He wanted to taste those tantalizing berries, but that would have to wait. "Now the skirt."

Without so much as blinking, she reached behind her and undid the button and zipper. The sound of it sliding down set off a burst of libidinous hormones in his body, making his muscles clench in primal preparation for taking his mate.

She shimmied it down her hips, and it, too, fell to the carpet, revealing curls more red than the hair on her head. They were fluffy from his earlier ministrations, and he knew if he touched them, she would quiver just as she had in the elevator.

He walked toward her, the draw of her body an irresistible pull. She wasn't the vulnerable one right now. He was because he needed to touch her more than he needed to breathe, more than he needed to eat to survive, more than he needed warmth, or shelter, or satisfaction in his job. He could live without those things, but he couldn't live without touching her.

When he reached her, he reached out and shocked himself by not touching the erogenous zones on her body, the parts of her now revealed to his gaze for the first time.

He cupped the side of her face with one hand and pressed his other one against her heart. "You are the most beautiful woman I have ever seen."

Five

Her eyes filled with tears, an inexplicable agony surfacing in their brown depths. "You said we would be honest."

Had he? Or had he said that his bluntness was a good counterpart for her honesty? It didn't matter. Either way, right now he was telling the absolute truth. "I mean it."

"You can't."

"Why not?"

"There are so many glamorous women in your world."

"And none of them come close to matching you for sheer feminine magnificence. How can you doubt my words? The inn could burn down around us and I couldn't let you go."

One tear spilled over and rolled down her cheek, but her sweet lips tilted in a smile that touched places inside him he didn't even know existed. "Oh, Blake . . ."

He kissed her and lost himself in her lips. He was kicking off his trousers before he realized he'd even started undressing, but he had to feel skin to skin, warmth to warmth.

The minute he was naked, she pressed herself against him, cradling his aching erection against the smooth softness of her belly and pressing her hardened nipples into his chest.

She moaned at the contact.

He groaned.

They fell on the bed, and he started touching.

Blake's hands were everywhere. Ivy loved it. He'd been so controlled in the elevator, but he'd lost that control now, and she reveled in his overwhelming passion.

One big hand cupped her backside while the other fondled her breast. His mouth was voracious on hers, and she responded with a renewal of excitement that made her ache for his possession. She hooked one leg over his thigh in blatant invitation and felt the head of his sex nudge her swollen folds.

She pressed forward, but he reared back, a loud groan issuing from his throat. "Wait a second, baby. We're going too fast."

Cooperation was all well and good, but she was done with games tonight. "Blake, I want you inside my body right now."

He laughed, the sound strained. "I wasn't going to make you wait, honey, trust me."

He was stretching toward the nightstand beside the bed. He pulled the drawer open and fumbled around inside, all the while keeping her from going anywhere with the hand still clamped to her butt. Like she wanted to. It would take a crow bar and a very powerful winch to get her from his side.

"Got one," he practically shouted as he drew back toward her, a foil packet in his hand.

"You brought condoms? To Delicious, Ohio?"

"I wanted you the first day I saw you. My self-control has been deteriorating ever since. I wasn't going to be caught flat-footed if it disappeared all together."

"Oh."

He ripped the packet open with his teeth and pulled out the condom with a shake that sent the packet flipping over his shoulder. "Can we talk about this later?"

"Yes, of cour—"

He surged into her with a thrust that stretched her, filled her, and took the last bit of breath from her body.

He pulled back, she sucked in air, he surged forward again, this time seating himself to the hilt. She cried out and instinctively tried to move back from the marauding intruder so intent on dominating her inner flesh.

He stilled, his body vibrating with barely suppressed savagery. "Are you okay?"

She couldn't talk; her lungs were still frozen, that one breath all she'd managed in the last few seconds.

He squeezed her, and she took a choking breath.

"You're big."

"Does it hurt?" His eyes searched her face with desperate appeal. "I didn't mean to hurt you. I'm sorry, sweetheart."

"It *doesn't* hurt. It's just . . . so much."

"Too much?" he asked, primal need lacing his voice, but concern for her was there, too. Sweat broke out on his brow.

"Not too much. I love it." *I love you,* she wanted to say, but held the words in check. Just barely.

"Good." He gripped her hip with strong fingers, adjusting her leg over him so she was blatantly open to his possession and then started to move.

His pelvis collided with her mound with every pounding thrust, and she knew another orgasm was not far off.

The pleasure built and built and built. He grunted with each thrust, the veneer of sophisticated businessman completely gone in the face of this primordial male so intent on dominating her body with his own.

He didn't have to be on top for her to feel like he was in complete control. Only she didn't mind. She wanted this no-holds-barred intimacy. She'd craved it forever, even if she hadn't known it.

"I'm going to come!" he shouted.

And then he started grinding his pelvis against her in a deliberate attempt to take her with him. It worked.

She screamed.

He shouted.

They shuddered together in sweaty, orgasmic bliss, but he wasn't done. He ground against her, groaning with another body-arching pulse from his sex. He did it again, and each one prolonged her own pleasure, the starbursts going off in her head in one pyrotechnic display after another until it felt as if her mind exploded. She gasped, her heart raced, her body locked in an orgasm that could have been measured on the Richter scale, and everything went black.

Blake could not believe it. Ivy was utterly limp against him. Her heart-shaped face had gone from tight with orgasmic tension to smooth and serene in the space of a heartbeat. He released her hip, and she fell onto her back in unconscious abandon.

He had never given a woman a fainting orgasm before. In fact, he'd sort of always thought that particular sexual myth was just that . . . a fairy tale. Sudden fear made him rear up and over her as he looked for signs of any kind of physical distress. What if it was more than her climax? What if she'd had a heart attack? Or an aneurysm? Or . . .

Her beautiful brown eyes slid open, and her swollen mouth creased in a gentle smile. "Hi."

"Hi, yourself." His voice was weak from the unexpected worry and scratchy from shouting his pleasure out loud enough to strain his vocal cords.

"That was pretty amazing."

"Yes. I lost control there at the end."

She arched toward him just the tiniest bit at the reminder, and his still semi-erect flesh slipped inside her slick opening. He couldn't help it; he pressed forward for total possession, or as much as he could achieve in his current state. She didn't seem to mind, but sighed out in what sounded like bliss to him. Then she tightened around him, and he grunted.

This woman was incredible.

"I didn't hurt you, did I?"

He'd pounded into her like a sledgehammer, and the fact he hadn't been on top of her hadn't stopped him from hitting deep with each thrust. In fact, the way her thigh had been hooked over his had laid her completely open to him.

"You might have bruised my hip a little, but I don't mind."

He looked down at her right hip. The soft white curve was such a perfect feminine shape, but it was marred by small blue splotches. He swore. "I held you too tight."

She touched his face, the feel of her fingers against his skin warm. "You held me just right. I loved it. Couldn't you tell?"

"I've never had a woman faint on me before."

"That makes us even. I've never fainted. Not in any circumstance."

Why that should make him feel so proud and primitively possessive, he had no idea, but the connection between the two of them seemed to be weaving tighter every second.

Pretty soon he was going to start pounding his chest and saying stupid stuff like, "My Ivy."

The fact those two words sounded anything but dumb inside his head was scarier than her faint.

He went to pull away, but her arms locked around him.

"I've got to take care of the condom."

"I know, but I don't want you to move."

But he had to, and they both knew it.

She sighed and let her arms fall back to the bed. "All right."

Holding on to the condom, he carefully slid from her tight heat and then rolled to his feet. He grabbed a tissue from the box on the bedside table and dealt with the condom. The wastebasket was in the bathroom; however, he didn't head there immediately. The view in front of him was too incredible to easily walk away from.

Her hair was a cloud of reddish brown silk against the white comforter. A sheen of perspiration covered her luscious body, her still erect nipples and scent telling him that she might be satisfied, but she wouldn't object to him touching her again.

"You're extremely sensual, Ivy."

"I never have been." She stretched languidly, her body twenty-two karat enticement. "Not with anyone but you."

He found himself swaying toward the bed in shock and renewed desire. He stayed upright purely by strength of will. She wasn't the only one their intimacy had laid waste to.

"You didn't enjoy sex before?" he asked, unable to contain his astonishment.

She was the most amazing lover he'd ever known and more responsive than he'd ever even fantasized about.

She didn't seem offended by his surprised reaction, not with that warm, sated smile still directed his way. "I've only ever made love with one other man."

"Who?"

"Doesn't matter; it was a long time ago."

"It couldn't have been that long. You're pretty damn young now."

"Been peeking at my employee records?"

"I'm the boss. It's my prerogative. Now stop trying to change the subject and tell me who it was. Did he hurt you? Traumatize you in some way?" She didn't make love like a woman who had had a bad sexual experience in her past.

She laughed, the sound soft and appealing. "No, nothing like that, and it happened my senior year of high school."

It happened? Had she only made love the one time? One man he could believe. One encounter? Impossible. "And you haven't had sex with anyone since?"

"No."

"Was it that bad with him?"

She came up on her elbows, striking a provocative pose. Her expression wasn't sensual, though; it wasn't amused any longer either. If anything, she looked thoughtful and just a little sad. "Making love with Danny wasn't like it is with you, but it wasn't terrible either."

"Then why?"

She sat up and slid her legs over the opposite side of the bed so her back was to him. "Because it hurt too much when he walked away."

"But everyone breaks up with their high school flame." And they didn't all stop having sex because of it.

She stood up and started hunting for her clothes. "Not everyone."

"Well, okay, a few end up getting married, but just because you didn't shouldn't have turned you off dating."

She spun to face him, the look on her face one of surprise. "I didn't say it put me off dating. I've dated plenty of men since high school."

"But you haven't made love with any of them." He tried not to make it sound like a question, but he was still having a hard time wrapping his mind around the idea of her years-long celibacy.

She cocked her head to one side and looked at him as if *she* was the one who needed to see inside *his* head. "Not everyone thinks sex is a natural component of dating."

Okay. Touché. "But if you were holding out for marriage, you wouldn't have made love with him, and you sure as hell wouldn't be here with me right now." He certainly hadn't offered her anything permanent.

She winced, and he realized how that had sounded, as if he was ruling out a future between them before the sheets had even cooled from the most explosive sex he'd ever had.

"I didn't mean—"

"Don't worry about it. I'm not looking for marriage or even a long-term relationship. I know that's impossible for us."

"Not impossible . . ."

She just smiled and shook her head. "I made love with Danny because I loved him. I *wanted* to marry him, but I knew he couldn't have his dreams with me around. He did, too."

"Are you talking about this moon thing?"

"Yes."

"Ivy—"

"I know you don't think it's real, but Danny knew it was. He wasn't ready to get married and start a family. Who is at eighteen? So, he had to move on, and so did I."

Blake didn't know what getting married had to do with her moon thing, but he understood the implication of what else she'd said. "So, he made love to you and then walked away?"

She shrugged. "Neither of us had a choice."

The little prick could have chosen to keep his dick in

his pants. It had to have been harder for Ivy to let Danny go after making love than it would have been before. She'd just said it had hurt, enough to make her very cautious about having another sexual relationship.

But she'd also said she didn't see making love as a given component to a dating relationship.

He was trying to get this, but it felt like one of those male-female things that he found incomprehensible most of the time. "So, tell me again why no sex since then."

She took a deep breath, as though preparing to say something that she rather wouldn't. She crossed her arms over her stomach and let the air out. "I've never loved another man enough to want to share something so intimate and sacred with him."

He felt like he'd just been gut punched. *"Are you saying you love me?"*

She winced again, her face pinkening with embarrassment, and she tightened her arms in a blatantly defensive move. "Yes."

He didn't know what to say. He wanted her like he'd never wanted another woman. Hell, his hard-on had grown to aching full mast again, and all they were doing was talking. About stuff that usually gave him a worse case of the jitters than a triple-shot espresso.

He hadn't considered the l-word, though. "Ivy, I—"

"Don't worry about it. I'm not expecting you to love me back." Her gaze flicked down. "Uh . . . are you going to take care of that?"

"I can't until I get rid of the condom and put a new one on."

Her mouth dropped open in an "O," and then she laughed. "I *meant* the condom."

He was still holding the tissue bundle. "We're talking."

"There's not much else to say, is there?"

He couldn't help feeling she was hoping there was, and he just didn't know if he could give her the words and mean them. If he didn't, he couldn't say them. She deserved the same level of honesty she had given him.

She could have lied and said she didn't love him when he asked, or that she didn't know, but she hadn't spared her pride at the cost of her integrity.

"I guess not. Not right now, anyway."

She nodded, the flicker of disappointment in her pretty brown eyes quickly masked. But he'd seen it and felt like a jerk for putting it there.

He turned and went into the bathroom without another word.

When he came back out, Ivy was dressing. She had her blouse on and the first several buttons done up.

"What are you doing?"

"Putting on my clothes."

"I can see that. Why?"

"Walking to my room stark naked doesn't appeal." She smiled, inviting him to share the joke. "I've never had even a slight hankering to streak naked down hotel corridors."

"Why are you going back to your room?" Was it because he hadn't said he loved her? Did she regret letting him into her body now because of it?

"You know the answer to that," she said lightly.

"If I did, I wouldn't be asking," he growled.

Her eyes widened at his tone. "Management Training 101: you're on duty even when you aren't." She finished buttoning her blouse and smoothed it down with a grimace obviously meant for the wrinkled condition. "If the staff needs me, they aren't going to come looking in your room. At least, I hope they aren't. That would be more than a little embarrassing."

"Oh."

She bent down and grabbed her skirt off the floor. It

was all he could do not to go over there and take her sexy butt in his two hands and squeeze. She was so perfect, shaped like a dream and as hot as reality could get.

She shimmied into the navy blue uniform skirt. "You could come with me, if you like." She said it casually, but her tense posture and the way she didn't meet his eyes when she asked gave away her nervousness.

"I like."

She looked at him then and smiled—a beautiful, happy, white teeth, lips bowed lusciously grin. "Good."

"You had to know I'd say yes."

"I thought me telling you I love you might have scared you off."

"Technically you didn't say the words," he said, apropos of nothing. He didn't want to hear them, did he?

She laughed, actually laughed. "No, I didn't, did I?" She didn't look heartbroken or miserable that he hadn't said he felt the same way, far from it, and how was he supposed to feel about that?

Her smile never faltered. "I love you, Blake."

Oh, man . . . that sounded good, too good.

It also turned him on. He started toward her, smiling with intent when her eyes widened in alarm. "We can go back to your room after."

"After?" she parroted, backing up a step.

"Yes, after."

"But . . ."

"I'm the boss, sweetheart, and right now your most pressing duty is to let me pleasure you stupid."

"Some duty." Her breath hitched, and her gaze grew hot. Just that fast.

"I think so," he said, forcing her back one more step, knowing it was the last one he needed to get her right where he wanted her to be.

Ivy backed into the bed and tumbled backward when Blake kept pushing forward.

Feeling the brush of his erection against her as she fell, she expected him to pounce immediately, but he didn't. Instead, he used his mouth and hands to sensitize her feet in a way that impacted every erogenous zone of her body as if each of her toes was some kind of remote control device.

The slow seduction of her senses had her begging for his possession before he'd even gotten her skirt off, but he showed with one tormenting caress after another that he was in no hurry to put himself inside her.

He slipped her skirt down her legs in an excruciatingly slow glide.

"Blake . . ."

"Shhh . . . honey, let me pamper you."

"Pamper me?" She gasped as he leaned over her naked bottom half. "You're driving me crazy."

He laughed, the warm air from his mouth stirring the sensitive hair on her mound. What was he doing? Her legs were pressed apart by strong hands, and then his mouth was against her most private flesh. His tongue swirled and dipped, making her arch toward his mouth in hungry, shivery excitement. He surrounded her clitoris with his lips, flicked it with the tip of his tongue, and started humming . . . not singing, but making a sound with his mouth that made her flesh vibrate. Then he slipped his finger inside her more than willing flesh. She clasped him as tightly as she could, moaning with the pleasure that inner clenching gave her. He pressed with his long finger against a spot that made her shudder and cry out.

He added a second finger, but kept up his attention to that secret spot she hadn't even been sure she had.

Without so much as a preliminary muscle rigor, she came. "Oh, Blake, oh, yes . . . it feels so good, so perfect. I love you, Blake." Having the freedom to say the words again intensified her pleasure, and her body continued convulsing around his fingers and arching toward his mouth.

The feelings grew unbearably intense, and she couldn't take any more. She tried to pull away while shoving at his head with her hands, but his grip on her was unshakable, and the pleasure that was close to pain continued to spear through her.

"Blake, please, you've got to stop . . . I can't stand it."

But he didn't stop, and she had another orgasm, this one even more intense than the first. Her whole body tightened to frozen immobility while her womb contracted and her inner core radiated the most amazing sensations outward she'd ever known. Then, again without warning, her body went limp, and every muscle that had been rigid was now totally incapable of moving or sustaining her in any way. Even her head lolled to the side in boneless abandon.

He kissed her, paying thorough homage to every centimeter of quivering nerves between her legs. Then he lifted his head, and she managed to turn hers enough to see him. Her essence glistened wetly on his mouth, and his blue eyes were dark with sexual pride. And hungry need. He'd given her pleasure; now he wanted to take his.

"You said it again."

"What?" she slurred.

"That you love me."

"Yes." And she'd liked saying it. Loved the freedom to express feelings she would get to revel in for a few short days at the most. There would be plenty of time to grieve his loss later, just as she had grieved Danny's, but right now she could do nothing but celebrate being with this man.

Instinctively, she knew Blake wasn't comfortable with emotion. It wasn't controlled enough for him, and this was one man who really liked to be in control. He'd given her a tremendous gift when he hadn't allowed her honesty about her emotions to drive him away.

He didn't say anything else, just started making love to her again, removing her blouse, caressing her, making her want him. Passion burned in his gaze like an inferno fed with gasoline, but his touch was gentle, and incredibly, he incited her own desire until it matched his once again before taking her with an excruciatingly slow, but inexorable thrust.

He filled her completely, and she wrapped her legs around his waist to keep him that way.

"It's not too much, is it?"

"No, darling. Not too much."

His eyes closed, and his head went back, a look of utter bliss on his features. "You can take all of me."

Their pelvic bones ground together. "Yes. I love taking all of you."

Then he started to thrust, each movement slow and measured.

"Blake . . . I want . . . I need more!"

"I was too fast the first time, but this time I'm going to be slow and careful. You're a lot smaller than me, Ivy."

"Just because you're some kind of freak of nature doesn't mean I'm a fragile midget. Go faster, darn it." She pounded his back.

But all she got for her trouble was another slow, deep glide.

She reached up with her mouth, latched on to a patch of skin just above his left nipple, and started to suck.

A strangled sound that could have been her name came from his throat.

She kept sucking and pinched his right nipple, then

played with it, delighting in the way the small, hard nub felt against her fingers.

Suddenly he was rearing back, breaking the hold her legs had on him and tossing her over onto her stomach.

"Hey," she yelled and then gasped as he slammed into her from the back.

He went so deep, he was touching her heart; at least that's how it felt. "You are a vixen."

"Vixen? Who says vixen?"

"I do. It fits the beautiful tease I've got in my bed."

"We aren't technically in your bed; we're on it," she panted.

"And I'm on you."

"Yeah, couldn't stand the heat, huh?"

"If you've only ever made love with one other man, where'd you learn that stuff?"

"I read."

A deep laugh rumbled against her spine. "I'll have to borrow some of your books."

"Any time."

"But right now, I want to love you without any of your little tricks, got it?"

If he'd said screw her, she would have said something equally sexy and tried to get the leverage to flip over, but he'd said love, and even though he didn't mean *love*-love, it still just melted her.

It wasn't a good idea to go gooey on him, though. That probably *would* scare him away. "Are we playing your game again?" she asked in an effort to keep it light.

"What would make you say that?"

"The fact you have me on my stomach and I can't do anything but what you want."

"Don't you like it?" He thrust deep and pulled out slowly only to thrust deeply again.

When she got enough breath to talk again, she answered. "I like it just fine, but I don't like you thinking you can always be in control."

"Would I think that?" he asked, reaching around and under her with one hand, his voice all rumbling innocence and his fingers a temptation to sin. The questing hand slid along her belly and down to her pubic hair; then fingers pressed between her labia and touched her clitoris.

"You might think it, but you'd be wrong." And she tried something else she'd read about.

He cursed, a word she never, ever said, but described spectacularly what they were doing.

She squeezed and released her inner muscles in a rhythm that matched his thrusts. Pretty soon the rhythm increased until all she could do was squeeze and hold the contraction for as long as possible, then release and start squeezing again.

Six

He panted in her ear, his fingers playing her sweet spot as though they knew her every secret. He did. More than any other person on the earth. Minutes later, she and Blake came together with lots of noise and passionately rocking bodies. Afterward, he collapsed on top of her, his weight warm and solid against her back.

He kissed her temple, her cheek, and her lips when she twisted her head at an uncomfortable angle so he could do so. Then he rolled off of her, but she couldn't move. She didn't even have enough energy to turn over. She felt him get off the bed, but she couldn't work up enough energy to wonder if he'd gone to take care of the condom again as her eyes slid shut.

She didn't go to sleep, but lay there in a state of semidoze until he came back. Without a word, he lifted her to cradle against his chest like something precious and carried her into the bathroom.

He stepped into the claw-foot tub with her still cradled in his arms and sank down until they were both submerged in the hot water. "There are times I positively love the quaintness of this inn."

She smiled and drowsily nuzzled his neck with the back of her head. "Me, too."

"Your words are slurry."

"Mmmm."

"You're so tired, you're barely awake."

"Mmmm."

"Go to sleep if you want. I'll take care of you."

But she didn't. No matter how tired she was, she wouldn't have missed the following half hour to save her life.

He washed her whole body. Using the glycerin soap the inn provided for its guests, he gently massaged muscles she hadn't known she had, or hadn't remembered. He also gently touched her between her legs, carefully cleansing her swollen vulva and opening. His touch was light, as if he was being careful not to arouse her again. It was pure tender care, and she adored every soothing caress.

When he was done, he lifted her out and dried them both off before carrying her back into the bedroom.

She looked at her rumpled clothes on the floor and shuddered. "I have to get dressed and get back to my apartment."

He put her down on the bed and then opened a drawer and pulled out a black T-shirt. "Put this on. It will cover everything, and it's clean."

"But—"

"It's late. Your apartment and this room are the only things on this floor. It's highly unlikely we'll run into anyone in the hall."

We? She hoped he meant that literally. She wasn't sure he remembered her invitation to join her for the rest of the night in her bed. She also hoped he was right about no one being in the hall, because the black T-shirt looked way more comfortable than her rumpled clothing.

He helped her pull the T-shirt over her head and tuck her arms through the big sleeves. She should feel like a child being dressed by a parent, but instead she felt cherished.

When the T-shirt hung on her like an oversized mini-dress, he went back to the dresser and got out a pair of shorts and another T-shirt. He pulled them on and then led her out of the room, one arm around her waist as if he knew that walking on her own would be way too much for her rubbery legs.

If someone saw them, the fact she was wearing his T-shirt wouldn't be the first thing that gave away their status as lovers. She couldn't make herself care. She wouldn't be working here much longer anyway, but even if she would . . . the prospect of having her employees know she'd slept with the big boss wouldn't have deterred her from taking him to her bed.

She loved him.

And he gave her more pleasure than she had ever believed she would feel.

When they entered her apartment, they went straight back to the bedroom, and he didn't even complain when he had to curl around her body to fit on the double bed.

Blake woke the next morning to Ivy's small hands exploring his body. He rumbled a good morning, she kissed him in response, and they made love, this time without any games or attempts at one-upmanship.

Then they showered together, and she experimented on him with soap, emulating something else she'd read in a book.

This time, he was the shaky one drying off. "I need to check my e-mail and get some work done before we drive into Cleveland."

She bit her lip as if worried about something, but nodded. "All right. We can have muesli and yogurt for breakfast, then. It will only take a minute to put together."

She made coffee to go with it, and he took his mug with him to his room.

He powered on the computer and left it to boot up while he shaved. He looked at the blond stubble on his face in the mirror and frowned, remembering the red spots on Ivy's delicate breasts and cheeks this morning. She hadn't seemed to mind the rough texture of his morning beard against her sensitive skin.

In fact, she'd gone a little crazy when he rubbed it over her nipples, but he still should have at least *thought* of shaving.

"Selfish bastard," he said to the man in the mirror.

And then remembering Ivy's screams of pleasure, he smiled. Maybe not totally selfish.

He came back into his room and went to check his e-mail and froze. The screen had a blinking white cursor and nothing else. He tried rebooting, but the same thing happened. It never made it past the bios commands. Damn it. It was a brand-new, state of the art laptop, and the hard drive had crashed. The manufacturer was going to hear from him.

Ivy came out of the bedroom after blow-drying her hair to find Blake at her kitchen table drinking more coffee. He was scowling.

"I thought you were going to check your e-mail."

She knew how slow the land line connections were. He could only be done if he'd gotten very few messages—unlikely—or hadn't been able to access them, which was all too likely considering how much time she'd spent in his room last night.

She bit the lip she'd been worrying all morning

since Blake had mentioned his computer earlier. Last night had been the full moon, a *blue* moon, and from the looks of things, her gift-slash-curse it-depends-on-how-you-look-at-it thing had run true to form. She'd wiped his hard drive clean.

"Stop biting your lip, sweetheart. It's swollen."

"Why didn't you check your e-mail?" she asked, feeling so cold even his endearment and indulgent smile didn't warm her.

"My hard drive crashed." His teeth snapped together in annoyance, all indulgence gone. "It's a brand-new computer."

"Blake . . ." She didn't want to say what had to be said. This was why Danny had left, and as long as Blake had believed she was superstitious rather than dangerous to hard drives and Swiss watches, he had wanted to be with her.

"Yeah, honey?"

She loved the way he called her sweetheart and honey. He'd even called her baby once, and she'd liked it, too. It meant she was unique to him, special. He didn't go around using endearments with anyone else.

"I was in your room last night."

His blue eyes warmed, the irritation melted away by male appreciation. "I know."

"It was a full moon."

"So?"

"Blake!" He wasn't stupid; he had to get the picture. "Are you trying to tell me you erased my hard drive?"

"Not *on purpose*, but yes."

He shook his head. "Hard drives crash."

"And watches break, even Rolexes. I know, but please think about this. What are the chances your computer, your watch, your cell phone, and your Palm Pilot would all break within the same twenty-four-hour period?"

"It could happen."

"You are a whiz with numbers . . . tell me the chances."

He looked disgruntled. "Not very damn good."

"And yet it happened."

"Yes."

"Because of me."

"N—"

"Yes," she hissed, tired of trying to convince the stubborn man of something she hated having him come to believe.

His eyes narrowed. "I know you believe—"

"Do you think I like living like this? No computer, no microwave, no cordless phone even?"

"I didn't say—"

"Stop being so stubborn." She gritted her teeth and counted backward from ten. "Granny Smith's Apothecary and Soda Fountain is right next door. They carry cheap watches that aren't anti-magnetic. Go buy one. Make sure it works and bring it back."

"Ivy, this is ridiculous."

"Just do it."

He could have argued they didn't have time, or that he had better things to do, but he didn't. He sighed and got to his feet, his expression disgruntled. "If it's that important to you, I'll do it."

She spent the next fifteen minutes trying not to dwell on what was going to happen once she convinced him of the moon magnetism.

When he returned, he walked into her apartment without knocking. He was carrying a small paper bag. "It's in here."

"Did you check to make sure it works?"

"Yes."

"Good. Take it out."

She was always more magnetic the days leading up to the full moon and during it than after. She didn't understand it, but she knew her body's cycle. To a point anyway. The level of her magnetism varied in intensity before and after the full moon, but she was guessing that since it had been a blue moon last night, she'd still be magnetic enough to prove her point.

He fished the watch from the bag.

"Look at it."

"What am I supposed to see?" He didn't sound irritated, or dismissive, just curious.

"The second hand moving. Is it?"

"Yes."

She put her hand out.

He gave her the watch.

She closed her fingers over it.

"I don't know what you're trying to prove."

"Oh, you know, you just don't want to deal with it."

He let out a frustrated breath, running his hand through his perfectly groomed blond hair and leaving it mussed.

The cold metal of the watch back warmed in her hand. She held on to it longer than she thought she needed to because when she let go, when she let him see, it would be over. Finally, she forced herself to open her fingers and let him see.

He looked down and scowled. "It stopped."

"Are you going to try to explain this away, too?"

He looked at her, and the expression in his eyes made her stomach knot. "It's true, isn't it?"

"I tried to tell you it was."

He nodded, but said nothing.

What was he thinking? That she was a freak? A weirdo? Definitely not a woman he could have in his world.

"What did your high school sweetheart want to be that he couldn't take you with him?"

"He works for NASA."

"You still talk?"

"Yes, he's the only person besides family who knows."

"I know now."

"True."

"You really can't manage a hotel with computerized check-in procedures and maintenance systems."

"No."

"Why not?" She opened her mouth to answer, exasperated by his willful ignorance, but he raised his hand to shush her. "I mean, why can't you just stay away during a full moon?"

"For one thing, I'm not always sure when the problems will start. Sometimes it's not until the day of the full moon; sometimes it happens several days before."

"But you know when the full moon comes every month."

"And you would be okay with your manager taking off for several days every month to cover my bases?" She shook her head, knowing the answer. "Even if that would work, where would I go? I can't exactly stay in a hotel."

"Where will you go when you leave here?"

The question sliced into her heart, slashing her deeply buried hopes. "I don't know."

The phone rang, and Ivy sprang to answer it. She'd convinced Blake about her moon magnetism, but now that meant he would leave, and she welcomed any interruption that would stave off the final break.

"Ivy?"

"Yes, Trudy?"

"The maintenance guy who is redoing the woodwork is here. He wants to talk to you."

"I'll be right down."

She hung up the phone and turned back to Blake. She couldn't read anything in his expression. "There's someone at the front desk I need to see."

"Ed?" he asked in a harsh voice, masculine hostility radiating from every pore.

"No. I told you, I'm not going to marry Ed, even if it would get rid of my gift-slash-curse it-depends-on-how-you-look-at-it thing."

"You stop being magnetic after you get married?"

She shook her head. "That's what the women in my family believed for generations, but I did some research. Pregnancy is what actually changes the chemical balance and ends the moon changes in our bodies."

"So, if you had a baby, you wouldn't have to worry about this anymore?"

"Right, but I'm not going to run out and get artificially inseminated just to change my body's chemistry. Children deserve a better start than that in life." She turned to go, trying really hard not to cry and afraid the wetness on her cheeks meant she wasn't succeeding very well.

"I could make you pregnant."

She stopped with her hand on the door. "What?"

He could not have said what she thought she'd heard him say.

She spun back around to face him, swiping at her cheeks. "What?" she asked again.

He came to her and laid his hand against her neck, his thumb brushing her pulse point. "I said I could give you a baby."

She couldn't help it; her eyes flicked down to the front of his pants, and he laughed.

"Not right this second, honey, but it wouldn't take much."

Despite the intimacy of the night before and that morning, she felt a hot blush stain her cheeks. "That's not funny, Blake."

"I'm not laughing."

"But you can't mean it."

"Why can't I?"

"You can't just give me a baby to change my body chemistry. You'd be a father. That's a lifetime commitment." And she had absolutely no doubt he would see it that way too. She'd known this man for three years. He took family seriously.

"So?" he asked, just as if the prospect of a lifetime tied to her through a child didn't upset him in the least.

The phone rang again. Ivy didn't have to pick it up to know it was Trudy reminding her to come downstairs. "I've got to go."

"Ivy—"

"I . . . we . . . let's talk about this later, okay?"

"Okay." He removed his hand from her, and she felt as if all the heat in her body had taken a vacation.

Cold loneliness rushed across her heart, and she shivered.

Get a grip on yourself, girl. He wasn't here two days ago, and he won't be two days from now. You survived then. You will survive later.

"Think about it," he said as she stepped out the door.

She rushed down the hall toward the stairs. If she appeared to be running, she could be forgiven. She was running, but leaving Blake physically behind didn't get him out of her brain.

He'd offered to give her a baby. He had to be losing his mind. Why else would he make such a preposterous suggestion? Did he pity her? Would a man make such a far-reaching suggestion based on pity? What else could it be? Blake wanted her, there was no getting around it, but she'd told him she loved him, and he had not said the words back to her.

He wanted to make love to her, not get saddled with her as the mother of his child for the rest of his life.

* * *

Blake stood in Ivy's tiny apartment, the shock of her revelations starting to wear off, but the seductiveness of his suggestion to give her a baby was not.

He got hard thinking about her swollen with his child. He'd have to marry her. She was right; a child deserved a better start in life than to be the solution to its mother's physical problems. He would love his child. Ivy would love the baby, too. She was good at loving.

The alternative—leaving and never seeing her again—was not one he could face. Not now. Not after he'd shared a level of trust in intimacy he'd never known with anyone else. Never wanted to know with anyone else.

He loved her.

Why had it taken him so long to realize it?

He'd fallen for her the first time he'd seen her. He'd avoided dating other women for the last couple of years and used work as an excuse. The truth was, he didn't want anyone but Ivy.

He had to tell her. She didn't know he loved her; how could she when he'd just realized it himself? She was going to say no to having his baby and marrying him if he didn't explain how he felt.

And he knew just the way to do it.

Ivy was sitting in her office chair, working on her ledgers, when Blake walked in. He'd left word with Trudy he was going to be gone for a few hours, and apparently Ivy had opted to put that time to good use getting some work done.

Her dedication to her job and to her employees was just one of the many things he loved about her.

He shut the door behind him.

Ivy's head came up at the click of the lock sliding into place.

His expression was as serious as a heartbeat; he knew because that's how he felt. "I think we need to have another lesson in cooperation."

She blinked, her mouth opening and closing, but no words came out. "C-cooperation? *Here?*" she finally stuttered.

He smiled, loving the catch in her voice, the feminine wariness combined with grudging interest in her beautiful brown eyes. "Here, sweetheart."

He crossed the room, just as he had the day before, but when he reached her side of the desk, instead of looming over her, he dropped to kneel in front of her.

"Blake?" Her voice was so tiny, almost scared, and he wanted to take her in his arms and tell her everything was going to be okay, but there were other things that had to be said first.

He took her hands in his. They were trembling, but then so were his. "I love you, Ivy Kendall. Will you marry me?"

Tears started sliding down her cheeks, and she shook her head. "You can't. You don't. It's just pity. Please, Blake, don't . . ."

He kissed her until her mouth went cooperative against his; then he pulled away. "I can. I do. It's not and I will, for the rest of our lives."

"But you didn't say anything when I told you I loved you."

He took a deep breath. "I'm stubborn. You may have noticed."

She laughed, a small, breathy sound. "Yes, I had."

"I didn't want to admit what I felt was love, not the times I was so disappointed I wanted to hit things when you didn't show up for the management training seminars, not when I realized my desire for you was out of control and spurring me on to fantasize about you in a way I hadn't ever done with another woman, not when you said you loved me and turned me on so bad, I lost what was left of my mind, not when seeing you getting dressed to go back to your room scared me worse than going sky diving for the first time, not even when you told me you couldn't be with me because of your moon magnetism. But, honey, when you ran away from me and my proposal, even I wasn't stubborn enough to keep denying my love."

"You didn't propose. You offered to give me a baby."

"Same thing. I'm not a sperm donor; I'm a man. If I'm going to give you a baby, you are going to be wearing my ring on your finger."

"Oh, Blake."

"Is that a yes?"

"I—"

Wait a second. He let go of her hands to dig in his pocket. He came up with a small black velvet box and flipped it open. The square-cut moonstone with diamonds on either side of it winked up at them.

He pulled the ring out and put it partway on her finger. "Yes?"

She grinned, her eyes glistening with tears. "Yes."

"Thank you, God."

She laughed, and he pushed the ring all the way on and then kissed her until she was plastered against his front, kneeling on the floor with him.

Then he gave her another lesson in cooperation and had to stifle her shouts of pleasure with his mouth.

Much later they were snuggled into his queen-size bed after Ivy announced their upcoming marriage to the staff.

Everyone congratulated them, but none of her employees were surprised. Trudy said it had been obvious to all of them for months that Ivy was in love with the big boss. They were just glad he had shown enough smarts to return her feelings.

"I'm not going to like being separated from you during full moons until I get pregnant," she said, rubbing her hand over his tight abdomen.

They had made love again, this time *her* giving *him* a lesson in cooperation. He'd even let her tie his hands to the old-fashioned bedposts to do it. He was free again, and his arms were locked around her as if he'd never let go.

He lunged up and over her, his face fixed in a scowl. "Who said anything about being separated?"

"You can't—"

"You've got to stop making erroneous assumptions, woman. They're going to get you into trouble one of these days."

"Thanks for the advice, but—"

"I've got a fishing cabin in Vermont, and we can retreat there for a few days every month."

"You can't leave your business like that."

"Actually, I can. I *am* the boss, but my plan is to work remotely. I've been thinking about it, and we can insulate the second bedroom against magnetic fields and make it my office. I'll do the same for my study at home as a safety precaution. You won't be able to go in those two rooms. I'm sorry about that, but it's better than being separated once a month."

"You would do that for me?" she asked, making no effort to hide the awe she felt at the prospect.

His scowl deepened. "Of course. I love you, or did you think saying that meant I just wanted to get you in the sack?"

"No, but . . ."

"Look, I want to be with you. Always. And I'd like to wait to have kids for a year or so. That means we need a solution to your monthly magnetic moments."

"You want to wait to have children?"

"Is that okay with you?"

"Yes. I'd like to be married for a while first, but I do want your babies, Blake."

"And the idea of you having them is the biggest turn-on I've ever known except for when you tell me you love me."

But waiting for a year or so sounded good. It meant he really was marrying her because he wanted to be with her, not because he was trying to help her fix her problem. The man had to love her a lot to have already worked out the solution he had.

She wiggled her hips against him. "You said me telling you I love you turns you on?"

"Yes," he growled.

"I love you, Blake. I love you. I love you. I love you . . ."

His laughter ended on a groan of desire, and they made love again, this time both of them totally secure in the knowledge this marriage was going to happen for all the right reasons and their love was real and strong enough to last a lifetime.

MOONSTRUCK

Dianne Castell

One

"How's it feel to be rid of a hundred and eighty pounds that was slowly ruining your life?" Bridget asked Julia as they made their way down the courthouse steps in Delicious, Ohio.

The clock on the spire chimed twelve, and Julia took off her wedding ring. She kissed it, tossed it high, sunlight sparkling against the gold band, and the fifteen-year symbol of her marriage to Frank Simons splashed into the fountain in the town's square. "Since I divorced his lying, cheating ass ten minutes ago, it feels great."

Bridget grinned. "'Bout time. You deserve better than him."

"Deception in a relationship sucks, and my dear ex is the king of deception. If I hadn't found his *other* credit card with charges for flowers I never got, fancy restaurants I never visited, and plane tickets to places where I never went, I wouldn't have known. I did the good wifey thing. I stayed home, did errands for his parents."

"While he did Club Med."

She watched water stream from the top bowl to the

second larger one, then overflow into the apple-shaped basin. "I wish Frank, that rotten pig, would wind up in that fountain with the ring. They belong together."

She turned as Frank Simons the third, bank president and son of the most prestigious family in town, strutted down the steps. He gave her the bird, snickered . . . then tripped and fell into the splashing water. Arms flailing, he slipped forward, then back, finally standing upright. He swiped his stunned face as water cascaded over his head. Then he *snorted?*

Bridget exchanged looks with Julia as she bit back a laugh. It felt good to laugh about something after the divorce from hell that kept the Simons' money with the Simons family and left the ex-wife with zilch. But that was okay because that *zilch* included Frank. "Sure wish I had a camera to immortalize this touching scene."

She watched her ex slosh his way down the tree-lined street, his five-hundred-dollar suit dripping, Gucci shoes leaving dark footprints on the sidewalk. "I wonder how Frank did that, fall into the fountain, I mean? He's been around it all his life. His great-grandfather donated it to the town, insisted the base be the shape of an apple to commemorate all the orchards in the area. How could Frank trip on a bright, sunny day in July? Doesn't that seem . . . strange?"

"What's strange is you didn't push him in." Bridget fluffed her frosted brown hair and grinned. "Maybe your luck's changing. You should help it along. God knows you deserve it."

"Maybe I'll go visit my parents in Cincinnati."

"I was thinking more like a new wardrobe. Maybe take a trip to Disneyland. Have great sex, and don't give me that wide-eyed look that says 'who me?' You're forty-one. *Cosmo* says that's a woman's sexual prime. I'm actually looking forward to turning forty next year. So, you don't want to waste it, you've done enough of that with Frank and his attack of mid-life, Viagra-enhanced puberty."

Julia wagged her head. "After this year I don't have a sexual prime. What about an apple pie prime? I'm definitely in my apple pie prime."

"That's the divorce talking. You're substituting food for sex. You need to get back on the horse. Go for a ride. Start to live again and do it right away, or you'll crawl back into that photography studio of yours and never emerge again. Not all men are Frank Simons, thank the Lord."

Julia twisted the handle of her purse and let out a sigh. "Wh . . . what if I don't know how to *ride*. Maybe I forgot. Frank and I hadn't ridden in a really long time."

Bridget held up her hand to silence Julia. "Course you know how to ride. That's what *you* tell women who've gone through what you have, right?"

She gave Bridget a sheepish grin. "Easier to give advice than take it yourself."

"Look, you're entitled to a new life now that this is all behind you, maybe a little sexual fantasy to boost your spirits."

She nodded at Julia's attorney coming down the steps. "What about Cal? Unattached. Attractive. He's been single for a long time. Bet he'd like a little fling in his life. And he's liked you since high school."

"That was a long time ago, and I think the *thing* was for you and not me. Cal and I are just friends."

Bridget's eyes rounded. "Since when? I could have sworn there was more."

"He told me six months ago he was glad we'd always been friends, and he shook my hand and kissed me on the forehead. If that isn't the friend approach, I don't know what is. I think I have a bad effect on guys lately. I have rotten male karma."

"What about that PI guy following Cal? Didn't Cal bring him in from Cleveland? He looks like a man who'd appreciate a little sexual fantasy."

"Marc Adams?" Julia rolled her eyes so far back in her head she saw where her ears attached. "Cal got him to follow Frank to Club Med and get the goods on him because thirty-five-year-old Mr. Studly Adams fits in the Club Med scene like a duck in water. Probably has a preferred customer card. I think he's way beyond me."

"Right now Barney, the purple dinosaur, is beyond you."

"Thank you very much for pointing that out," she whispered as the two men approached. "So how could I wish for Marc Adams to want wild, hot sex with me?"

Cal pulled up beside her and loosened his tie, yielding to the noonday heat. "Well, it's all over with, Julia. You can get on with your life."

He took a camera from the suddenly dazed looking Marc Adams and handed it to Julia. "Marc happened to have this in his pocket, tools of the PI trade. He snapped a picture of Frank in the fountain." Cal winked. "I think you should cover it in Plexiglas, put it on the floor of your photography studio. Walk all over him for a change."

Julia glanced at Bridget and said, "This is really strange. I wished for Frank in the fountain and for the picture, and both happened."

"All sorts of things happen in divorces." Cal turned to Marc. "Right?"

Right? Right about what? Marc felt totally dumbfounded, in a complete state of physical shock. One minute he'd been taking pictures of Frank-the-jerk in the fountain snorting, and the next thing Marc knew he had a hard-on for Julia Simons that was so intense he could barely walk. *What the hell!*

"Marc?" Cal asked, looking concerned.

"Sure," Marc answered, not having the slightest idea what he'd agreed to, his sudden boner for Julia boggling his mind and other over-active body parts.

Oh, he'd admired her flame red curls, flashing green eyes, resilience, and good sense, but deep down inside the woman scared the hell out of him.

"You okay," Cal asked, giving him a curious look.

"Busy." He caught Julia looking at him and buttoned his sports coat to hide his dick straining against his zipper. Sweat prickled his body. He shouldn't have buttoned his coat, but if he didn't . . . Shit!

He raked back his hair. "Much busier day than I expected." Julia Simons now Dempsey was not his type. She was one of those feisty, sassy, take-no-prisoners types. Started MRS, Men Running Scared, a support group for wives who vow to take action against their cheating husbands. Didn't she sell Frank's Jag on eBay, give his custom-made titanium golf clubs to the Boy Scouts for their putt-putt golf course?

She was justified in her actions, but she was *not* the easy-going, fun-loving, live-for-the-moment type of gal he dated. Not the type who turned him on. But if that was true, what was happening to him now?

Cal gave him a curious look. "Busy? Aren't you done for the day?"

Yeah, he was *done*. His brain was cooked oatmeal. All he could think about was Julia's nicely rounded breasts hidden under her gray silk blouse. How they'd feel all warm and full in his hands, how they'd taste sweet in his mouth, how his tongue could tease one nipple, then the other, making them hard and taking them deep into his mouth and—

What the hell am I doing! He wanted to have hot, wild sex with Julia Simons. Take her to bed and do things to her Frank probably never dreamed of. Marc sure as hell couldn't *say that* to Julia, but he wasn't about to let her walk out of his life, either. "Would . . . would you like to go to dinner tonight?"

"Me?" Julia's eyebrows arched to her hairline, and she looked around as if searching for someone else.

Marc swallowed. His common sense yelled *run, run, run;* his dick demanded *sex, sex, sex*. His dick won. "To, ah, celebrate a new beginning . . . for you." Sounded lame, he needed more. "I like to take my clients to dinner after the case ends."

Cal's forehead furrowed. "You do?"

Marc gave his old friend from their police department days in Cleveland a butt-out look, then said to Julia, "Seven? I'll pick you up? The Old Orchard Inn? I'm staying there, the food's great. Terrific apple butter, apple fritters, apple pie. I'm sure they have other great apple things; I just haven't gotten to them all."

Damn, he was rambling. He never rambled. He was a focused get-the-job-done kind of guy, till he got an unexplainable hard-on for Julia Simons.

Her fingers twisted the handle of her purse. "Well, I—"

"She'd be delighted," Bridget answered with a big grin. "Julia loves the Old Orchard Inn. They're remodeling it, you know. I hope they don't ruin the charm. She's restoring the historical photos to hang in the hallways. She's a terrific photographer, expanded her hobby into a career."

Marc returned her grin. "Great."

"I have a shoot at seven." Julia countered, looking relieved. "Jeffery Blum's seventy-fifth birthday party, I'm committed. Sorry, I can't make it."

"Nine, then?" Marc offered, his dick refusing to take no for an answer.

"Ah, sure." Julia looked like a woman who'd just run out of excuses.

"Great."

She held up the camera. "I'll develop the film and return the camera to you tonight."

"Great." All he could say was great? His erection had corroded his brain. At the moment one head completely controlled the other.

He fell in step beside Cal as they left, and Cal said, "You don't take clients out, especially forty-one-year-old clients who have a backbone. Thought you were heading back to Cleveland tonight."

"Changed my mind."

Cal stopped under the green-and-white-striped awning of Granny Smith's Apothecary and Ice Cream Parlor, making Marc stop, too. "What's going on with you? Are you sick?"

Marc put his hand to his forehead. "Maybe."

"Go to the doctor."

He considered his present physical state. "Not now." He shook Cal's hand. "Don't worry about me, I'll be fine. Glad I could help on the Simons' case. Deception has no place in a relationship; I learned that from my parents' disastrous marriage many years ago. Anytime I can help someone out of a mess like that, just give me a call."

"You're hanging around Delicious for a while?"

Marc puffed out a deep breath and thought of Julia, her creamy skin, rounded hips that would fit perfectly against his hips. His physical condition wasn't improving. "I'll be around for dinner."

Cal put his hand on Marc's shoulder. "You'll be fine, just hang in there."

That's the trouble, at the moment he wasn't *hanging;* he was stiff as a frozen fish. "Maybe things will get back to normal after tonight." *Somehow.* "I sure as hell hope so."

"What's that supposed to mean?"

Marc looked Cal dead in the eyes. "It's really complicated."

Bridget walked with Julia toward her studio, a slight breeze the only break in the summer heat that kept most people inside by the air conditioner or swimming down at Golden Lake. "Marc Adams asking you to dinner is definitely the way to start your new life. How terrific is that?"

"The question is *why?*"

"Are you kidding, because he's handsome with incredible brown hair with gold highlights that weren't put in by some salon. And his blue eyes make me feel faint, not to mention his build. Batman would kill for that build. That's why it's terrific."

"Not the terrific part, the dinner-date part." Julia stopped by the big picture window of Mom and Pop's Diner. "Why did he ask me out? Doesn't that seem a little weird to you? We're not exactly a match made in heaven. I'm six years older, newly divorced. He's a big-time player and likes it that way. Why me?"

"Maybe he's due for a change. Maybe he's looking for something more than a hot date."

"Gee thanks."

"I mean the *more* part. And now's not the time to second-guess the situation; you accepted and you have to go. And you need this; you need a connection with a real man, someone who'll remind you that you're a woman."

"I know I'm a woman; men don't get cellulite. *You* accepted the invitation; *you* should go."

"I have a boyfriend; Jerry would not be thrilled." She batted her eyes. "He's very possessive. Besides, you have Marc's camera. You can't just drop it off and break the date. That would be rude after he did you a favor taking that picture. Go, have fun. Wear something sexy, black, low cut, high cut. Strappy shoes. Men love strappy shoes. With beads. They go ape-shit over beads."

"I'm on the board for the library and the apple heritage museum. I'm on the town council. I have suits and sensible shoes and . . . damn if McGuffy didn't park his truck in front of my studio again."

Bridget's nose wrinkled. "How'd McGuffy get into this?"

Julia pointed to the next block. "Every day for the last two months he's parked his big red truck in front of my studio. How's anyone supposed to see Photos By Julia when McGuffy Movers blocks the way."

"I take it you asked him to park elsewhere?"

"I'd like to tell him to park it where the sun doesn't shine. But he likes that spot, says it's a good place for advertising since it's across from Stan's Garden Store and next to The Book Nook. I just wish McGuffy would park somewhere else."

Bridget turned back to Julia. "Would you forget McGuffy, for crying out loud, and think sexy, naturally potent younger man."

Julia sneered at the truck. "I have a business to think about. I have to make a living, and I have a nice summer navy linen suit that will do just fine—*ohmigod!*"

Bridget grinned. "You're going to do it, aren't you? You had an epiphany, an estrogen awakening. I knew you'd cave, no scratchy linen, but soft sexy silk. Marc's such a hunk. Make him drool, make him hard as a rock, make him—"

"He's moving?"

"Marc's moving here?"

Julia turned Bridget around and pointed a shaky finger down the street. "Look. McGuffy. He's moving his truck."

"I'm glad that you're glad, now about the drool and the hard-on."

Julia huffed. "Don't you see a pattern? All the crazy things that have happened today? There's something going on, Bridge."

"Yeah, you got divorced, and you got a hot date with a *Playgirl* centerfold all in the same day. Life is good, better than it's been in a really long time for you. No one's getting their picture taken today, too hot. Get your nails done, buy condoms, do you have a garter belt?"

"It's only a date!"

"The man looked at you as if you were the last woman on earth. He buttoned his coat."

"So? He's a professional, probably has a gun."

Bridget winked. "Yeah, I just bet he has a gun. A nice big one—"

"Bridget! I can't just jump into the sack with someone I don't know anything about."

"He's a friend of Cal's, he seems like a good guy, and he's smart, and God knows he's handsome enough. The guy's hot for you. Go for it. Go for *him*." She kissed Julia on the cheek. "I've got to tutor a kid on ancient history or he's not going to be a senior come September." Bridget started off and called over her shoulder. "Think hot chickie."

Julia watched Bridget leave and thought, *I'm nuts for going on this date. The only thing I know about hot chickie is barbecued wings on the grill. What the heck have I gotten myself into?*

TWO

At ten o'clock as Julia gazed across the table bedecked in white linens and pretty china at the Old Orchard Inn to oh-so-handsome Marc Adams in a taupe sports jacket and cream shirt, she knew *exactly* what she'd gotten into . . . *the most boring date on the face of God's green earth.*

"The baked chicken was very tasty," she said as she sipped her decaf cappuccino, her cheek muscles aching from the smile plastered on her face through salad, entrée, and coffee.

"Yes," Marc replied, his own fake smile starting to quiver.

What the heck *was* she doing here? She'd been divorced only ten hours. Didn't she need some downtime? Time to rebound? A time without a man in her life? Actually, she'd been doing that for over a year now. And not associating with men more had been a really bad idea because now she had no idea what to do on a date, especially a date with Marc. They had nothing, *not one darn thing*, in common. Why couldn't Marc be a woman? They could talk fashion, diets, Oprah. She had completely lost her other-gender communication skills.

"The coffee is . . . fresh," Marc added to their attempt at conversation.

"The espresso is wonderful. Was your apple pie good?"

"Yes, very good."

Well, they exhausted the pie and coffee subject. Now what? She'd never been to Cleveland or been a PI; he'd never been married or lived in a small town. After their discussion on cameras that lasted ten minutes, and Delicious and Cal that lasted five more, dead silence had followed them on their short walk from her apartment over her studio to the inn.

Marc might be giving her his best fake smile, but under it he looked pained, as if sitting on a tack. First time she ever had that effect on a guy. Even Frank never looked that uncomfortable; he just looked apathetic. She should give up guys. Julia Dempsey was not the Marilyn Monroe of Delicious, Ohio.

Marc put his napkin on the table. "Are you ready to go?"

About an hour ago, she thought and said, "Yes," trying to keep the eagerness out of her voice.

She didn't wait for him to slide back her chair. She stood, needing to get this torture over as quickly as possible for both their sakes.

Then he put his warm hand to the small of her back, guiding her, and she suddenly felt . . . tingly? Maybe body parts had fallen asleep during dinner. Except she also felt . . . excited? Really excited. Indigestion? Indigestion never felt like this.

A waiter passed, and to avoid him Marc stepped closer to her. His thigh brushed hers, his firm chest connected with her shoulder, and his arm slid farther around her waist. Heat pulsed deep inside where nothing had pulsed for a really long time. Truth be told, she thought her pulsing days were over, no matter what *Cosmo* said.

She felt totally off balance and light-headed. She tripped, and Marc caught her. Her legs refused to work, and her body sagged a little closer to his. He asked, "Are you okay?"

His breath fell gently across her face, and the aroma of his after-dinner brandy filled her head. *No, I'm not okay at all!* "Yes."

He smiled a really great, sincere smile that curled her toes into her sensible pumps.

"Too much froth on the cappuccino?"

Too much froth between her ears. She'd just met Marc Adams, they had a date they'd both like to forget ever happened, and suddenly she wanted to tear his clothes off and salivate over every lovely inch of his naked body.

She shook her head, hoping thoughts of Marc and sex would dislodge. She straightened her linen suit. Then she straightened his tie.

Why'd she do that? Her fingers lingered at his throat, the heat from his skin warming hers. He swallowed, she did the same, and her gaze went from his well-defined, clean-shaven chin, over his seductive lips, his slightly crooked nose and locked with his . . . blue, dark as night, sensual, back-lit with passion.

Holy crap! "Thanks. I'm fine now."

What a whopper! She was . . . *horny?* As if over a year of sexual deprivation suddenly caught up with her all at once. Marc looked as if he felt that way, too, though she seriously doubted the cause was the same. What did cause him to look like that? Her? How could that be? But there sure didn't seem to be anyone else around for Marc to get the hots over. Their waiter was sixty and bald.

Now what? What should she do when they got to her apartment? Marilyn Monroe would know what to do. Too bad the only thing she and Marilyn had in common was they both wore a size fourteen.

Sweat beaded across her lip as they started for the door until a young woman in a flowered dress approached. She blocked their way and nervously pushed a strand of long blond hair from her face. "Julia? Julia Simons?"

"I was . . . until this afternoon. It's Dempsey now. Do I know you? I'm sorry. My brain's been a little scrambled today." *And tonight*, she added to herself. *Especially tonight.*

"I'm Sally McLean and live over in Harvest Grove, but I'm here visiting friends." She shifted from one foot to the other. "I joined MRS. I thought it was a good idea but now . . ." She licked her lips. "Larry's come back again and . . ." She spread her hands wide. "I don't know what to do."

Her eyes clouded. Julia knew this feeling and this look. Could have been part of her autobiography. She turned to Marc. Now was her chance to get rid of him and avoid any complications at the apartment when he dropped her off. That was good because now there'd be *no* complications, and that was bad because now there'd be *no* complications. Was being single always this difficult?

She said to Marc, "I had a great evening." *At least the last minute or so was pretty darn great. Confusing, but still great.* "I want to talk to Sally for a few minutes, and I can walk myself back to my studio and—"

"Has he done this before," Marc asked Sally, ignoring Julia. He nodded at the table they'd just vacated, then put his hand to the small of Sally's back and led her in that direction. Julia followed, eyeing Marc's strong hand to Sally's narrow waist. Julia's jaw clenched, and her eyes narrowed. She gulped back a little growl crawling its way up her throat. Wait, she didn't growl. Even over Frank at Club Med, she didn't growl. She cussed a lot and sold his Jag that he'd put in her name for some tax reason, but she didn't growl.

Marc swiped a chair from another table for Sally as Julia reclaimed her own chair, feeling a little left out. That made no sense at all since Sally came to see *her*, not Marc, right? Hey, if she were Sally, which one would she rather see? Julia eyed the most gorgeous hunk of man north of the Ohio River. What a dumb, dumb question.

"Is he cheating on you?" Marc asked. "How many times do you intend to take him back?"

Humm, Julia thought. *The direct approach, the manly way of doing things.* Julia opened her mouth to say something, but Marc said, "Do you have any children? Have you done counseling?"

Julia wondered why Marc Adams was so into this, and Sally said, "Larry's taken off twice before, then says he's sorry and that we're okay so he doesn't need counseling. We have a baby."

Marc drummed his fingers on the table. Sincerity and concern lined his face. "How long do you think it will be before he takes off again? Think what kind of message this sends to your child? Do you want it to be 'mates can come and go at will and that's fine'?"

Julia added, "You need to show Larry that the front door is not a revolving door for his convenience."

"I told him that, but he says this is his house, too. Where he lives."

"Show him he doesn't live there just because his things are there. Get rid of them. Give away his golf clubs. Nothing tells a man he doesn't live here anymore like tossing out the golf clubs."

"He doesn't golf, but he has a riding lawnmower he loves."

Marc said, "You might need that."

"Fishing rod?" Sally offered.

"Bingo," Julia said. "I suggest my personal favorite place to get rid of things, eBay."

Marc gave Sally a dazzling grin that made Julia think, *Smile at me like that*.

Sally fiddled with the napkin on the table. "What if he has a fit?"

Marc said, "He'll know you mean business and that you're not sitting back and doing nothing so he can have his way. Marriage is a two-way street, and he can either shape up or ship out."

"But I love him?"

Marc leaned forward and gave Sally a long, hard look. "Can you really love someone who treats you like this? You have to love yourself and respect yourself first."

Julia said, "It's your call, but think if waiting for Larry is how you want to spend the rest of your life."

Sally looked from Julia to Marc and back again. "I knew the answer before I even came to you; I just needed to hear it out loud." She smiled at Julia. "It's great you have a boyfriend who understands you so well and what you do. You make a great team, and a great couple. You both have that same hungry look. Larry and I used to have that, but we don't anymore."

Her eyes brimmed with tears, and Julia said, "Try and get Larry to counseling, but if he won't go, you go, then decide what's best for you and your baby." Julia opened her purse and took out a business card. "Call me."

What hungry look, Julia wondered as she watched Sally leave. Probably caused from passing up the apple cheesecake for dessert. Then she cut her eyes to Marc, and the hunger in her gut had nothing to do with cheesecake and everything to do with the yummy man across from her.

"I didn't know you were into the problems of divorce," she said, trying to keep impure thoughts out of her brain at a family restaurant.

"My dad told my mom one lie after another to serve his own purpose. She finally learned the truth and divorced the bastard." He sent her one of his incredible smiles, the kind she wished for. "Everyone deserves the truth; it's one of the reasons I went into the PI business."

Marc took her hand, his strong fingers wrapping gently around hers. "I respect what you do, Julia. You help people get through rotten mates and difficult times." He leaned toward her, his lips not far from hers. "I find that totally refreshing. Something I don't run into very often." He kissed her hand. "Ready?" he asked in a quiet voice.

Her brain fogged from his nearness, making thought processes impossible. Until the last ten minutes the only thing between them had been strained conversation. Then he touched her, making her senses come alive. The brass chandeliers overhead gleamed, the food smelled heavenly, the flowers on the tables radiant. Sally showed up and the connection grew. Marc was more than a PI; he was a PI with heart and a lot of soul and compassion . . . not to mention a killer smile. "Ready for . . . ?"

He gave her a suggestive look through lowered lids. "Are you ready *to go?*"

"Oh." They stood, and he didn't release her hand. *Now* what was she going to do when she got back to her apartment? A kiss? Marc Adams looked like a man who had more than a kiss on his mind, and right now she wasn't sure she had a mind.

Never, in all her life, had she felt so strongly attracted to a man in such a short period of time. Maybe because she was divorced today, or maybe because she'd been *manless for over a year.* Or maybe because any woman with an ounce of estrogen in her veins would have the hots for Marc Adams.

She followed him into the entrance hall, empty at eleven-thirty, but instead of going outside into the muggy July night, he stopped in front of the coatroom. "We should get your coat."

"I didn't bring one. It's July. No coats. There's a folding screen in front of the room in case someone forgets. Are you okay?"

"We should check anyway. Maybe you brought a coat and don't remember." He gave a quick look around, then took her hand and led her behind the partition.

"What the heck are you doing?" she whispered as she looked at tables, chairs, rugs and furniture stacked in storagelike confusion, nearly filling the small room.

"Losing patience," he whispered back as he slid between two tall highboy dressers. Then he stopped and pulled her into his arms and gave her a quick kiss. "God," he said on a ragged breath as he rested his forehead against hers. "I've wanted to do that since we talked at the fountain."

She felt her eyes widen. "You have?"

"Sort of." He took her face in his hands and kissed her again, slower this time, seducing her lips into an erotic dance she didn't realize she knew, making her heart pound in time with a sensual rhythm.

"Now, *that,*" he said, his voice even more ragged than before, "is *really* what I wanted." His lips caressed hers, kicking the rhythm up a notch. "But without clothes."

Her mouth went dry. "This is a little sudden."

"You're not the one who's been in a state of debilitating lust since noon."

Her eyes widened to her hairline. "For me?"

He kissed her again, coming closer as he wrapped

his arms around her, his erection pressing hard into her belly. *Yikes, question answered.* Been a while since she felt one of *those*.

"What . . . what if someone comes in?"

"You just said no coats this time of year, and this place is obviously used for storage during restorations." He nipped her bottom lip. "No one's restoring anything tonight."

That's what you think, she said to herself. Frank had left because she wasn't exciting, because she bored him. And after hearing that enough times, she believed him . . . until right now as Marc's warm hands slid under her sensible cream blouse, making her quiver head to foot.

Suddenly she didn't give a rat's rump what Frank thought, because, according to the incredibly handsome and dynamite kisser, Marc Adams, Frank was dead wrong.

She dropped her purse on the floor. This time she kissed Marc, loving the feel of his mouth on hers. No one had ever made her feel the way he did. Not just with his body against hers, but the way he held her, complimented her, lusted after her, all making her feel like a real woman again.

Her hips arched against him, her body having a mind of its own that completely lacked basic common sense and wallowed in sexual decadence. It had taken forty-one years and Marc Adams for her to realize she even *had* sexual decadence.

Her breasts swelled full and sensitive against his chest. Her nipples hardened, begging to escape her bra and have Marc's bare skin against hers.

He caressed her breasts through the satin material, and the sheer delight of his hands on her made her weak. He whispered, "I want to make love with you, Julia."

Her insides melted.

"More than I ever wanted to make love in my life and that's going some."

His dazzling blue eyes met hers. "The question, Julia Dempsey, is *what do you want?*"

Three

Having sex with Marc Adams was not on her list of things she wanted to do at forty-one, but it sure as heck should be. "You really want me?"

The faint light spilling over into the oversized coat-room from the hallway cast shadows across his face. He gave her a smile that looked wolfish in the dim light, and he said in a husky voice, "Oh, babe."

Babe? She was a forty-one-year-old babe! His erection pressed more intimately against her middle, and she marveled at the strength of the zipper keeping it in check . . . then she considered it *not* in check. A fast pulse beat at the juncture of her legs. Prickles of heat ran up her spine and neck. She gulped. "In a coatroom?"

He kissed her, his tongue tangling with hers, the bra unsnapped. *Holy smoke! In a coatroom!*

"If we use my room upstairs or your apartment," he said against her lips, "the whole town's talking by morning."

Her heart knocked against her ribs. He undid her blouse, popping two buttons. Ann Taylor had not designed for rapid stripping in a coatroom.

He pushed her bra up over her breasts, taking her breath away. "Oh, babe," he said again, this time in a worshipful voice as he gazed at her. He cupped one breast, then the other, his thumb fondling her sensitive nubs. She bit back a whine, his touch obliterating every thought from her mind except Marc Adams and the feel of him. She barely resisted the urge to tackle him to the floor and tear off his clothes. Was this what divorce did to a woman? Or was this what Marc Adams did?

"God, you're beautiful."

She looked down to see what miracle had befallen her not quite so perky boobs since this morning. Nope, same pair, until Marc kissed them, setting her completely on fire. She sighed and nuzzled her face in his hair, loving the texture against her cheeks, inhaling his heavy male scent. Everything about him mesmerized her. "I know this is crazy and irrational and much too fast, but I can't help it. I really really want you . . . *now!*"

Marc's insides tightened into a hard knot. "Thank God. I didn't want to finish this alone."

He looked up, her face flushed with excitement, turning him on even more. He undid his belt and watched as Julia kicked off one shoe, then the other, then paused.

"The only men I've ever taken my clothes off for are Frank and my gynecologist, and I think the gynecologist appreciated it more."

"Does that mean you're having second thoughts?"

"No. No second thoughts. Not tonight." Her gaze fused with his. "Not with you." She hiked up her skirt, revealing lovely feminine thighs. She reached under her skirt, squirmed her hips left, then right . . . *what the hell* . . . then peeled off her undergarments and kicked them into a little heap.

She righted herself and swept her hair from her face. "Shew, that's hard work!"

He snagged the garments and held them up for inspection. "What's *this?*"

She snapped them back and tossed them to the settee behind him. "Girdle, panty hose. I didn't dress for seduction. I dressed for linen."

"I think I hate linen." He unzipped his trousers.

Her eyes rounded. "Oh, hell."

He swallowed hard. "Let me guess, now you're having second thoughts?"

"Protection."

"Oh." He brightened. He fished out his wallet and held up a condom. "Not to worry."

She looked from it to him, her brows furrowing. "You had this *planned?*"

He waved his hand over the cluttered coatroom. "Babe, no one on the face of the earth could have *this* planned." He tore open the package and covered himself, her eyes following his every move.

"Oh . . . damn." This time her voice was a smoky whisper as she stared at his dick. Was this a good *oh, damn* or a bad one?

"You're . . . so . . . *big*. Frank wasn't . . ."

Marc grinned. *Definitely good.* He tangled his fingers into her luscious hair and kissed her hard, tasting the sweet sexy heat of her mouth and listening to her short gasps of mounting excitement. He toppled her onto the maroon settee, then followed her, bracing himself on his elbows, looking down at her. "Stunning full breasts, pink nipples, you're—"

"Marc!" she said, passion filling her eyes. "Inventory later. *Hurry now.*"

He felt her tug her skirt up to her thighs. She stopped and bit her lip in hesitation.

"Are you okay?"

"I just need a minute here."

"Babe, I don't think I have a minute." He gritted his teeth, fighting for control. "What you do to me . . ."

Get a grip, Adams, he thought to himself. *It's not like you haven't done this before.* Except with Julia it was different. *She* was different. He kissed her, her eyes darkening to jade, and he felt her skirt again slide up, exposing soft curls, the heat from her silky mound now surrounding his pulsing dick. The smell of sex hung heavy in the room, her shallow breaths the only sound. She wrapped her legs around his back, and his dick touched her swollen, wet lips.

Every muscle in his body throbbed with wanting, and he slowly eased himself into her, knowing the instant he touched her clit because she bucked against him. "You're so ready, Julia," he said in a ragged voice. "So sweet, so hot, just for me."

Her eyes glazed, and she widened her thighs, opening herself more to him. He wanted her to get the feel of him a little at a time . . . until she arched against him, taking his shaft deep inside her, nearly making him come. *"God, Julia."*

"Make love to me, Marc."

He pulled out just a bit, and she whimpered in protest till he plunged back into her. He did it again, then again, farther and faster, her fingers digging into his shoulders, her body meeting his thrusts making him delirious with pleasure.

Her legs tightened, and he drove into her once more as she gasped, throwing her head back in pleasure. He kissed her, swallowing the sweet sound of her crying out his name as his own explosive orgasm racked his body in the pure ecstasy of making love to Julia.

He sagged on top of her, sinking them both into the soft cushions. "Incredible," he whispered in her ear. He gulped in deep breaths, trying to calm his racing heart, then raised his head and gazed at her. He brushed strands of damp hair from her temples. "Sorry we didn't take more time."

"Hello?" came a female voice from the entrance to the coatroom.

Julia's eyes cleared instantly and rounded to the size of softballs. She gave him an oh-shit look. He pulled out of her, trying to take his time and knowing they had no time. He rolled onto the floor, took off the condom, wrapped it in his handkerchief and stuck it in his pocket. He slipped under the settee, dragging her suit jacket with him. Damn, where was Julia?

He reached around the cushions and curled his finger for her to follow. In a second she was beside him, facing him, as they heard the old floor creak. Someone was coming toward them.

"Anyone here?" The lights came on.

Julia mouthed, *girdle, panty hose*. She pointed up to where they'd been. He knew those damn things were no good.

He felt along the back of the settee, connecting with a silky leg. He tugged, bringing down the girdle, too. Julia snagged her shoes. He grabbed her purse.

"Hello?"

A pair of Doctor Scholls came into view at the side of the settee. Marc held Julia tight, mostly to keep any body extremities from protruding, or maybe he wanted an excuse.

"Margaret," came another voice from the hallway. "We're locking up the restaurant. Cook's almost done. There's no one there, let's go home, I'm beat. Did you see that PI stud with Julia? He can park his butt in my bed anytime. Bet he's hung like a damn horse."

Julia grinned, and Marc didn't know whether to be embarrassed or proud.

"I thought for sure I heard something."

"Probably mice."

"Don't think I ever heard mice moan before."

"You're absolutely right," the owner of the Doctor Scholls declared. "Mice. Nothing but mice."

Instantly, she retreated toward the entrance. Marc exhaled in relief, and Julia did the same. The lights went out in the coatroom and then in the entrance hall, leaving only the glow of red from the emergency signs. He waited, listening for the all-clear sounds of locks falling into place and the dead quiet of no footsteps. Besides, lying next to Julia was not exactly a hardship. He loved the feel of her body next to his. A wood floor was not the best, but he'd take it all the same.

Finally, he wiggled out from under the sofa, and Julia followed. He stood and helped her up. Trying not to giggle she whispered, "A horse?"

"Just couldn't let it go, could you?"

"I just wonder how she knew?" Julia grinned, then slid on her shoes. "We were almost on the front page of the *Apple Bee*." She stuffed her girdle and panty hose into her purse.

"I can see it now, *Town council member found doing the nasty in the coatroom at the* Old Orchard Inn."

Her eyes met his, and she framed his face with her cool hands and kissed him, her lips puffy and slick from his kisses. "It was not nasty," she said. "It was great."

"Yeah, me, too." He kissed her back. "We have to get the heck out of here unnoticed. You just got over one mess; you don't need to be the center of gossip again. The emergency exit should work. If we're seen together, especially with you looking like this, people will talk."

He wagged his head, a devilish grin spreading across his face as he straightened her blouse, trying to pull together the material where buttons were missing. He helped her on with the jacket. "I think we killed your suit."

She stood on tiptoes and kissed his top lip, the bottom lip, then both together. "It was for a good cause." Her words and kisses made him hard for her again. How could that happen?

He gathered her close so she'd feel how she affected him, her eyes brightening in surprise. He nodded at the settee. "If I wasn't worried about your reputation . . ."

"You mean the merry divorcée of Delicious, Ohio?"

"I'll call you tomorrow night. I'm helping Cal with another case, so I'll be out of touch till then."

"Oh my, more scandal? How can this be?"

"Let's just say it's amazing what goes on in little towns in Ohio." He grinned. "And I'm happy to do my part as long as I'm with you."

He took a penlight from his inside pocket, shined it on the floor, took her hand, and made his way to the red exit sign. "I'll check the alley." He gave her one last kiss. "In Cleveland this wouldn't be a problem."

"Welcome to Delicious."

By the next evening Julia had accomplished zip in the photography studio. All day . . . and all last night . . . she'd thought about nothing but Marc, the inn, and a certain maroon settee in the coatroom.

This is crazy, she decided as she leaned back in the chair, her scheduling book spread out on the round oak table in front of her. How could she be so attracted to a younger man who was not her type at all? A city boy, a PI, a player. Then again, she had thought Frank was her type and look where that got her.

Frank wasn't always a jerk, of course, just the last few years. After he hired that blond bombshell teller with the big fake bazooms, things were never the same. Julia just hadn't faced it till she'd come across that credit card and gotten Cal to do some investigating. Frank? Club Med? What a joke.

Or, maybe *she* was the joke. She caught her reflection in the glass framing the Ansel Adams poster on the wall. She bunched her hair on top of her head and stuck a pencil through to hold the loose knot in place. More youthful, definitely more sexy. Though Marc seemed to like her just the way she always looked.

Last night was fabulous. *He* was fabulous, and it took more than sex to get her to have that opinion of him. He was smart, funny, compassionate, caring, selfless, *and* hung like a horse. What more could she ask for? *Nothing.* That's why she had sex with him. Men like Marc didn't come along every day.

She knew him, because of the divorce. But she'd never known this fun, sexy side of him.

Concentrate, Julia, concentrate, and not on Marc. She looked back to the cluttered table. She had three weddings in August to arrange, the Ziglers' twenty-fifth anniversary party, the yearly group picture of the Historical Society, and the senior pictures for the high school yearbook. And she wanted to take some artistic shots of the Abernathys' sunflower farm in bloom and this week's full moon reflecting on Golden Lake.

"Julia," came Bridget's voice from the doorway of the studio. "I'm glad I found you. I should have known you'd be working late. I have news." She stared at Julia and paused for a second. "You look . . . different."

"Exhaustion. I've got a killer schedule ahead of me."

"Nice hair." She sat in the chair across the table and gave Julia a sassy smile. "Word has it something's going on over at Old Orchard Inn besides renovations. Something that goes bump in the night."

"Mice."

Bridget arched her left eyebrow. "Condom wrapper on the floor of the coatroom."

"Active mice." Julia willed herself not to blush.

"You wouldn't know anything about this?"

"Trojan found a niche market?"

"You old dog." Bridget sat up, grinning at Julia. "How could you not level with me; I'm your best friend, the one who got you into that coatroom? You are one fast woman."

"I'm forty-one, my fast days are over."

"Your secret's safe with me."

"What secret?"

Bridget didn't seem to be listening and continued, "This is perfect, an affair without strings."

"What affair! Did I mention affair?"

She hunched her shoulders in a dismissive way. "If you're interested, I know why this is going on, why all that strange stuff happened yesterday."

She looked Julia dead in the eyes. "I know why Marc's attracted to you. It's a fluke. Your wishes are coming true." She leaned across the table. "Think about it. You wished Frank to fall in the fountain, which he promptly did."

"Coincidence," she said, but suddenly didn't believe it as strongly as she wanted to. She'd had an icky feeling all along things were screwy.

"And," Bridget added. "Frank snorted, what about *that?* You said he was a pig. You wished for a picture, and Marc took it. Then there was the McGuffy truck episode. That man drove you nuts for two whole months. And what happens yesterday? You *wish* he'd move and he does, within minutes."

Bridget grinned at Julia, leaned back, and crossed her legs under her long blue cotton skirt, looking very pleased with herself. "Then there's the clincher. The wish for hot sex with Marc Adams."

"*That* was sarcasm."

"It seems wishes have no sense of humor."

Julia tapped the pencil on the table. An eerie feeling crept up her spine. "Today I wished Linda Farmer and Belinda Snow would pay their bills for their First Communion pictures."

"And?"

"And they did."

"Holy shit." Bridget bolted straight up in her chair. "Look, you said yourself something's going on, and you were right. *You get your wish.* It's like having a birthday, except you had a divorce and now your wishes come true for real."

Julia leaned across the table. "Lots and lots of people get divorced, and they don't get what they wish for."

"Yeah, but you divorced Frank, and the angels rejoiced. So, maybe they're giving you a little gift."

"And how long does this wish thing last?"

"Who knows, who cares? Take it for what it is and have fun. Least you're not seeing dead people like that poor little kid in the movie."

"Gee, Bridge, I feel so much better now." Julia shivered.

"You should wish for a bunch of other stuff, see if it happens."

"No way. I've read Stephen King. A person can get into a heap of trouble messing with the cosmos like that. So, you really think Marc's under some kind of influence because of me?"

"Why else would he come after you?" She held up her hand. "I didn't mean it that way," she rushed on. "But this is not a match made in heaven, your words."

"You think Marc Adams is attracted to me because I wished it?"

"And until it ends take it for what it's worth, and that means great sex for Julia Dempsey with Marc Adams.

No permanent attractions and no one gets hurt. What could be better than that?"

Bridget cocked her head. "Unless, of course, you're falling for him. You're not doing that, are you?"

Julia tisked. "Of course not. We had dinner, a really boring one. We have nothing in common."

"Except a coatroom?"

"Mice." Julia tapped her pencil again. "Nothing but mice."

Bridget winked. "Think about Marc and enjoy your freedom." She glanced at her watch. "Yikes, I've got to run, I have a date with Jerry. His crew's building an addition to that motel by the expressway, so he's been putting in a lot of extra hours. But we're getting together for . . . uh, dinner." She grinned.

"Set a wedding date yet?"

"Next summer. Definitely next summer. He promised."

Julia smiled, wanting to kick Jerry in the butt. He'd kept Bridget waiting for two years already. An engagement of convenience; all the perks and none of the responsibility.

Bridget winked. "Marc's the right guy at the right time, Jules. He's here for now, then goes back to Cleveland. You'll find another guy who's really for *you;* you don't have to wish it, and you'll live happily ever after."

Julia watched the door close behind Bridget, then focused on the big full moon glowing creamy white outside the store front window of her studio. Marc Adams' attraction to her was nothing but a wish? *Impossible.*

Then she thought of their lovemaking and the greatest sex she'd ever had. *Some wish.*

She thought of Marc's compassion for Sally and other divorced women. Of his humor, his fun, his ability to not take himself too seriously and laugh at the situation they'd gotten into. She thought of the way he'd made love to her and how he treated her and made her feel alive and wonderful and how this would all end unexpectedly.

Marc Adams might be under some kind of wish influence, but the only influence she was under was Marc Adams. She threw her pencil across the room. "Well, hell. Now what?"

When it came to men, she sucked. She'd fallen for Frank, who cheated on her, and now Marc, who would go back to Cleveland and forget about her. She should do herself a really big favor and join a convent or at least stay away from Marc until he left town.

Four

Marc slapped on mosquito repellent, then laced up his running shoes. The full moon glowed overhead in the clear night sky, casting a ribbon of silvery light across the lake. Fishing boats with lanterns and a few rowboats dotted the calm water. A night for lovers, except Marc's *lover* was nowhere to be found.

Frogs and crickets chirped their mating calls as he hit redial on his cell and listened to the continuous ringing at the other end followed by Julia's voice requesting a message. He had a message for her all right, *Where the hell are you?*

He'd said he'd call, and that's exactly what he'd been doing for the last hour and a half. He wanted to see her, and he just plain wanted her. But since that wasn't going to happen, he'd run off some of this frustration. He sure as hell had to do something with it.

He stretched, then jogged down the gravel path that disappeared into a thicket of apple trees. He came out the other side by the docks, where vendors sold refreshments and rented boats during the day. At night it sat deserted . . . except for Julia.

He stopped, watching her hair play catch with moonbeams while she disassembled her tripod and camera. His breath caught, and it had nothing to do with running—thirty seconds was not a run—and everything to do with Julia.

Damn, he'd missed her. He missed the way she walked, the sophisticated tip of her chin, her clear voice, her gentle laugh, her wiseass comments. He'd thought about her all day and how he wanted to be with her all night. Sure the sex was good. Hell, it was beyond good, but most of all he just wanted her near.

He walked in her direction, calling her name so as not to sneak up on her in the dark and scare her half to death.

"Marc?" Her eyes rounded, but she looked more apprehensive than happy to see him.

He pulled up beside her. "I've been trying to get ahold of you."

She picked up the camera cases and headed for her car parked by the docks. "I got some shots of the moon and lake to frame up for the tourists." He snatched the tripod and followed as she added, "You know, *A Delicious Moon*. Make some note cards and stationery to sell at the studio."

He put the tripod next to the cases in the car while Julia rambled, "Think I'll get some other shots from the other side of the lake. A little cash is always good and—"

"What's wrong?" He cupped her shoulders and looked into her eyes, but she refused to meet his. She seemed nervous, unsure, like they'd just met. "Have I done something to upset you?"

"No." This time her eyes met his.

In desperation, he bent his head and captured her lips in a heated kiss, the luscious feel reminding him of last night. At least the kisses were the same, the feelings the same, but something was going on. "We have to talk, Julia. I'm no good at mind reading, and we're too old for games, what gives? Something's off, like you don't want to see me. Is that it?"

She gave him one of those forced grins he hated and that she'd assumed over dinner last night when they were bored to unconsciousness. "I have photos to take, you're out for a run, and I don't want to interrupt that so—"

"Bullshit. You want to get rid of me, and I have no idea why."

"You're one damn stubborn man."

"I think I met my match with you. The Julia of last night was too wonderful to let go without finding out what the hell happened to her."

She raked her hair back from her face. "You just didn't see me for who I really am, Marc. Last night was sort of a . . . fluke. I just divorced, you were there all handsome and gorgeous, we found a settee—"

His left arm snagged her waist and led her behind the boathouse. Sound carried over the water, and this discussion did not need to be rehashed tomorrow morning over every neighbor's fence. "I'm not leaving till you level with me. Something's going on that you're not telling me about, and it's not that you don't like me. If I have to camp outside your damn studio, I swear I'll do it. I've never fallen for anyone as fast and hard as I've fallen for you. Whatever's bothering you, we can fix it, Julia. Together we can fix damn near anything; that's the kind of people we are. We make things right. That's why I'm a PI and you started MRS. You just have to give me a chance, give *us* a chance."

Except there is no us, Julia thought to herself, looking into his eyes full of sincerity and true feelings for her. Damn her wishes for getting her into this mess and damn Marc Adams for not letting it go.

He kissed her again and slid his hands under her

T-shirt, heating her skin already damp from the July evening humidity. His lips were even more delectable than she remembered, and she'd remembered the whole blasted day.

"Ah, Julia." He breathed her name softly into the night and wrapped his arms around her, cherishing her close. "Now, *this* is the woman I remember."

Moon glow reflected in his clear blue eyes. Her breasts suddenly felt heavy, the juncture at her legs moist, anticipating their lovemaking. *Damn traitorous body.* Her brain knew this was all wrong. Then he wedged his leg between hers, parting them. His thigh rubbing against hers, then higher, her brain surrendering to her heart.

How could she let him go? *Just a little more time,* she thought, desire eating at her like some out-of-control fire. *Just a day or two.* She felt like Cinderella in Nikes except she'd never get the prince, and she had no idea when he'd just ride off into the sunset, or sunrise.

"The boathouse." She nodded at the gray-and-white clapboard building with neat flower boxes. "Can you do some trick and get us in there?" She wrapped her arms around his neck and gave him a long, steady look. "I want to make love to you, Marc."

"In there?"

"Hey, you dragged us into a coatroom. The sheriff just came by here, making his rounds of the town so no surprise visits."

His brow furrowed in question. "Okay, first you wanted me gone. Now you don't. You're not the fickle type, Julia. Tell me what's upsetting you."

She could just imagine saying, *Oh, Marc, I just wished all this and you don't really care for me.* Or something like that. Yeah, he was sure to believe every word.

Instead she said, "Nerves, work, divorce, my car needs

an oil change. Life's catching up with me, that's what's wrong. But I'm better now." She gave him a genuine smile. "Having you near makes everything better."

He pulled her to him, her cheek against his broad chest, his steady heartbeat a balm to her frazzled state. He massaged the back of her neck and her shoulders, the knots of tension melting away as he applied gentle pressure. His breath tangled in her hair, the heat from his body mixed with hers, and his arms felt secure, trusting, dependable.

A night breeze wafted off the shimmering water. The scent of apples surrounded them as Marc kissed her hair. He tipped her head back and kissed her eyes, then her mouth. It was one of those perfect nights, the kind a woman remembered all her life . . . and Julia would remember.

"I'm not hitting you up for sex, you know. We can go for a walk, talk, and look at the moon." His hands massaged her spine down to the small of her back.

She closed her eyes, reveling in his touch. "I've had my fill of this moon. And I'd rather spend the night with you . . . *really* with you . . . while we have the time."

"You're acting like there won't be other nights."

She opened her lids, and he looked deep into her eyes, her soul. "I'm not leaving you, Julia," he said with conviction and promise. "Cleveland is two hours away, and I plan on hanging around here for a while."

His expression morphed into a sensual grin. "And if you want to make love with me tonight, I can't imagine a more wonderful way to spend an evening."

He went to her car and tossed in his cell phone. He snagged a blanket from the backseat. She looked at the blanket and frowned. "Last time I used that I had a picnic with Frank. Told him I was divorcing his lying carcass."

"You did it over a picnic? That was very civilized."

"I needed to do it myself, not through an attorney. I packed sandwiches, no sharp or blunt objects around so I wouldn't do anything I might regret later, though strangling his fat little neck had definite appeal. I felt betrayed. I should have known things between us weren't right, but I thought it was one of his little phases. Frank had a lot of phases. The sushi phase, the wine phase, the opera phase—I really hated that one—and the Viagra phase, though I only knew about that one by rumor."

"How could he need that kind of help with you around? Just seeing you and being near you is a turn-on, Julia. Your scent, the spark in your eyes, the curve of your hips." He ran his hand over her and gave her a half grin. "Damn, woman, I'm turning myself on just talking about you."

He took out his wallet and selected a credit card. He wedged it between the doorjamb and the lock of the boathouse, gave it a little nudge, and the door sprang free.

"Thought that only worked in movies."

"And old locks in Delicious, Ohio." He pushed the door open and spotted a desk in the corner. Rowboats, canoes, paddles, and other boating paraphernalia were scattered about. He swept her into his arms, his eyes smoky blue. "I'm making sure you don't change your mind again."

"I won't." She kissed him and kicked the door shut with her toe. His breathing accelerated; his arms held her tighter. He nearly tripped over a trashcan in the shadows. She dropped the blanket onto a pile of boat cushions by a window, and he toppled them both into the heap.

She laughed as she landed on top of him. "You win." She smoothed back his hair and memorized his eyes, nose, mouth, and chin. She kissed his cheek, rough with late-night stubble. "The settee was more comfortable than this." She sat up, straddling his hips.

His eyes, dark as the night sky, widened a fraction. "What are you thinking, babe?"

"I'm thinking about you, all of you. Especially the part I haven't seen . . . yet. Though the part I have seen is pretty impressive."

Was that a blush creeping across his face? Even in the dim light she knew it was. Marc Adams, super-stud, may have a wilder reputation than he deserved. She smiled to herself, liking him all the more. Then she slowly slid up his shirt, taking in his trim waist, firm abdominal muscles, and fine broad chest. She ran her hands over him, the curls of sandy hair tickling her palms, his bare skin making her heart thud. She bent her head and kissed one hard flat nipple, then licked it, making it wet and shiny.

"Julia," Marc said in a deep, throaty voice as she did the same to the other nipple. She edged backward now, straddling his thighs, and spread a line of wet, tantalizing kisses across his torso, his solar plexus quivering, her kisses stopping at the waistband of his shorts. Then she French-kissed the indention of his navel.

His chest expanded as he sucked in a quick breath. His fingers tangled in her hair. "You're playing with fire. I think I should take over from here."

"Fat chance." She eased his shorts over his hips and gasped. "A jock strap? And I got all that grief over a girdle? What's *this?*" She snapped the waist band.

"Ouch. I was running . . . least I intended to . . . what did you expect?"

"Bounce?"

"I'm supposed to just lie here and let you make fun of me?"

She grinned and gave him a sultry look. "Oh, absolutely."

"Amazing how wrong you can be sometimes." He yanked up his shorts and flipped her on her back, pinning her under him, grinning ear to ear.

"I wasn't finished."

"Depends on your point of view. He sat up and pulled off his shirt, then tossed it into a rowboat, at least she thought that's where it landed. She was too busy ogling him to be positive. He tugged her T-shirt over her head and sent it flying. "I think this society has way too many undergarments. It's amazing that anyone ever has sex with all this *stuff* in the way."

He reached behind her and unfastened her bra. Her eyes glazed as he peeled it over her shoulders. Looking his fill, he let out a soft whistle, his appreciative gesture making her nipples hard and her breasts swell. "You were gorgeous last night. In the moonlight, you're astounding."

He fondled one breast, then the other, making her crazy for wanting him. "Oh, Marc," she exhaled as he suckled her nipples, taking them deep into his mouth.

She closed her eyes, enjoying the moment, the incredible sensation . . . till he stopped to slide off her shorts, taking her panties in the process. Her eyes flew open. "Oh, Marc!"

He knelt by her feet. "I can't decide which *oh, Marc* I like better."

"I'm . . . naked."

"You have shoes." He took them off. "Now you don't." He spread her legs just a bit and kissed her ankle, the sensation reverberating up her legs, pooling where they met, making her weak and glad she was lying down. He kissed the inside of her calves. "Where exactly are you going with this?" She struggled to form words.

"Up." He parted her knees and gave her a heated look. "This was your idea, remember?" Before she could think of some wiseass answer he kissed the inside of her thighs. Her body temperature soared, and she trembled as he ran more kisses . . . up.

The sight of his head at the apex of her legs made her weak, and when he licked her intimate folds, swollen and tender with anticipation, she nearly swooned . . . or whatever women do when they almost pass out.

"Bend your knees for me, babe. Your body was made for this. It was made for me to love. I want to taste all of you."

"Taste? Marc? I—"

His mouth covered her, and she gasped, her hips arching off the pillows and losing all control. His tongue and lips explored her, sucked and teased her, then took possession of her again and again, sending her into a rapid explosive climax she never expected.

"You are so wonderful, Julia," he whispered as he held her in his arms and kissed her face. She looked at him through a hazy fog, realizing he was beside her now. "How'd you do that to me?"

"Making love to you is an out-of-body experience for me. You respond to my every touch, every caress. A man couldn't ask for more."

Her eyes finally focused on his. "But that wasn't the plan."

"Plan?" His eyes opened wide.

She bit her bottom lip. "Well, not exactly a plan, but I want you *in* me, *with* me. I want to give you pleasure, too."

He smiled. "Oh, babe, we can do that." He reached into the back pocket of his shorts, snagging his wallet.

Taking advantage of the situation, she pushed him onto his back and slid her body on top of his, the feel of her bare breasts against his chest hair nearly making her come again.

He stared up at her. "I was off balance. That was sneaky. Didn't we start this way?"

"But *we* didn't finish."

His look turned heated. "And you had clothes on."

"The important word is *had*. Now, where was I before I was so rudely interrupted." She pushed her-

226 *Dianne Castell*

self up and skimmed her breasts sensually across his chest, his abdomen, his navel, her nipples teasing and seducing him. "Julia," he ground out. "What are you doing to me?"

She kissed him. "Doing to *us*."

She straddled his knees, and he could feel her feminine heat on his bare skin, tormenting him beyond his wildest imagination.

"I think I was here before you upended me." She laid her hand possessively over his arousal, gently pressing through his shorts. "My, my, what is this?"

"In about one second I'm going to show you what *this* is."

She pressed her finger gently across his lips to silence him. "Patience is a virtue."

"Screw patience."

"I'd much rather you did that to me." She let her palm linger, the warmth and her touch making him crazy. Then she eased his shorts down over his bulging erection. "Nice package." She carefully took off the jock strap and tossed it into the air while taking in every long, hard, thick pulsing inch of him. Then she bent her head and tasted him with the tip of her tongue.

"*Julia!*" He sucked in air through clenched teeth, his whole body tensing into one hard mass. "You can't . . ." But he seemed to lose his train of thought as she took his engorged penis into her mouth.

Marc felt all the air rush from his body. He fisted his hands, fighting for restraint as her sweet tongue licked and tormented him like he'd never been tormented before. "God, Julia. No more."

She took the condom and smiled sweetly . . . much too sweetly. Then winked. "Oh, there's more."

She tore the package and rolled the latex over his dick, slowly, provocatively, letting her fingers linger and stroke and massage.

"Dammit, Julia!" He tumbled her on her back, keeping himself positioned over her. "You're too much."

Her face flushed, and she ran her hands over every inch of his solid torso. "I want to remember you hot and sweaty and sexy, just as you are now."

Her eyes glistened; his knees spread her legs wide. Then he fused his hips tight to hers, his dick tight to her swollen wet lips, open for him. "I'm not going anywhere, Julia. You're going to have me around for a long time."

She framed his cheeks in her delicate hands, the moonlight falling across her lovely face. "You're terrific, Marc. I didn't know God made men like you for real."

Her words and her searing look and possessive touch took him over the edge. He thrust himself hard and deep inside her. Her eyes widened and glazed. Her breathing stopped, and her legs tightly embraced his hips. She met his every move, every thrust, as he plunged into her again and again, harder and faster, both of them reveling in a climax that captured her body and shook his very being.

His head sagged beside hers, his heart nearly bursting from his chest. He could feel her pulse throbbing as he stroked her graceful throat. "It's never been like this for me, Julia. Not even close, I swear."

She fondled his hair, her fingers trailing across his shoulders. "*You?* I was the one married to needle-dick Frank for fifteen years. I had no idea sex was like this. I can't believe I just said needle-dick."

He chuckled and wagged his head. "One minute I'm having the orgasm of a lifetime, and the next minute you've got me laughing over Frank."

She sobered. "That's the way life is. Just when you think you've got things figured out, something happens, turning your world upside down and setting you right on your ear."

He levered himself up on his elbows and gazed down at her. "What's that supposed to mean?"

She didn't say anything for a moment, as if weighing her words. "Incredible as you are, and you are totally incredible, doesn't this attraction between us seem a little . . . *odd* to you? It's all kind of sudden. We just met."

He grinned. "You think I'm incredible?"

"We just proved that beyond a shadow of a doubt. So, why me? Why now?"

Five

"My attraction to you is not just lust, if that's what you're thinking," Marc said as he gazed down at her, stroking her cheek. "Last night I was ready to walk away from that . . . painfully walk away, but walk all the same."

He smiled and kissed her eyes. "But then I got to know you. You're no wimp. You're not shallow or uncomplicated. You're interesting as hell and always have something going, and you make me laugh. Until now I thought uncomplicated girls were the types of women I liked. But I was wrong. God, was I wrong!"

He kissed the tip of her nose. "*You're* what I like in bed and out of bed . . . or settee or boathouse or wherever the hell else we wind up."

He combed his hands through her curls, loving the silky feel of them sliding over his fingers. I don't know where we're going from here, Julia, but we're going together. And not just when we leave the boathouse."

She pulled in a ragged breath.

"You don't believe me?"

"Of course. I do." She kissed him. "But right now

we better get out of here. Someone may see the car and go snooping for me."

"I think snooping's the pastime of choice around here."

"It comes with knowing everyone and everyone knowing you. The good part is if you've got a problem, everyone helps. The bad part is if you've got a problem, everyone talks. There's no place to hide in a small town. Not even in a boathouse for very long."

Marc stood. He wrapped the condom in paper from the desk and threw it in the trashcan. "Next time we're doing this in a real bed where there are no gossips or snooping people hovering about and where we have facilities."

"Yes," she said, staring at him through the dim light. "Next time."

He detected a touch of sadness in Julia's eyes. After a wonderful night of making love what caused that?

But the look left as quickly as it came, or maybe he just imagined it in the first place. She stood and reclaimed her clothes, the moonlight glistening off her delectable skin as she moved about the boathouse. "You're a goddess, Julia. I couldn't wish for more."

"Wish!" She sounded less than thrilled. She faced the window, hands on hips, the heavenly light pooling around her naked body. "I hate wishes. Why does anyone make them without considering just what they're getting themselves into? Wishing on stars and at birthdays and at wells is stupid. People should put their money in the bank, not a puddle of water in the ground."

He came to her side and turned her to face him. "What's wrong with wishing? It's just for fun."

"Fun? Did you say fun?" she ground out, then stepped back from him and kicked one of the pillows where they'd made love. "Let's just forget wishes. Let's go have apple pie at Mom and Pop's."

"I could do with a piece of pie."

"Piece? I was thinking the whole thing. I'll eat with a spatula; I'm in the mood."

"You're getting a little irrational here, babe."

"I know, that's the problem, nothing makes sense." She yanked on her clothes.

"With a little luck Bridget will be at Mom and Pop's, *without* her fiancé. I don't think I'm up to dealing with Jerry Price tonight."

"You don't approve of him?" Marc asked, thinking a change of subject was a really, *really* good idea and wondering how Julia could eat a whole pie. The divorce had obviously stressed her to the brink. He snagged his shirt from the rowboat and found his jock strap in a canoe. It was like a damn scavenger hunt.

"Jerry Price is out for Jerry Price. A little too slick, too many answers that don't answer anything at all, and Bridget is much too good for him."

"Does Bridget know how you feel?"

"What am I going to say, *'You're dating Jerry-the-Jerk'*?"

"That bad?" Marc pulled on his shirt, then folded the blanket.

"Let's just say never in a million years would I wish Bridget to fall head-over-heels in love with Jerry Price. Or . . ." Her eyes covered half her face, and she slapped her hands to her cheeks. "Ohmygod! Ohmygod!"

"What?"

"I wished Bridget would fall in love with Jerry!"

"So?" He went back to straightening things up. "It's just a wish, Julia, a verbal token of good karma, or in this case not so good karma. You're obsessing."

"You have no idea what I've done. This is a catastrophe!"

"You haven't done anything, unless you're referring to what we did here, and that was pretty damn good in my book." He put his arm around her.

She wiggled out of his embrace. "This is awful. Now Bridget will be more in love with Jerry than ever. Me and my big mouth."

He wagged his head. "You're going ballistic over nothing, Julia. It's the stress of the divorce talking. Listen to me. *Wishing* is a figure of speech . . . right? Besides, you prefaced with *never in a million years*. That made it a negative wish."

Her expression turned frantic. "It doesn't work that way, Marc."

"What doesn't?"

She spread her arms wide. "The wishes, dammit. The wishes!"

Marc took Julia's hand and led her out the door, then closed it quietly behind them. "Take a deep breath and let it out slowly. You need fresh air, lots and lots of fresh air. Maybe a glass of wine . . . or three. Your divorce has really done a number on you, babe. You can't let it get to you like this."

He put her in the passenger side of her car. "Where are your keys?"

"In the ignition."

"Good grief." In Cleveland her car would have been stripped and camera equipment stolen all in about five minutes. Guess that's why she lived in Delicious. Smart girl, though at the moment she could do with a little therapy.

He turned the ignition, and his cell phone chirped. He snagged it from the dash and listened to Cal give info on the case they'd been working on. Julia stared out the window bug-eyed, her brain somewhere else besides the car. Marc disconnected and turned to her.

She still stared straight ahead. "How could I do this to Bridget?" she muttered. "She's my best friend, has been since freshman year in high school when we fought over the same boy, then realized he wasn't worth it."

Marc took Julia's chin and turned her face to his. "I'm working on a case with Cal, and I have to go. I'm going to drop you off at Mom and Pop's for pie. Are they still serving at this hour?"

"If I go to the back door and beg."

"Good. Eat, then go to bed. You need sleep."

"I can't sleep. What about Bridget?" She gasped, her eyes covering half her face. "Oh, crap. She's out with Jerry tonight. What if she does something . . . stupid. What if they elope?"

"Bridget can take care of Bridget."

"No, she can't." Julia banged her head against the dashboard.

"Julia, get a grip. Until she asks for your help she's not going to listen to you no matter what you do or say. People in love are like that."

But Bridget has to listen, Julia thought as she watched Marc jog off after leaving her parked in front of the diner. She's the one who messed this up. She had to get to Bridget and confess all. Or if that didn't work, lock her in a closet till the wish lost its power . . . whenever the heck that was.

Julia slid into the driver's side and headed down Jonathan to Bridget's house, saying little prayers she was home and not with Jerry. Julia parked the car at the curb behind Bridget's. Lights blazed inside the white frame bungalow. *Good.* Bridget was there, but now what?

Bridget loved Jerry already, and this wish would make the devotion more intense. What to say? *Hi, Bridge, I'm the dumbass who wished for you to love the biggest louse on earth . . . besides Frank.*

Not coming up with anything better, Julia headed for the house. She'd just spill her guts and hope it made sense. She walked up the path lined with red hibiscus plants, orange and yellow daylilies, and zinnias. She clambered across the wood porch as the wicker swing and hanging baskets swayed gently in the humid evening breeze. She knocked, wondering how things could look so peaceful when, thanks to her, all hell was breaking loose. Bridget answered, a big sappy smile covering her face, a dreamy look in her eyes, and knitting in hand.

"Is Jerry here? Kick him out. What in the world are you doing with the knitting stuff?"

"Jerry, my dear darling man, isn't here." A forlorn look replaced the sappy one for a moment, then disappeared. "But I'm knitting him socks. Isn't that a great idea?"

"You don't know how to knit. And why socks?"

"I'm learning because I love Jerry so much I can hardly stand it," she said on a deep sigh that made Julia think *damn, damn, damn.* "I never knew I loved him this much till tonight. I was just sitting here on the sofa after he dropped me off, watching *Survivor,* and *bam,* I fell more in love with him than ever. Even though we had another fight over setting a wedding date. In books they knit their man socks when they're in love. So I am, borrowed stuff from Ms. Greeley next door. She's always knitting something."

Julia took Bridget's hand and led her inside and closed the door. "You've been reading those Regency romances again, haven't you? Those are old books, women don't knit socks anymore, and you don't love Jerry, least not as much as you think you do."

Bridget's expression turned pouty. "Of course I love him. I love him to death. How can you say such a thing?" She grinned hugely. "But since you mentioned books, I have big news to tell you."

Julia slapped her hand to her forehead. "Dear God, you're pregnant."

Bridget looked at her as if she'd lost her mind. "What's that got to do with books?"

"I don't know. It just seemed like the next logical catastrophe, though right now I don't think logical exists."

Bridget patted Julia's shoulder. "Well, I'm not pregnant yet, but I'm going to get my big stallion"—she growled deep in her throat and wiggled her brows—"to work on that." She giggled.

"Forget pregnant. I could do with some good news right now. What is it?"

Bridget tapped a history book on her coffee table. "Yesterday when I was tutoring I came across something that got me thinking." She brought her hands to her breasts and let out a deep sigh. "Yesterday I could think about things; now all I can think about is my beefcake."

Julia spread her hands wide. "Bridge, get a grip."

"I'll try, but it's hard, let's see now. Oh, yeah, history. The ancients had calendars pretty much like ours and planned their whole civilization around the sun and the moon, especially the phases of the moon. When it's full, usually once a month, they had rituals and sacrifices and did a bunch of other stuff—"

"Just get to the point."

"Two nights ago the moon was full."

"And this all means . . ."

"A double whammy, because this month there are *two* full moons, a blue moon." She exhaled noisily. "Jerry loves full moons. Once he—"

"Bridget!"

"You don't have a romantic bone in your body, I swear." She swept her head back, for a moment looking like Ms. Piggy does drama queen. "Two full moons a month don't happen very often and ancients believed it made them able to do things they normally couldn't do, make things they did *special*. Yesterday you got divorced."

She held out her hands in surrender. "I don't get it."

"You took off your ring, kissed it, and threw it over your shoulder into the water exactly at noon, directly opposite midnight which is when the full moon is most powerful. After the toss, you immediately started wishing about Frank, then the snort, then the picture, and then hot sex with Marc. I love hot sex with my honeybun." She blushed, then continued, "Just think of all the wishes you made and how they came true. Something caused that, Julia. It doesn't just happen for no reason."

Julia dropped onto Bridget's sofa, remembering making love to Marc at midnight in the coatroom and it being the most astounding sexual experience on earth. "My wishes coming true is because of the moon?"

"It's too much of a coincidence. And, that makes for good news and not so good news. Tomorrow the moon passes into the next phase, taking its influence right along with it."

She looked into Bridget's eyes. "Do you believe in this?"

"I teach ancient history. There's a lot there we don't understand today. They lived closer to the earth and understood it better than we do."

She rested her hand gently on the book. "I just know if my Jerry lived then, he'd be a god."

"Holy cow."

She nearly swooned. "I agree."

That meant Marc would come to his senses tomorrow at midnight. Her heart dropped to her knees. She knew it was coming, that her wish for him couldn't last forever, but now she knew when it would end, and she wasn't ready for that at all. Well, she'd deal with that later; right now she had to keep Bridget away from Jerry till midnight tomorrow.

She tugged Bridget down beside her, then knelt on the floor so they'd be eye to eye. "Bridge, you got to listen to me. This is important. I did a really stupid thing. I *wished* for you to love Jerry. Actually, I wished you *didn't* love him, but that's not the way it worked out. But you understand now because you just told me all about the moon and the wishes and how it all works, right? That's why you love Jerry. You don't really and truly love him you just *think* you do. Do you understand me?"

Bridget nodded, looking a little spacey. "I think I'm going to get him to elope tonight."

"No!"

"And I think I'll lend him the money for his new business. That's why he won't set the wedding date. He doesn't think I believe in him since I won't lend him more money."

"More!"

She batted her eyes. "Isn't that sweet; he wants me to be a part of his life. Why didn't I see this before? What was wrong with me?"

"You had a brain then. You can't do this, Bridge. You're under the influence of something I wished for. We just talked about all this. Your idea. I wished you to fall in love with Jerry; that's why you're feeling like you do."

"I can use my teacher's retirement fund. I can get the money tomorrow."

"Listen-to-me!" She took Bridget's shoulders in her hands. "Don't do anything tonight or tomorrow. It'll be a disaster. You have to wait. You have to trust me on this."

Bridget gave Julia another dopey smile. "I'm so in love."

Julia plopped down on the floor and leaned back against the couch as Bridget took up her knitting and hummed "The Wedding March."

Things had gone from bad to much worse. Marc trying to jump her bones because of a stupid wish and her falling for him big time, and that had nothing to do with a wish at all, and now Bridget intended to ruin her life by marrying Jerry. How could she get herself and everyone else into such a mess?

A knock at the door made Julia's hair nearly stand on end. *Jerry?* Bridget put down her knitting that looked more like a series of really strange knots and grinned. She straightened her blue skirt. "It's my man, I just know it." She put her hands to her cheeks and sighed, "I'm coming, lover-boy. Your hot mama's all ready and waiting for you."

Julia threw herself in front of the entrance ahead of Bridget, flattening herself against the door, arms and legs spread for maximum blockage. "You can't do this. It's a huge mistake!"

Bridget went to the window, undid the screen, and hitched one leg through the opening. A woman obsessed!

"Oh, hi, Marc," Bridget said, retreating back into the living room, her face pulled into a deep frown. "I was hoping it was my Jerry, my man, my honey-stud." She growled and wiggled her hips.

Bridget went back to the sofa and resumed knitting and humming. Julia unlocked the door and stepped onto the porch.

"We've got a problem," Marc said and pulled her onto the swing.

"No more problems. I'm all problemed out." He'd changed from his running shorts into khakis and a polo shirt. The man looked great wearing anything . . . or *not* wearing anything.

He gave her a hungry look. "I need a kiss." He wrapped her in his arms and leaned her back into the swing, it creaking with the motion. He laid claim to her mouth, and for a second, she forgot about Bridget and

Jerry and the moon . . . until she caught more strains of "The Wedding March" coming through the open window.

She pushed Marc away and sat upright. "We don't have time for this."

"Babe, the way I feel right now it won't take much time. Something about midnight around here and you and being here with a full moon really turns me on. Like I have no control over myself." He pulled her back into his arms, his tongue reacquainting with hers. "Maybe Bridget has a room we can borrow, just for a few—"

"Marc!" She gripped his shoulders and looked deep into his hungry eyes. She gave him a little shake. "You've got to snap out of it. We've got things to deal with here."

He gave her a quick kiss. "I want you right now. I want your legs over my shoulders, and I want you open wide for me, and I want to bury myself deep—"

"Why are you here?" She slid under his arms and stood, taking calming breaths to get her heart rate back to normal. Fat chance that happening with Marc around. She peered down at him as he said, "I'm here because you're here. Saw your car and I really want you. How about the backseat? We can do it in the backseat."

He cupped her hips and brought her midsection opposite his lips. He inched up her blouse and kissed her navel, taking tiny bites at her waist.

"Marc!" she stage whispered and tried to step back, but he held her in place. At least the bushes blocked this front-porch seduction from the street. "As good as you feel, and you really feel good, by the way, we have a situation, and I'm not referring to your horny state . . . though I'd rather be thinking about that." *What am I saying?* "Bridget wants to elope with Jerry tonight."

That seemed to get his attention. He looked up at her.

"That's not good," he said. His hands circled around her bare thighs right below her shorts. Her heart raced back into the danger zone, and her mouth went dry.

"I'm working on a case for Cal; that's where I was tonight. His client owns the motel by the expressway, and things are getting stolen. New hot tubs, in-room refrigerators, light fixtures, and things like that."

His hands inched inside her shorts, and she nearly swallowed her tongue.

"Jerry's the one doing the stealing, and he's screwing around with the night desk clerk. Guess that's how he finds where stuff is and what's coming in."

"He's cheating on Bridge?"

Marc cupped Julia's derriere in his palms, and she gasped as his fingers pressed into her soft cheeks. His eyes brightened with passion as he continued, "We have to tell Bridget. She deserves to know."

Bridget? Who's Bridget?

His fingers hooked under her panties, connecting with her bare flesh and setting her insides blazing. "Bridget's not going to believe you," Julia said, forcing her brain to function. "She's in love with Jerry more than ever. Maybe I can lock her in a closet till she gets over it, and *ohmygod,* Marc, what are you doing?" she gasped as his palms held her bottom but his fingers met at the juncture of her legs.

"Kidnapping's against the law." His fingers stroked her sensitive lips, opening her as she bit back a moan of pure delight.

"Even for a good cause?" she managed to get out as his fingers pressed inside, making her legs part and her insides shiver with each stroke.

"The courts won't see it that way. We'll talk to Bridget together. I'll lay out the facts." His fingers found her clit, and she nearly collapsed into his lap. "You're so wet for me, Julia. So ready. You want me as much as I want you." He gently stroked her swollen folds. "I want to finish this for you, babe."

"But Bridget. We have to think of her and—"

"Jerry's preoccupied right now with the desk clerk. We have . . . time, and we won't need all that much of it."

"Garden shed?" She panted, her brain surrounded in a cloud of Marc and sex and one hot summer night. "Around back."

He took his fingers from her, making her fragile from unfulfilled desire. He grabbed her hand and led her down the steps. Keeping to the shadows, they made for the back of the house. Julia opened the door to the green shed, the smell of rich soil and plants washing over them. Moonlight filled the room. She closed the door quickly as Marc worked the button and zipper of her shorts, then dropped them to the floor in a soft swoosh.

She undid his trousers, and he sat down on a bench. Their gazes fusing, desire was nearly palatable in the little space as he slid on a condom. She straddled him, bracing her arms on his shoulders. Her heart hammered, his hands stroked over her hips, and she slowly eased herself onto him.

She gasped, his eyes blazed, his breathing harder, faster, her insides melting.

"Oh, Julia." He whispered her name as his erection opened her, taking possession of her.

She paused, and his eyes widened. "Julia?"

She straightened her legs, taking herself from him. "What are you doing?" he asked on a ragged breath, running the words together.

"I'm giving us pleasure. Making this last."

"I don't think I can make anything last right now."

"Try." She lowered herself again, her own climax mounting with every movement, every inch of him penetrating deep inside her. She pulled back again, her body aching for his return. His jaw clenched; sweat glistened across his forehead. His hands at her waist tightened; his eyes dilated. "You are an incredible lover."

She brought her mouth to his, savoring his tongue and lips while she lowered herself yet again. Marc filling her, completely overwhelming her as all her senses now focused on him and making love with him. Inch by inch, his throbbing hardness slid into her, soft, wet and hot, sending orgasms pumping through her as they finally came together.

Her head slumped onto his shoulder, her heart thumping wildly. She gulped air to calm it as Marc stroked her hair and her back, his own breathing tattered and shallow. Heat from their lovemaking filled the shed, making her slick with perspiration and dizzy from the experience.

"I can't get enough of you, Julia. After I make love to you, all I can think about is doing it again and again." His gaze met hers. "In all my life, I've never been this obsessed with a woman." He pressed his lips to hers. "And I don't want it to end."

She kissed him back, her heart squeezing tight knowing it would end very soon. "We have to help Bridget. She's planning on giving Jerry money for his business. Her retirement fund. She already gave him some of it."

"Will there ever be a time when we can make love and not have to go running off someplace right afterward?" He looked around. "How do we wind up in such bizarre places?"

"Frantic desperation." She grinned and brushed her lips over his, then stood, easing herself from him, already missing the connection, the lovemaking.

She looked back to Marc. His eyes wide, a wolfish grin on his lips, obvious desire mounting once more.

Holding up her hands she took a step away. "Don't even think it!"

"You're right," he said on a dejected sigh. "We have work to do, and it can't wait. After Bridget hears what we have to say she'll change her mind about Jerry."

"No, she won't."

Marc gave her an incredulous look. "Why not? She's smart; she'll get it."

"It's a moon thing."

He shook his head. "What's the moon got to do with anything except tides?"

She raked her hair from her face and paced the little room. "I should tell you what's going on. You have a right to know what's happening to you and why. It'll make it easier for both of us. I know it's not going to make much sense, and I didn't mean for it to happen, but it did. I have no idea why, not really, but it works, and now you're in a mess and so is Bridget and it's all my fault and I haven't the faintest clue what to do about any of it, or how to get out of it right now, so we're stuck till tomorrow at midnight." She stopped pacing and held out her hands. "Now you know."

"Have you been drinking?"

"That's one solution."

He stood and took her into his arms. "I have no idea what you just said, but we'll work it out together, I swear it. All I know is I want you to be part of my life, Julia, and I don't care who knows about it. No more boathouses, no more coatrooms. Just us together."

"You don't know what you're saying."

"You're right. I'm under your influence, and it has nothing to do with the moon. It's all you, and I can't even think straight. I care for you, Julia." His eyes darkened, and a soft smile touched his face. "I'm falling in love with you."

She froze, his words crashing down around her like

a bucket of ice water poured over her head. With all her heart, she wanted to believe him because that's the way she felt, too. But it was a lie . . . one big fat moonstruck lie . . . at least on his part. She'd wished for sex with Marc, not love, but how could he distinguish between the two? He didn't know what was going on. In twenty-four hours he'd go running back to Cleveland, wondering what happened to scramble his brain in Delicious, Ohio.

"Did you hear what I said? I love you. I've never said that to a woman before."

Her heart cracked a little. "We'll talk later."

"Later?" He looked into her eyes. "I pledge my love and you say *later?"*

"It's the moon, Marc."

"Bullshit. I know how I feel, and the moon has nothing to do with it."

This was crazy. He was not listening to her. She needed something to put him off until he wised up on his own. The more they were together, the deeper their attraction, and the more it would hurt when he left. "I just got divorced. I have a lot going on in my life. I need time to adjust to your feelings for me. You caught me off guard. Can we discuss it later? Bridget talked about eloping with Jerry."

He pulled Julia into his arms, her damp, naked body tight to his, the sensual experience the stuff dreams are made of. "This isn't over, Julia," he ground out, a no-nonsense look in his eyes. "You love me, too. I can feel it with every part of my body and my heart. But something's in the way, and you passing it off on the moon makes no sense at all." He kissed her, then let her go.

An uneasy silence stretched between them as she pulled on her shorts. She hated that silence. She wanted the camaraderie, the easy talk and banter they shared.

It's what made the relationship unique and special. And when he left her for good, she'd miss him terribly.

Julia followed Marc back across the yard to the porch and peeked in the window to check on Bridget. Knitting lay on the sofa, no humming, all lights on, door ajar.

She turned to Marc. "Good grief, *Bridget's gone! What the heck do we do now?*"

Six

"We'll find her," Marc said, moonlight slipping through the leaves, falling around him in a soft halo, making him more handsome than any man has a right to be. "If she's as crazy about Jerry as you say she is, she's probably gone after him."

"To ruin her life for evermore," Julia huffed. "I bet she's on her way to that motel site right now. She thinks Jerry's working late on a job and that's why he doesn't spend more time with her."

Julia grabbed Marc's hand. "I just hope she doesn't have much of a head start on us. We have to save her."

What to do? Julia wondered as she and Marc made for the car. She could wish Jerry *not* in love with Bridget, but it wouldn't matter. He didn't love her anyway or he wouldn't be cheating. He'd just keep faking that he cared about her till he got his grubby hands on her money.

"I'll drive," Julia volunteered. "I know the roads better."

"And I can call Cal and tell him what's going on. The motel owner is his client. He can catch Jerry red-handed and consider pressing charges. That should make Bridget see Jerry for a sleaze."

That's it, Julia realized. The answer to her problems. She turned the ignition, and Marc punched the numbers on his cell. She did a u-ee in the middle of Jonathan and tore down the street.

If good old Cal fell for Bridget, at least for the next day, maybe he could keep her from marrying Jerry and handing over her savings. If he really, really had the hots for her, he'd at least get in the way of her plans, right? Maybe scare Jerry off. Cal was handsome enough and a good attorney. Very persuasive. With all that going for him he'd have no trouble convincing Bridget she was in love with *him,* not Jerry, and Cal could talk her out of the money fiasco. It was worth a try. Julia couldn't think of anything else at the moment.

She drove faster. Marc still talked to Cal. Besides, what was the harm of one more wish? This time tomorrow everything would get back to normal. Bridget would be rational, and Julia could reason with her. Cal could go back to being friendly old Cal, and Marc would still turn her on with one look, but he wouldn't care because he'd be back in Cleveland.

Course *she'd* care a heck of a lot, but this whole mess was her doing in the first place, so there was no one else to blame. She'd have to deal with the consequences as best she could.

Marc continued his conversation, both hands in a white-knuckled grip, one on the phone and the other on the door handle, his version of city boy does two-lane country roads. Julia glanced at the moon. Okay, it was now or never. She muttered, "I wish Cal would fall head over heels in love with Bridget right now and pursue her till he had her for his own."

She let out a hopeful sigh as Marc's eyes widened

and he said to Cal, "Really? I had no idea you cared for Bridget in that way."

He took the phone from his ear and stared at it. "Cal cut me off. Said he was going after Bridget. Was going to have wild unbridled sex with her if it took him all night to persuade her he was the man for her."

Marc wagged his head. "I didn't know Cal felt any of those things for Bridget."

Neither did he, Julia thought, keeping it to herself since Marc was in no mood for her moon theory. "Gee, this is a lucky turn of events," she said innocently, dodging a deer bounding across the road. "With us telling Bridget about Jerry and all his shenanigans, and Cal making amorous advances to Bridget, maybe she won't sign over her life's savings to Jerry or marry him."

"And," Marc added, leveling Julia a steady look. "After we take care of Bridget and her problems, we'll deal with our own." He gritted his teeth as she dodged an opossum glaring into the headlights. "Course, it would be nice if we lived long enough to have that conversation."

Marc dropped his phone on the console so he could hold on with two hands as Julia fretted. "What if Bridget and Jerry already eloped to Vegas and we're too late?"

"It's not going to happen till she forks over the money and probably not even then. From what I could see through binoculars tonight, old Jerry and the night clerk were going at it pretty hot and heavy in the lobby. I can imagine what was going on behind the desk. Marriage to Bridget is not on that man's mind, but money and sex sure are."

"I'm going to kill him dead! How could he do that to Bridget!" Julia seethed. She swung into the parking lot at the lit sign by the red brick motel, her headlights picking out Bridget and Cal standing close. They both looked around as Julia pulled the car to a screeching stop beside Cal's car—lights still on and door wide open—parked in the middle of the lot beside Bridget's car.

Marc said, "Does everybody around here drive like a lunatic?"

"It's in all Midwest genes." Julia threw open the door and ran for Bridget, getting between her and Cal. She gave Bridget a hug and said, "I'm so glad to see you. I thought you might have eloped."

"See," Bridget said to Cal, pointing at Julia after she let her go. "It's like I've been telling you for the last five minutes; everyone knows I'm crazy about my stud-muffin, Jerry. I'm flattered you find me attractive and want to get to know me better, but I already have my big hunk-of-man just waiting for me here hard at work."

Cal looked totally forlorn, then rallied and assumed his best lawyer stance. "I object. I'm the man for you, Bridget my love. I didn't realize that till tonight. It just dawned on me, but you must give me a chance to prove myself. I can be a stud-muffin, too."

Cal the stud? Marc had never heard him talk like that, even during their days on the force.

"But I'm engaged to Jerry," Bridget implored. "Surely you understand that?"

"And where is exhibit 'A'?" Cal asked with an edge of courtroom authority as he held up Bridget's left hand. "No ring to submit in evidence. Your protest is overruled, my most lovely Bridget."

Julia added, "Listen to him, Bridge. Cal's really crazy about you. Jerry's just after you for your money."

Bridget gasped, looked horrified, and gave Julia a squinty-eyed look. She wagged her school teacher finger. "That's not true. How can you say such a terrible thing? Jerry loves me, wants to marry me and—"

"And wants you to withdraw your savings and give it to him?" Julia added.

Cal said, "Bridget, please don't give your money away. If you would allow me to take you to dinner and discuss profitable investments and then—"

"I need to find Jerry." Bridget glanced around as the short, blond, twenty-something clerk came out of the motel lobby. She looked from one to the other. "Hi, I'm Dolly Mitchell. Can I help you all with something? Even though we're under construction we are open for business, and we have some vacant rooms and a very nice breakfast bar in the morning."

Bridget said, "I'm looking for Jerry Price. He's the foreman for this job." Bridget sashayed her hips. "He's my fiancé. We're going to be married tonight. We're going to elope."

Dolly took a step back, her cheeks pale. "Fiancé? Jerry? You can't be serious. Wh . . . where's your ring?"

"I rest my case," Cal said, looking totally pleased.

Bridget tisked. "Okay, so I don't have a ring. Big deal, but I love my honey-lamb." She said to Dolly, "Do you know where Jerry is?"

Dolly's eyes narrowed, and she folded her arms, matching Cal's stance. "More than I want to. He's in room 309 . . . getting a shower."

Bridget giggled like a schoolgirl. "Guess he needs it from all our *excitement* earlier. He sure knows how to pleasure a woman."

"Pleasure, *you?*" Dolly huffed, her eyes angry.

"And there is my dreamboat now," Bridget cooed as Jerry rounded the building. He spied the gathering and stopped dead in his tracks. Then he turned and ran in the opposite direction, and Marc gave chase.

"Now you all went and scared him," Marc heard Bridget say as he took off. *How could she be so damn gullible?* She was a teacher, an educated woman. Marc poured on the speed and cornered Jerry by his truck. "Going somewhere, Price?"

Jerry raked back his still-damp hair. "Let me go, man. Those women are going to eat me alive."

"I know. And I'm damn happy to be here to witness it. Should be quite a show."

Jerry took a swing at Marc, but he snagged his arm, turned Jerry around, and put handcuffs on him.

"What the hell's this for?" Jerry bellowed as Marc marched him toward the others. "Screwing two bimbos at once is no crime."

"Bimbos?" Marc felt his blood pressure jump. "I'm sure Bridget and Dolly will love to know what you *really* think of them."

"Hey, give me a break."

"Think I'll leave the breaking to the ladies." Marc led Jerry around front and presented him to Dolly and Bridget. "Meet the man who's been keeping *both* of you happy. I'm calling the owner to see what he wants to do with this guy."

Julia watched Marc get his cell phone from the car. Bridget went all goo-goo eyed and wrapped her arms around Jerry's neck. "There you are, my little sugar snap. Now, tell this young lady we're going to be married. We can elope tonight."

"Yes, tell me," a totally pissed off Dolly said to Jerry.

"I object again!" Cal said. "Bridget cannot marry Jerry, when I'm so deeply in love with her."

"Why does this woman"—Bridget pointed to Dolly— "seem to know you so well? Is she from Delicious?"

"I'm from Wakefield, just down the expressway, and Jerry said *he'd marry me.*"

"Just let me guess," Julia said. "He'd marry you if you lent him money for his construction company. That *is* what he said, right?"

"So we'd be a team," Dolly beamed. "That makes him mine, all mine. And we don't need anyone else on our team." Dolly pulled on Jerry's left arm, bowing it out since his hands were still cuffed behind his back.

"No, he's not. He's going to marry *me*," Bridget insisted, snagging his other arm, it also bowing, looking as if Jerry suddenly sprouted wings. *Fat chance, that*.

"But you're mine," Cal insisted to Bridget. He snagged her away from Jerry, and she stumbled into his arms. He gazed deep into her eyes. "My dearest darling, Bridget." He dipped her back and kissed her while her arms flailed and she muttered protests between his kisses.

Dolly wrapped her arms around Jerry's neck and kissed him hard, and Julia felt her last nerve snap. "Dolly, he's not the guy for you. Bridge, Cal, I got you into this, and I'm sorry but you're all adults; act like it for Pete's sake. *Think* about what's going on here." She threw her hands in the air and wailed, "I just wish you'd come to your senses."

Bridget and Cal froze. Cal carefully brought Bridget back up and set her on her feet. He smoothed out her dress and gazed at her as if seeing her for the first time. "Wh . . . what am I doing?"

Bridget blushed and said, "I'm not sure but . . . but I think I really liked it, once I got used to it." She gave him a shy smile. "I had no idea you were so romantic, Calvin."

"Neither did I." He gave her an uncomfortable grin. Bridget smiled at Cal, then said to Dolly, "You should know Jerry also wanted money from me. I came here because I thought he was working hard to make a success of his company and not visiting room 309 with you. I wanted us to get married right away."

Bridget looked at Jerry. "How could you do this to me? Promise to marry me for almost a year, then go out and cheat on me? *And* take my money? Why didn't I figure this out before?"

Dolly said to Jerry while pointing to Bridget, "*She* really was going to give you money, too? For your business, though I doubt any of that money would make it there. You promised to marry me, *and* her? She's not just making all that up?"

Jerry gave Dolly a sexy smile and shrugged. "Hey, girl. All the babes dig me. I'm irresistible, what can I say?"

"How about *ouch!*" Before Jerry could figure out what she meant, Dolly doubled her fist and socked Jerry square in the jaw, sending him stumbling backward, landing flat on his butt on the asphalt.

Dolly glared down at him and dusted her hands together as if getting rid of something nasty. "You bastard!"

Marc slid his phone into his pocket and said to Dolly, "You should know he was using you for information. He was the one robbing the motel. Probably looked at the shipment records while you were checking people in and knew when to expect deliveries."

Dolly rolled her eyes. "Great, I'm probably out of a job because I believed this jerk." She glared at Jerry.

Bridget sighed. "How could I have been so blind? I wanted to marry him, and I never would have believed he'd cheat on me till I saw it with my own eyes." She held out her hand to Dolly. "I'm glad we both escaped."

Dolly took Bridget's hand. "Me, too. I'm calling the sheriff. Jerry's not getting away no matter what." She turned for the motel lobby.

Marc looked down at Jerry. "You're going to jail. I wonder how irresistible you'll be there?"

"You have nothing on me but the word of two lovesick females who are upset that I don't want to marry either of them."

"Bet if I look in the back of your truck, I'll have more evidence than I need. Or maybe I'll look in your house or garage for all the stolen merchandise?"

Cal said to Bridget, "Can I call you sometime?"

"How about tonight." She slid her arm through Cal's, and they turned for their cars. "Would you like to see my knitting?"

Marc said to Julia, "I can't believe those two hit it off so well."

"Yeah, funny how that turned out." She felt a blush creep across her face and hoped it didn't show in the dim light of the motel sign. "I think they were always drawn together, but with Cal being older they never connected in school. Then they fell for other people, until now. They needed a little push to get them together, and tonight they got it."

Marc hooked his arm around Julia. "I've got to wait for the owner and the sheriff. There'll be paperwork, and I want to try and convince the owner not to fire Dolly. After that I can meet you. Your place?"

"I'm really tired, Marc. It's been a long day. I'll meet with you tomorrow." She gave him one of those fake smiles she hated. But what else could she do? Get even more involved with Marc only to have him walk out on her tomorrow at midnight? The more they were together, the more his leaving would hurt. "We can talk then."

She started to walk away but came back. She placed her palms against his cheeks and looked into his dark blue eyes. "I've had a great time these last two days. The best ever, I want you to know that." She brushed her lips across his and walked toward the car.

"Julia?" Marc called after her. "I'll see you in a little while. Don't make it sound like forever."

She stopped and faced him. "Nothing's forever, Marc. No matter how bad it is or how good." Then she got in her car and drove slowly out of the lot.

Seven

The next evening Marc walked down Jonathan Street as the clock on the courthouse chimed eight. He spied Cal in Mom and Pop's and went inside. Cal looked up, a happy smile on his lips. "Hey, Marc. How're you doing? Last night sure was something, wasn't it?"

He gave Marc a sly grin as he sat down. "Sorry I didn't hang around to help you out." He fiddled with a napkin on the table. "But I figured you and the sheriff could handle things. Did Dolly lose her job?"

"The owner put her on a six-month probation, but she's still employed. Jerry's in the slammer as we speak. Need any clients? Or is there a little conflict of interest involved after last night?"

Cal took a long drink of iced tea and stared at the ring of condensation on the tabletop, then back to Marc. "When I think how that jerk sweet-talked Bridget and lied to her the way he did . . . Me defending Jerry Price is out of the question."

Marc leaned back, studying his friend. "Thought legal representation was the basis of the defense, not if you believed your client innocent or guilty."

"I wouldn't be much good at defending Jerry if I

wanted to punch his lights out every time I looked at him."

"You got it bad?"

Cal's gaze met Marc's. He gave him a lopsided grin. "Actually, I got it good. I always liked Bridget but never thought she liked me other than as a friend. She thought I felt the same about her, and then last night I got this notion, like a bolt of lightning out of the blue, that I wanted more. The feeling was really intense at first; then it wasn't, but Bridget was still there, and I knew I didn't want her to go."

Cal took another drink of tea. "Something happened to me, I don't know what, but I'm damn glad it did. She's the gal I've been looking for all my life, and she was right here in Delicious all the time." He shrugged. "Sort of like what's happening between you and Julia."

"Julia?" Marc wagged his head. "Right now I don't know what's going on with her. I can't even find her. She's been gone all day."

"You know, Cleveland's not the only place a PI can make a living. This area's growing, and I know lawyers in the surrounding towns could keep you busier than you want to be . . . just in case you have the need to leave the big city and move to the boonies."

Cal suddenly focused on something beyond Marc. His whole face brightened, and his eyes danced. He stood, and Bridget sallied up beside him. He looped his arm around her, drawing her near. A perfect fit. Like two pieces of a puzzle joining together, or two lovers who'd found each other.

Cal gazed at Bridget and said to Marc, "Want to join us for dinner? The roast beef sandwich and apple pie special is legendary."

"Think I'll pass." Getting between these two would be criminal. "Have either of you seen Julia? The note on her studio door said she went to some farm to take pictures, but she should be back by now. I haven't seen her car."

Still looking at Cal, Bridget let out a dreamy sigh and said, "She's back. Parked her car behind my house so you wouldn't see it, so you'd think she wasn't home. But she is, and she's on her roof hiding out."

Bridget's head snapped around, and she stared at Marc. "And when you find her, I'm not the one who just told you that. She'll wring my neck."

"The roof? What's she doing on the roof, and why doesn't she want me to know where she is? What's this all about?"

Bridget raised her hands in surrender. "She just doesn't want to see you till after midnight. And you'll have to get her to tell you what it's all about. You'd never believe me if I told you. You may not believe her, but it's up to the two of you to work this out." She kissed Cal's cheek. "Just like we are, at least I hope so."

Marc said to Cal, "Do you understand what she said?"

"Not one word. But we have all night for Bridget to explain, and I suggest you let Julia do the same."

Marc left the diner, pie box in hand. He could just pick the lock on Julia's apartment and let himself in, but her lust for apple pie might get him legal entrance. He walked down the street, past The Book Nook where Jenna Rowan was closing up after an evening book signing at her store. It promised to be another perfect summer night in small-town, USA. Clear skies, the moon full, though not as full as two days ago.

A car stopped to let a dog cross, and the driver waved to the elderly couple sitting on a bench eating ice cream with their grandkids. A young couple strolled with their baby and stopped to talk to another couple doing the same. Things were different here.

Marc climbed the wood steps on the side of the

clapboard building that housed Photos By Julia. He knocked hard at the apartment door, and when Julia didn't answer he peeked around the white curtains. No movement, no Julia. The roof? How the hell was he supposed to get there? He looked up. He couldn't climb; the roof was too high.

He went back down the steps, shaded his eyes against the setting sun, and called, "Julia? Julia, I know you're up there. Bridget ratted you out. You better talk to me or I'm going to be yelling here all night. I'll sing, drive you nuts. I can do 'A Hundred Bottles of Beer on the Wall,' bet you'll love that. Ninety-nine bottles of beer on the wall, ninety-nine bottles of beer," he sang off key until Julia peered over the side.

"Shhh. Be quiet."

"Let me come up."

"There's no reason for you to."

"We have to talk. And, I have pie."

"What kind?"

"Apple. From Mom and Pop's."

"Go back to Cleveland, leave the pie."

She disappeared back over the top, and Marc kicked a rock. "Damn, stubborn woman."

He felt someone's hand on his shoulder and turned and faced Jenna Rowan. "A fire escape's around back if you think that might help. There's a garden area on the roof so fire regulations made the escape mandatory."

"Thanks, I appreciate it."

She smiled. "My pleasure. I just went through a similar experience."

"You hid on the roof?"

She laughed. "Not quite, but it took my fiancé to straighten things out. I wish you luck. Julia's a nice person."

Jenna crossed the street to Stan's Garden Center, Stan waiting for her in front, a big grin on his face. Something was going on in the little town of Delicious, Ohio. Bridget and Cal, Jenna and Stan. Now, if he could just persuade Julia to . . . To what?

He watched Stan drape his big arm around Jenna and bring her close and kiss her cheek. That's what Marc wanted. He wanted Julia close and he wanted to kiss her and he didn't want to stop.

He rounded the building to a grassy backyard with huge old oak trees and a detached garage off an alleyway. He got a rake from the garage and snagged the bottom rung of the ladder of the fire escape. He yanked, and it creaked as it dropped down.

Julia appeared over the edge of the roof. "Now what *are* you doing?"

"Coming up."

She spread her arms wide. "Why are you so pigheaded?"

"Why won't you give us a chance?"

"Like I've said, there is no *us;* you just think there is, but by midnight you won't, so what's the point?"

"We'll find out." He gripped the old iron ladder with one hand and climbed on, his other hand holding the pie box. Flakes of black rusted metal showered down around him as he progressed from one rung to the other till he reached the first landing, stood, and put his foot through the decayed grating.

He exchanged looks with Julia, her eyes huge.

"Go back. You'll die."

"I think it's safer to go up."

"Try my window."

He gave it a tug, shaking the whole fire escape. "Locked, and I don't think I want to wait on this death trap while you unlock it." He stepped onto the next ladder. More rusty flakes fluttered around him as he climbed, bringing him to the rooftop.

He passed Julia the box, then vaulted himself over

the ledge and into a garden area. Flowers, roses, a patio complete with a little fountain. There was a lounge chair on some grassy carpet, half shaded by the big oaks from below, stretching their branches overhead. Julia's camera sat perched on a tripod in the middle. "Where'd this all come from?"

"Stan across the street has such wonderful plants and flowers. I can't resist. And, I needed somewhere to get away from things during the year I was separated from Frank before our divorce became final. One of the reasons I bought the building with some money my grandmother left me is because of this roof. No phones, no in-laws blaming me for everything that went wrong, no Frank. It's the highest roof in town, so no one's looking over my shoulder."

"It's great, just don't use the fire escape."

"You could have been killed."

"You could have avoided this by just letting me in."

Her brow furrowed. "You could have avoided it by going back to Cleveland."

"Yeah, but then you wouldn't have pie. Look, I've made up my mind; I'm not going back, Julia." He took the pie from her hands and put it on a table, then snagged her around her waist and kissed her. "I'm staying in Delicious with you. Cal said there is business enough in the area if I want to relocate. I love the town and the friendly people. And, I love *you.*"

He shocked himself with his admission, but every word was true. He was absolutely sure of it. "I want to be with you forever, Julia."

She bit her bottom lip, looking totally despondent. "You didn't give up your job in Cleveland yet, did you?"

"I will. Did you hear me? I love you."

She pulled him onto the lounge chair and sat down beside him, folding her hands matter-of-factly in her lap. "You have to listen to me, Marc. And understand. that what I'm telling you is true. After midnight you'll go running back to Cleveland and wonder what you ever saw in me, or Delicious."

"Not a chance."

"You're under the influence of the full moon, a blue moon. I brought on this situation by tossing my ring into the fountain. I know that sounds insane, but it's not. Too many things went nuts without any explanation. I wished for Frank to fall into the fountain, and he did. And not only that, he snorted because I said he was a pig."

"It's called coincidence."

"I wished for a picture of Frank in the fountain, and you took it for me. I wished McGuffy would move his truck, and then, I messed up and wished for Bridget to fall for Jerry—you were there for that one—and she did, and then I had to wish for Cal to fall for Bridget to distract her from Jerry."

"You need therapy, babe."

"It's true, every word. I did all the wishes without knowing what I was doing, except the wish for Cal to fall for Bridget. That was on purpose to get her away from Jerry. I was desperate."

"I've got news for you, Bridget and Cal are in love, and it has nothing to do with you wishing it that way."

"That's because I wished everyone to come to their senses, and they did. Bridget and Cal have been attracted for years, so they came to their senses and realized they were in love."

"What the hell does any of it have to do with us?"

"I wished to have wild sex with you."

He grinned. "You did? Well, damn."

"Actually, I did it as sarcasm, because I knew I wasn't your type. But then it happened for real. You fell for me when you normally wouldn't."

"You really think I'm in love with you because of the influence of the moon?"

"And by tonight it will all be over with, because the moon passes into the next phase, at least that's what Bridget said. Think about it, Marc. I'm older, live in a small town, and take local pictures. You're a city boy, on your own, and enjoy the single life. We have great sex together, but we don't *belong* together."

"We have fun, can talk about anything, like helping people, adore apple pie. The sex is damn terrific. A lot of relationships are built on less, Julia. I've dated more than my share of women, and I've never felt the way I do about you. For me, you're the one."

He tucked a strand of hair behind her ear. "How do you feel about me? Do you love me? Or is that part of the moon influence, too?"

She looked him in the eyes, hers sad and confused. He wanted nothing more than to take her into his arms and reassure her. But that wasn't the thing to do right now. She had to see they were right for each other on her own or she'd always wonder if he'd pushed her into the decision.

Twilight canopied the garden, now in shades of gray and black, the moon inching its way across the sky. The hot steamy night swirled around them, reflecting how he felt for her.

She let out a deep sigh that seemed to come from somewhere deep inside and said, "Yes, I love you. I think I have since you arrived here. You were compassionate and caring and thought Frank was a jerk for cheating on me. You're a great guy, and that's probably why I made the wish to have great sex with you in the first place."

She kissed him, her lips mating with his. "I'm glad it happened, if only for a little while."

He took her in his arms, no longer able to resist the urge to hold her. "This isn't a little-while relationship, Julia. I've had those, and what I feel for you is way beyond that."

He lay back in the chair, taking her with him, cuddling her close in the moonlight. "There's only one way to settle this. We'll spend the night here under the moon that's caused all these problems. Together we'll wait for midnight."

She gazed up at him, so handsome, so sure he was right while she knew at midnight he'd leave. But he was here with her now, and she loved him more than she thought she could love anyone. "Make love to me, Marc. One last time."

She sat up and pulled off her blouse and bra. "I know this isn't a good idea because I'll miss you all the more, but I want to see you naked in the moonlight. When I come up here I want to remember you with me."

"You'll remember me because I'll be right next to you always." He sat up beside her and stroked one breast, the heat from his hand intoxicating. He cupped her other breast, held it tenderly and kissed it, his lips on her skin making her dizzy with wanting him.

He stood and slid off his pants, his male physique taking her breath away, his aroused condition fueling her own passions. She unsnapped her shorts.

"Let me do the rest. I want to see you one inch at a time, like unwrapping a wonderful package."

He laid Julia back and bent over her. Her insides quivered as he eased off her shorts, leaving her thin pink panties as her only covering. He spread her legs and lay between them, making her blood rush in anticipation for what was next. Then he kissed her mound through the thin silk barrier, the pressure of his lips, the wetness of his mouth, taking her over the edge. She gasped as an orgasm shook her. "I want you in me, now."

She heard a rip and felt the silk barrier that separated her from the man she loved give way. Then he was in her, filling her completely with himself and making love to her one last time before he left her forever.

"I love you," Marc whispered as he climaxed, taking her with him. Then he held her close under the moonlight, the sweltering night mingling with the heat of their lovemaking.

"I love you, too, Marc." She kissed him, then let herself fall asleep in his arms, knowing when she woke, he'd be gone.

And as early morning sunlight flooded the garden, she knew she'd been right because she felt for Marc and he wasn't there. Slowly, almost painfully, she opened her eyes, feeling more alone than she'd ever been before. She'd known all along that he wouldn't be here. She'd even prepared herself for the moment, though some part of her had prayed all night she'd be wrong. But wishes were wishes and reality something else entirely . . . like the creak of the fire escape?

She held her breath and went to the edge of the roof. She nearly fell over the edge with relief when she saw him, flowers clamped between his teeth as he climbed toward her. "You're back!"

He mumbled something around the flower stems but she couldn't understand what he said. Were the flowers to wish her a nice life before he left her for good . . . or something else?

Marc heaved himself over the ledge and held out the flowers. "I wanted to get back before you woke, sorry I

didn't make it. I had to get Stan out of bed for these."
He nodded at the flowers. "He and Jenna are not happy
with me at the moment, and you've got to give me a
key. I'm getting too old for fire escapes."

She held her breath, summoning all her courage to
ask, "And you brought me flowers because . . ."

He gave her an incredulous look. "Because I love
you, of course."

He grinned and got down on one knee and pulled a
little black velvet sack from his shirt pocket. He said
something about Cal selling the ring as part of settling
an estate, but his words barely registered. Pure happiness bubbled through her, the kind of happiness a
woman feels once in her life and drowns out all the sad
times.

He undid the drawstrings and slid an emerald and
diamond ring into his palm, then held it up to her, the
morning sunlight making it sparkle like the stars at
midnight.

"Marry me, Julia Dempsey. I may be moonstruck,
but it's because of my love for you. I don't care if it's a
Blue Moon, or because pigs fly or hell freezes over; I
love you, and it's not going to go away. I love you for
the rest of our lives, and no phenomenon in nature is
going to change that."

She knelt down beside him. "I wish this moment
could last forever."

"It will, I promise, Julia. And the next time there's a
full moon I get to do the wishing."

"What will you wish for?"

He kissed her and tumbled them both back onto the
rooftop. "You and a big, big bed."

Get more Lori Foster!
Here's a sneak peek at
MURPHY'S LAW,
available now from Zebra . . .

With building impatience and anticipation, Quinton Murphy leaned against the cinderblock wall and checked his watch for the tenth time. How pathetic for a grown man to go to such lengths to talk with a woman.

A woman who had refused him—*after* kissing him senseless.

He didn't leave. He *wouldn't* leave. Not until she showed up and he had a chance to set things right with her.

Loosening his tie and pulling at the collar of his dress shirt, he cursed the unseasonable warmth of the October night and the stifling stillness of the parking garage. He checked his watch yet again, and then, finally, her yellow Civic pulled through the entrance.

Headlights flashed around the gray, yawning space, now mostly empty except for his Porsche Carrera and the vehicles of the night shift workers. Her brakes sounded a little squeaky, and she parked with a jerk of the gears that shook the aged automobile.

Always in a hurry—that described Ashley Miles. At least from what little he'd seen of her. He had to wonder if she ever relaxed or took a day off to laze around.

As soon as her engine died and her headlights went dark, the driver's door swung open and she stepped out. Quinton soaked in the sight of her, letting his gaze meander along the length of her long legs, her trim midriff, and the understated curves of her small breasts before settling on her face.

Once again, he mulled over her startling effect on him—and wondered at it. At thirty-three, he was hardly a monk. He'd had infatuations, relationships of convenience, and once he'd even been in love.

But something about Ashley, some indefinable nuance in her nature got to him in a most unusual way.

Pieces of her were perfect: her dark eyes, her long silky hair, and her mouth . . . God, he loved her mouth.

She smiled easily, had a sharp tongue, and said no far too often.

But she kissed with an enthusiasm and hunger that made her impossible to dismiss, almost as if she'd never kissed before and the sensation of it overwhelmed her. He wanted more. He wanted everything. Until he had her, he wouldn't be able to get her out of his thoughts.

Put all together, Ashley made a mostly average appearance. But when she spoke, all that sassy attitude came crashing out, and it made her seem appealing yet unattainable, brash yet vulnerable.

She said things he didn't expect, behaved in ways unfamiliar to him. She smiled, and he wanted to strip her naked.

Her car door slammed hard and she looked around the garage behind her, talking to herself in low mumbled words that reeked of irritation and disgust.

Unaware of his presence, she said, "For God's sake, Ashley, get a pair, why don't ya."

Never taking his gaze off her, Quinton pushed away from the wall. Patience, he told himself. He'd have her, and soon.

"A pair of what, Ashley?"

She screeched. The high-pitched yell of panic bounced around the cavernous garage in deafening force, causing Quinton to wince. "For God's sake, it's me."

Eyes wide, she whipped around, zeroed in on him, and went from startled to furious in a heartbeat. The change was something to see.

And she looked as desirable pissed as she did impatient.

After stomping across the concrete floor, she thrust her chin up close to his face. Since this was the second time he'd startled her in the garage, he felt a little guilty. Holding up his hands in concession, he said, "My apologies."

She didn't soften a bit. "You're making a habit of this, Murphy, and I don't like it."

Quinton gave in to a half smile, gently touched her hair, and lied through his teeth. "Not on purpose. I just finished some late business. Since I knew you were due in soon, I decided to wait to say hi before heading home." The last time he'd seen her, he'd been with a client. A sexy, blond, female client, and though he knew Ashley wouldn't admit it, she'd misinterpreted the situation.

Now he needed to make her understand his interest for her and her alone.

For a single suspended moment she stared at him, mostly at his mouth, her expression soft and giving . . . then with a frustrated growl she strode away from him.

Damned contrary woman. She wouldn't make this easy for him. But she did make it interesting.

Quinton propped his hands on his hips and watched her long-legged retreat, undecided on whether or not he should say anything more.

But after only three steps she halted. Her straight, stiffened back still to him, she snapped by way of explanation, "I usually don't scare so easy."

An olive branch? He gladly accepted it. "I gathered as much." He hadn't known Ashley long, but already he accepted that she wasn't a timid woman, definitely not a woman who jumped at shadows. In fact, he'd have described her as ballsy beyond belief. "So what's going on? Why are you so jumpy?"

"It's nothing."

She shut him out and he didn't like it.

Don't miss Dianne Castell's
HOT AND BOTHERED,
out this month from Brava . . .

His neck snapped as someone grabbed his tie and yanked him inside the carriage house, the dark interior making it impossible to see who did the yanking.

"What the—," he gasped as the wood door clicked closed. He stumbled, his body flattening a woman's against the wall, giving him a soft landing that made the choking worth it. He caught the faint aroma of coffee and doughnuts as breasts swelled against his chest, his body reacting as if he hadn't had sex in months. Hell, maybe he hadn't. "Charlotte?" he croaked through a shrinking trachea.

"We need to talk."

"Wish I could." He loosened his tie and gave a quick glance around the narrow hall, his eyes adjusting to the dim light. "Consider using a telephone?"

"Someone might overhear and I know you don't want that, and I was heading for my house to change and I saw you coming, and . . ." She took a deep breath, her face scrunched in question as she peered up at him. "So why did you really come to the office?"

"The will? The missing daughter? Keeping things quiet? Stop me if you've heard this before. You sure you didn't whack your head when you fell off that chair?"

Her breath came fast and was getting faster. Her eyes lit with fire—even in the dim light he could tell. "Why me?" she whispered, the implication having nothing to do with the case but with the two of them together now in this hallway after all these years of dancing around.

His brain refused to function, probably because the part of his anatomy below his belt was overfunctioning. "You run an ad in the yellow pages." Maybe? He had no idea about anything right now except Charlotte and wanting to kiss her and knowing he shouldn't. Things between them were complicated—always had been and getting worse by the minute. He studied her delicious mouth, wanting and waiting for his lies. Make that getting more complicated by the second, and if his plan worked, *complicated* would be a huge understatement and their lives would be totally fucked.

He touched Charlotte's cheek, her skin soft and smooth, as her body leaned into his, setting him on fire. "We don't have an ad." She bit her bottom lip. "You're right, I should have phoned," she said with a shiver. "But we're here now." She yanked his tie again, bringing his face to hers, and she kissed him right on the mouth, her lips full and moist and delicious and opening. Did they have to open? Closed lips were a lot easier to dismiss, but this was not a dismiss kind of kiss, especially since he'd wanted it for so many damn years he'd lost count.

She released his tie, her arms sliding around his neck as his tongue touched hers and he lost his mind. Dumbass!

Their tongues mated, and his hands dropped to her sweet round bottom, pressing her softness to his hardening dick. There'd always been an attraction between them, but this was pure jump-her-bones-and-do-her-right-now lust . . . and he liked it more than he ever imagined.

She sucked his bottom lip into her mouth, the motion suggestive as hell as her legs parted, nesting his erection tight against her heat. God, she had great heat! He slid his hands into the waistband of her skirt, her firm rump fitting so well into his palms. His mind warped, there was a ringing sound . . . no kiss or ass-grabbing had ever made his head ring before, especially to the tune of "Moon River" . . . a Johnny Mercer song . . . his favorite. Ah fuck! His cell!

And keep an eye out for
Lucy Monroe's newest book,
THE SPY WHO WANTS ME,
coming from Brava
in January 2009!

According to her files, the tall, muscular scientist was Frank Ingram's right hand man as well as the project manager on the antigravity experiment that had been compromised, leading to TGP's interest in ETRD. Any other professional information regarding his role at ETRD was sketchy. TGP only knew what they did about his role on the antigravity project because his name had been on the intercepted plans. Frank had offered the information that Dr. Beau Ruston was his second-in-command when he hired Elle for the security consultation.

Other than that, she knew that the young PhD had begun working for the company as an intern while pursuing his doctorate. He'd been hired on in a full time capacity even before he'd successfully defended his doctoral thesis. Other than the antigravity experiment and the projects that had gone public, TGP had no information regarding what the man did at ETRD.

The company was better at keeping secrets than the Pentagon. Much better. Hence the need for an agent on sight to determine the lay of the land.

She wasn't here to investigate Beau Ruston per se,

but he was certainly someone she was interested in finding out more about.

She turned and leaned back into the car to grab her briefcase, giving the string man a view of her toned backside in the tailored slacks. Being a good agent meant using all assets at her disposal to do her job. If that included flustering a man by exposing a little thigh, then she did it. If it meant bending over to offer a glimpse of a body she used as a tool for her job, she did it.

And her instincts told her that she wanted this particular man as off-kilter as she could get him.

She locked the car and headed toward him, noticing that he had not moved from his spot in front of the building. So, he knew who she was too and he was waiting for her.

As personal greeters went, she'd take him.

His expression neutral, he put his hand out when she was within reaching distance. "Ms. Gray? I'm Beau Ruston."

Her hand was engulfed in the warmth and strength of his. For a split second she saw something in his Hershey brown eyes and tension-filled square jaw that found a corresponding response right in her core.

Desire. Hot. Urgent. Primal.

And wholly unexpected.

Oh, she was used to being admired. Even wanted. But that flash of sexual heat went beyond the surface physical reaction of a man and a woman meeting for the first time. And the fact that it mirrored her own response was as close to frightening as facing down the wrong end of her own favorite Ruger P95 semi-automatic.